SAVE
THE
QUEEN

An ALEX HALEE Thriller
With
JAMIE AUSTEN

TERRY TOLER

Save The Queen
Published by: BeHoldings Publishing

Copyright @2021, **BeHoldings, LLC, Terry Toler**

Cover and interior designs: BeHoldings Publishing
Editor: Jeanne Leach
For information, address support@terrytoler.com

Our books can be purchased in bulk for promotional, educational, and business use. Please contact your bookseller or the BeHoldings Publishing Sales department at: sales@terrytoler.com

For booking information email: booking@terrytoler.com
First U.S. Edition: March, 2021

ISBN: 978-1-954710-01-6

BOOKS BY TERRY TOLER

Fiction

The Longest Day
The Reformation of Mars
The Great Wall of Ven-Us
Saturn: The Eden Experiment
The Late, Great Planet Jupiter
Save The Girls
The Ingenue
The Blue Rose
Saving Sara
Save The Queen
No Girl Left Behind
The Launch
Body Count

Non-Fiction

How to Make More Than a Million Dollars
The Heart Attacked
Seven Years of Promise
Mission Possible
Marriage Made in Heaven
21 Days to Physical Healing
21 Days to Spiritual Fitness
21 Days to Divine Health
21 Days to a Great Marriage
21 Days to Financial Freedom
21 Days to Sharing Your Faith
21 Days to Mission Possible
7 Days to Emotional Freedom
Uncommon Finances
Uncommon Marriage
Uncommon Health
Suddenly Free
Feeling Free

For more information on these books and other resources
visit TerryToler.com.

PRAISE FOR THE JAMIE AND ALEX SPY SERIES

"Lots of action and dangerous situations kept my interest. I thoroughly enjoyed it."

"I want Jamie on my side."

"I could not put this book down. I read into the early morning until my eyes couldn't hold up. As soon as I woke up the next morning, I picked up my phone and started reading again."

"What a great and exciting book."

"A female Jack Reacher."

"Very interesting and intriguing stories."

"Would make a great movie."

"Great book. It was a page turner."

"A 'WOW' of a thriller!"

"Toler proves that one doesn't need gutter language or sex to write a great story."

"A truly gripping read. "

"While reviews of other author's books claim to be gripping, this novel sets the benchmark."

"I'm a sucker for thrillers with a happy ending."

"I was not disappointed."

"Love that Jamie Austen is a top-notch, take no prisoners kind of woman."

"What a ride!"

"These books keep me on the edge-of-my-seat."

"This series gives insight to current issues in the world."

"Heartwarming!"

"I want to believe that the good that can be accomplished in these stories could be real."

"When I finish a book, I think about it for days which is the characteristic of a great author."

"I can't wait to see what you come up with next."

"I love the characters. They draw me in, and I find myself rooting for them."

"Very entertaining."

"A perfect read that projects just enough suspense. Adding a young innocent in a tough situation who becomes the hero of the story makes it extraordinary."

"This is an exciting spy thriller with complex, interesting characters."

"I would definitely recommend these fantastic books."

"I love the message of these books."

"Love Toler's stories! Suspense and romance combined."

1

London Tube

J amie saw the man before I did.

"Alex," she whispered, "when you can, look at the man three seats ahead of us on the left. He's acting strange."

"We're in England. I suspect we'll see a lot of people acting strange on this trip."

Jamie let out what seemed like an obligatory laugh but kept her steely demeanor. I'd seen it many times on a mission. Seeing it on our honeymoon was something I'd hoped to avoid.

Her instincts were right, more often than not, so I did look more out of curiosity than anything else.

"What do you think?" she asked. "I think he might be a terrorist."

"We're not on a mission, Jamie," I said. "I think you should relax."

"He's wearing a jacket. It's August. And ninety-five degrees outside. Who wears a jacket in August unless they're up to something?"

That did cause me to look more carefully. I studied the man to see if there were any signs that he had a bomb strapped to his body. Even though he was wearing a jacket, it wouldn't conceal the bulges of a homemade bomb. Sticks of dynamite made obvious indentations pressing against a shirt, and we were trained to spot them.

After careful examination from a distance, I was convinced he wasn't carrying a bomb.

"He's sweating," Jamie said.

"He's sweating because he's wearing a jacket."

"It's more than that. His right hand is in the right pocket of the jacket. He hasn't taken it out the entire time since we got on."

"There could be any number of reasons for that. He could have his wallet in his right coat pocket. Maybe he's carrying drugs. Some important papers."

Jamie let out a sigh. "You're probably right. I'm being paranoid. The CIA report filled my head with thoughts of knifings, acid attacks, and bombings. It's easy to profile a man, just because he's Muslim."

Jamie had spent most of the flight from Washington D.C. to London poring over the threat assessment report. That and griping about everything that went wrong at our wedding.

I wasn't sure about the man, so I didn't respond right away. He was acting strangely. Nervous tics. Sweaty brow. Leaning forward in his seat. His hand firmly planted in his pocket. All tell-tale signs of a terrorist. A quick scan of the subway car confirmed that there weren't any authorities nearby to notify.

The car was three quarters full, and I did a quick assessment of potential targets for a terrorist. To our immediate left, one row ahead sat a woman with a child. The boy looked to be five or six years old. Further ahead, across from suspicious guy, was an older couple. American. She was chatting away. He seemed to have tuned her out. I wondered if that was what Jamie and I would be like fifty years from now. That thought brought a smile to my face. We were already that way!

The car was a target-rich environment for a terrorist. But he didn't have a bomb. Not much he could do with whatever he had in his right pocket. At least, not on a large scale. I tried to tamp down the analysis and clear my thoughts of him. Five minutes later, I hadn't been successful.

The suspicious man left me with a nagging feeling inside which was always what I relied on in the field. I wanted to let it go but couldn't. I finally figured out why. One final tell was clearly bothering me.

The man was staring straight ahead. Avoiding eye contact with anyone. Even though I was purposefully staring at him, he didn't look my way at all. Like he was forcing himself to keep his eyes fixed on a target ahead of him. Like he knew me and didn't want me to know he was targeting us.

Why would a man on a London subway car be targeting us? That was beyond what my mind could possibly imagine. No one knew we were in London, not even Brad, our CIA handler. If the man was randomly targeting us, then why me. I was the biggest guy on the subway car. By far.

"I can't wait until we get to the hotel," Jamie said, bringing me back to reality.

"Me either," I replied. My heart skipped a beat at the thought of finally being alone with my wife. Although, I wasn't sure if she was thinking the same thing I was thinking. Right after the wedding, we had to rush to the airport to catch our flight. We never had a "wedding night" per se.

"I'm so tired, I'm going right to bed." Jamie let out a huge yawn.

My heart sunk a couple inches in my chest as her statement was explained. Clearly, I was going to have to wait a little longer to consummate our marriage. We'd been married for nearly twenty-four hours and still hadn't had sex. I had a lifetime of lovemaking ahead of me, but for whatever reason, I was obsessed with the first one.

Maybe since I'd been thinking about it almost since the day we met. We mutually agreed to wait until we were married. While I was glad we waited, I wasn't glad we were waiting now.

Neither of us said anything for a good five minutes. Jamie finally broke the silence.

"I know I told the florist Tuesday," Jamie said, picking up where she had left off on the plane. Griping about the wedding. At least her mind was off suspicious guy.

"We should just drop it. It doesn't matter now."

When we had arrived at the chapel for our wedding ceremony, there were no flowers. Jamie called the florist. When she hung up the phone, she asked me, "What day did we tell the florist to have our flowers? Today right?"

"Yes," I said reluctantly, not fully processing the problem.

"They have it down for tomorrow. Tomorrow we'll be in London. I think I would know my own wedding date."

"You told them today," I said. "I remember."

"I have my something blue. Something borrowed. I have a white dress. I have everything except my bouquet." She'd said each word passionately, for emphasis.

"Another thing we don't have is Curly. He's not here yet," I said reluctantly, not wanting to upset her even more. "We can't get married without him."

Curly was the minister. I use the term loosely. Normally, he was ten minutes early to everything. He was also our trainer at the CIA. Turns out he also had a license to marry people that he got off the internet. While Jamie wanted a traditional wedding in a church, she didn't seem to mind that Curly wasn't a real minister.

"Did you tell Curly the right date?" Jamie had asked.

"Of course. I think I would know my own wedding date!"

Curly never did show up. Turns out he thought the wedding was for Wednesday as well. The associate pastor at the church was there and reluctantly agreed to marry us. The thought of the ceremony brought a smile to my face. Then I remembered what happened afterward.

"I know I told the limo company Tuesday," I said angrily.

The limo was to be a surprise for Jamie. A driver was to take us to the airport to catch our flight. When we walked out of the church to leave for the airport, the car was nowhere to be found. I called them. They insisted the reservation was for Wednesday. I distinctly remember making the reservation for Tuesday, August 15th. Watson Community Church. Two o'clock in the afternoon.

It was all disconcerting. First the flowers. Then the minister. And finally, the limo. We were bewildered as to how all three important parts of our wedding got messed up.

Twenty-four hours later, we still had no explanation.

That wasn't even the worst of it. When we arrived at the airport and discovered our business class seats had been changed to coach, I went ballistic.

"There's been some mistake," I said to the flight attendant. "We should be in business class. I used my frequent flyer miles to book it."

"I'm sorry, sir. But your boarding pass says coach. You need to take your seat. The captain is preparing to taxi for takeoff. He can't move as long as anyone is standing up."

"I need to speak with someone. They gave me the wrong boarding pass."

I could see two seats open in business class.

"Those are supposed to be our seats," I said, pointing at them. "The wrong boarding pass somehow ended up on my phone. Look up our reservation. You'll see I'm right."

"We aren't privy to the reservations. The gate agent handles that. I'm sorry, but you're going to have to take your seat."

I was prepared to make a scene if I had to.

Jamie tugged on my shirt. "Let's just go sit down," she said. "People are staring. We're holding up the plane."

"I'm not sitting ten hours in coach when our reservation was for business class!"

Jamie pulled harder on my arm. I jerked it away, roughly.

"Don't make a scene," she whispered. "They'll kick us off the plane."

Jamie was right. Every flight had air marshals on them. If I protested too much, they'd have us arrested and thrown off the plane. Starting our honeymoon in jail in the US was not a pleasant thought.

The reservation mix-up still had me fuming.

"I think we should check that man out," Jamie said, bringing me back to the potential problem at hand. "The more I look at him, the more I'm convinced he's planning something."

"Like I said, we're not on a mission," I said strongly. I hoped Jamie didn't think my angst was directed at her. Neither of us had been able to sleep on the plane. We were both squished in coach in middle seats between two people. So much for best laid plans.

The plan had been for us to sleep the entire night in beds on business class and hit the ground running in London after some passionate love making at the hotel. Truthfully, now I needed to crash in the bed as much as she did. The long-awaited physical union would have to wait. One thing I knew was true. Things would go a lot better if we both got some rest first. You only get one first time. I was determined to make it special, even if we had to wait.

That didn't make it any easier.

I almost wished suspicious guy was planning something. I could take out all my frustrations on him. An impulse hit me to go and talk to him and see what was in his pocket. Then I realized he could delay us getting to the hotel even longer if we got involved. So, I decided not to confront him and put him out of my mind.

Jamie clearly hadn't. She kept staring his way.

It wouldn't do any good for me to try and stop her. She'd only get mad at me. Getting sucked into a mission was not on the itinerary. Neither was fighting with Jamie.

But... if I had to be in a fight, I'd choose suspicious guy over Jamie any day of the week.

* * *

Ten minutes later

"London isn't such a safe place anymore," Jamie said soberly.

The ride to central London was forty-five minutes and I'd pulled out my laptop. I stopped typing to give her my attention. Jamie had the CIA report out again.

"What does the report say?" I asked.

"Terrorist attacks are up 112 percent."

"That's a lot."

"They aren't big things. More along the lines of knifings and acid attacks. Can you imagine that? Somebody throwing acid in your face. London is averaging two acid attacks a day."

"I can't. The pain must be excruciating."

"The victims are blinded. Permanently scarred. Some die. Maybe they're the lucky ones. The survivors are usually in for a long recovery."

I shuddered at the thought and glanced over at suspicious guy. There didn't appear to be any way he could be hiding acid on his body. It could be a knife in his pocket though.

"Well... hopefully, none of that will happen while we're here," I said, still eyeing the man warily.

"Let's hope not. Security is tighter. There's a royal wedding on Sunday. The day before we leave. It's going to be a zoo in London. I guess we didn't plan our trip very well."

"It could go either way. Increased security reduces the threat, but a high value target like a royal wedding with lots of people increases it at the same time. Anyway... not our problem."

I leaned over and gave Jamie a kiss. "You're sexy when you talk about knifings, and bombings, and terrorist attacks."

Jamie gave me a faint smile and returned the kiss, but her focus was clearly on the report. "Listen to this. Seventeen people were arrested in London two weeks ago on sex trafficking charges. Thirty-one women, ages twenty to forty were rescued. Three of those arrested for trafficking were women."

Jamie made a sound of disgust. She worked in the sex trafficking division of the CIA. Her job was to go into the seedy underworld and rescue girls. Something she was extraordinary at doing. By most metrics, she was considered the foremost lethal female operative in the world. She could kill a man with her bare hands in a hundred different ways.

"It infuriates me that women would be involved in sex trafficking," she continued. "How could they do that to other women knowing what they put them through?"

"Doesn't make any sense to me," I said. I had to let Jamie rant, but I didn't want her to go too far into the abyss. If I let her, that's all she'd talk about for hours. I knew that fact well. If she got me started talking about Pok, I wouldn't shut up. Pok was a cybercriminal I'd been tracking for several months. I got close to him once and was determined to get close enough to him again to put him out of business.

"They were from Romania."

"At least they caught them," I responded supportively. "Sounds like the Brits are serious about combating it."

"Thirty-one girls are a drop in the bucket. There are thousands of them in England."

"I suppose. When we get back home, we'll get right to work on it. We have a lot more freedom now. We can choose our own missions."

Ironically enough, yesterday, we'd both been let go from our jobs at the CIA. Not fired as such. Our handler, Brad, had set up a new corporation for us called AJAX. Named for Alex and Jamie. Letters of our name. We were given full operational control. We could set up offices, hire employees, and go on missions. Completely off the books. Funded by money we confiscated from an Arab oligarch named Omer Asaf on a previous mission to Belarus. When we got back, we had a lot of work to do to get operational.

Jamie brought up the knife and acid attacks again. Then she mentioned suspicious guy three or four more times before we got to our stop. Each time, I shot her down. If I didn't, she'd spend the entire honeymoon scanning every place we visited for threats.

Still... I kept my eye on him.

2

Somewhere in Iran

G I Man Pok sat in front of a computer screen in a newly constructed cyber warfare lab just outside of Zahedan, Iran, near the border of Iran and Pakistan. A huge smile dominated his face like Big Ben in London dominated the Parliament building.

London.

Alex and his wife Jamie were now in London.

For the last couple days, he'd been having some fun with them. The idea came to him when he inadvertently came across an email from Jamie to her maid of honor, Emily. Through a secured system. Not secure enough for a man of his hacking abilities. The subject matter was an outline of her wedding plans to Alex Halee. Every detail was listed. The florist. The church. The minister.

The date.

It wasn't hard to hack into the florist's computer and change the date from Tuesday to Wednesday. The limo wasn't hard either once he found the company. There were six of them in the area. He had to hack into three of them before he found a reservation for Alex Halee.

He didn't even know that Alex would hire a limo. It's just something he'd heard Americans did. When he found the reservation and changed it, he almost doubled over in laughter.

Serves them right. Such extravagance. Didn't they know there were starving people in the world? Not that he cared about starving people. His bitterness was directed toward Alex. He hated the man.

Changing the reservations were as easy as a couple of keystrokes. Child's play. For a man of his skills. Pok was considered in some circles as the best hacker in the world. Alex Halee believed he held that title, but Pok was out to prove him wrong.

The only regret he had was that he couldn't see their faces when they found out about the change in plans. What he'd done was nothing more than a teenage prank, he admitted to himself. Still the thoughts were cracking him up, and he couldn't stop laughing. He'd stolen billions of dollars from financial institutions over the years, and nothing was as satisfying as this. Ruining Alex's wedding day. While he wouldn't normally bother with such frivolities, he did it to prove to himself he could.

Not for payback. That would come later. Alex would have to suffer a lot more than this before Pok would feel like he had avenged Alex fully.

In fact, revenge wouldn't be complete until Alex was dead.

His hatred for the man ran deep.

When Alex had infiltrated his cyber lab in North Korea and shut it down with a lethal virus, he'd begun to doubt his own abilities. Maybe Alex's claim of being the best hacker in the world was true. Pok refused to accept it, even though he nearly lost everything. Almost his own life. Halee embarrassed him in front of the Supreme Leader. Now, he would prove to the world that he was the best.

Alex is good. But I'm better.

"I'm the best," Pok said emphatically even though no one was in the room to hear him. He pounded his fist on his desk.

He'd kicked himself mercilessly for months, for being so careless that Alex could actually infiltrate his lab. A mistake he'd never make again.

Hopefully, their wedding day was ruined. He'd never know, but he allowed himself the satisfaction of pretending it was. Maybe his wife, Jamie, would even blame Alex and start an argument. Pok's mind was out in left field.

What did they think when they got to the airport and found out they were booted out of business class back to coach?

"And they were in middle seats!"

His handiwork. Pok was laughing so hard his side hurt.

Will they know it's me?

50-50.

Maybe they will. Maybe they won't. More than likely, they'll be second guessing themselves.

Doesn't matter. If his London plan worked, Alex would definitely know it's him. He would rain down terror on the British city unlike anything anyone has ever seen before.

Right under Alex's nose. And Alex would get the blame.

And... there's nothing Alex Halee can do about it.

* * *

Pok couldn't have carried out what he was plotting from his home country—North Korea. His cyber lab was decimated by Alex Halee's virus and wasn't yet back to full capacity. Further, it didn't have the broadband speed, sophisticated computer systems, and access to technology the Iranian lab had. It also didn't have the one thing he needed most: Men and women willing to blow themselves up. Something vital to his upcoming plan.

When Pok told Iranian leaders that Alex Halee was the one who stole the nuclear codes that Iran had paid North Korea for, they gained a mutual enemy. Iran opened their lab and all their resources to him. Pok now stood at the front of the lab to address their workers and present the plan which became operational as soon as Halee arrived in London.

"Salam," Pok said, giving them the traditional greeting of peace from a non-Muslim.

"Wa Alaikum," they responded in unison. *And the same unto you.*

"Thank you, my friends," Pok began. "We're going to make history over the next few days. With your help, we'll bring the west to its knees and avenge the crimes Alex Halee has perpetrated on your great country. In front of you is our operational plan. You may turn to it now."

He'd made sure the plan had been handed out to each participant. Pok waited until the rustling of papers died down.

"We'll carry out this plan over five days, beginning today."

A bank of televisions was on the wall behind Pok. More than a hundred. He turned and looked at them.

"Pull up the video feed," Pok said to his North Korean assistant. One of a dozen experts he brought with him from North Korea.

Each television had a different real time view of a street in London.

A murmur went up among the crowd.

"The city of London is the most heavily monitored city in the world," Pok explained. "The government has installed more than six hundred thousand CCTV cameras around the city. Including private cameras which they have access to. You literally can't walk or travel to any public place in London without your image being captured. Everything flows through one central location. I hacked into that system and can now see everything they can see."

He paused for a moment to let that sink in. Actually, to give them a chance to marvel at his capabilities. He'd been working on infiltrating the system for months. A breakthrough gave him access just a few short days ago.

Pok reached down and typed a few keystrokes, changing the images to various recognizable locations.

"This is the corner of Parliament. Here is Westminster Abbey. London Bridge. The Tower of London. St. Paul's Cathedral. Trafalgar Square. Piccadilly."

He hit more keys.

"Here's the subway system. It's called the Underground. Or the Tube. There are cameras throughout. All monitored by British authorities."

He hit another key, and the image of Alex Halee and his wife appeared.

"This man is our target. And his wife. They just arrived in London. Your job is to track their every move and follow them around London on the system of cameras. When they leave the view of one camera, you'll need to quickly move to the next camera in the direction they're headed."

The room was staring intently at the pictures. Some leaned forward in their seats, straining for a better view.

"From the moment they got off the airplane today, we've been following them," Pok said, the bitterness rising inside of him. "Your job is to keep your eyes on them, everywhere they go. Is that understood? It won't be easy. They could get on buses. Take taxis. Ride the Tube. Go inside and outside of buildings. I'm counting on you not to lose them. Can you do that?"

A chorus of agreement went up among the crowd.

"Turn to page two in your handout," Pok said. "I'm going to turn the floor over to Adil Niazi."

Niazi was the assistant to the commander-in-chief of the Iranian Revolutionary Guard—second in command. He would oversee the military aspect of the operations.

"*As-Salamu-Alaikum,*" he said with the traditional shortened Muslim greeting. Allowed when time was short. A non-Muslim was not allowed to use it. Pok didn't understand all their religious rules but kept his mouth shut.

"*Wa alaikum assalaam,*" the Muslim's in the room responded. *And upon you be peace.*

Niazi began discussing the plan. "We'll carry out attacks each day for five straight days," he said in Persian, the official language of Iran.

"Each day will escalate in scope and intensity. That's by design. Thirty-five of our brothers are in London and are prepared to launch fury on the infidels."

"*Inshallah*," a chorus resounded. *God be willing.*

Pok looked down at his copy of the notes.

Day One: Knife attacks.

Day Two: Acid attacks.

Day Three: Suicide vest bombings.

Day Four: Car bombings.

Day Five: Dirty bomb. Launched at the royal wedding.

Niazi explained each day's attacks even though they were self-explanatory. When he was finished, Pok was called back to the front to explain the coordination of the attacks and what they had to do with following Alex Halee.

"These attacks won't be random. They'll be launched in the proximity of Halee. That's why we're tracking him. Once we have eyes on him, Commander Niazi will move his men into position. Upon his command, they'll launch their attacks on targets near Halee."

Niazi had questioned the plan. Why wasn't Halee the target? Niazi wanted to kill Halee at the first opportunity. Halee couldn't be killed in the attacks. Pok had his reasons which he wasn't ready to divulge. It had to appear that Halee happened upon them. Eventually, he might make the connection that the attacks weren't random but not until it was too late.

Pok had considered messing with Halee's hotel reservation and cancelling it altogether. He had resisted the temptation. This way he'd know where Alex was at least twice a day. When he left in the morning and when he came back in the evening. They would always have a starting point. Then they could follow him all day, springing attacks along the way. If they did lose him, the camera system had a face recognition program. If someone was on camera, they had a way of finding them.

Pok marveled at the technology. Also, at his own skills. Alex might suspect Pok was behind the attacks, but he wouldn't know for sure. He had no way of knowing Pok had hacked into the camera system until later, when Alex hopefully figured it out.

"Halee is on the Tube from the airport to his hotel with his wife as we speak. They boarded the subway to central London about fifteen minutes ago and will get off at the Piccadilly stop. Commander Niazi has a man on that subway car. When they exit in central London, his man will launch a knife attack on a target in close proximity to Halee. Commander Niazi will coordinate subsequent attacks. Your only job is to not lose Halee. Can you do that?"

A resounding yes went up in the room.

Pok put another picture on the screen. The subway platform at Piccadilly station.

"You'll want to keep your eyes peeled to this screen. In less than thirty minutes, all hell is going to break loose."

3

The brakes of the subway car screeched to a halt at our stop. By that point, I'd decided that suspicious guy might be a threat, but my mind was focused now on finding our hotel. We'd exit the subway car, go to the top of the stairs, and make the three-block walk to our hotel. To the right at the top of the stairs if I had my bearings right.

Once there, we could check in and get some much-needed rest. If all went well, we'd wake up, make love, take a shower, and begin our sightseeing. Jamie wanted to be awake in time for three o'clock tea. She insisted that we had to have British tea at midafternoon on our first day. That meant we needed to wake up by one-thirty or two. That would give us a good three or four hours of sleep and enough time to carry out my plans. Not ideal, but we were on vacation. A good sleep would come later. We'd be back to the hotel early enough tonight to get a full night's sleep.

I was sitting on the aisle seat out of habit. For quick maneuverability. Just because I was on my honeymoon, didn't mean I could easily ignore all my operational training. Jamie was on the inside seat, so I could protect her if necessary. Truth be known, she could protect me as much as I could her. Still, it made me feel more like the man of the relationship. Her knight in shining armor, so to speak, which was a very British thought to have.

As soon as the car stopped, I stood and immediately walked to the door to get there before everyone else. Not to get off first, but to let the suspicious guy see me. He was hanging back which was fishy to me. I was tall and an imposing figure. Intimidating to most people. Standing at the door, he wouldn't act with me there. I could also control the order in which people exited.

I didn't want him exiting after me. No way was I going to let him get behind me. Keeping him in front would allow me to act if he indeed were planning something. While I repeatedly told Jamie to ignore her suspicions, my threat radar was on full alert. I could tell she was still on edge as well.

The older American couple exited first. Suspicious guy motioned for me to go ahead of him. Our eyes met. I could see the hatred in his eyes. Even if he wasn't planning anything now, he was capable of it. I knew that look. His right hand was still firmly planted in his jacket pocket. He motioned again with his left hand for me to exit the car.

Not going to happen.

"I'm waiting on my wife," I said sternly. I think that was the first time I'd said that. Called Jamie my wife. My heart warmed as I looked at her.

I motioned for the mother and young boy to go in front of us. Jamie was behind them. She had the same thought as me. Keep the threat in front of us.

The mother thanked me. She seemed nervous as well. Probably because she was on a subway traveling with a small child.

Once she cleared the step off, I motioned for suspicious guy to go. He hesitated. Then went. I followed right behind him. In front of Jamie, so she exited after me. Not in an unchivalrous manner, but so I would be her first line of defense. If the man were planning an attack on us, he'd have to go through me to get to Jamie.

The thought occurred to me that I was being extremely paranoid. More so than Jamie had been. But... Curly drilled in us that we could never be too careful.

The platform was packed with people coming and going. A throng of people were gathered a few steps back from the door, waiting for us to exit so they could board. The sign for the stairway was to our right. We had about a thirty-yard walk to get to it. I noticed several security cameras in various locations. That made me feel better. Suspicious guy wouldn't do anything with all those cameras around.

Mother and small child were ahead of us. The man was behind them. We were right behind him. Nothing out of the ordinary was happening. A good configuration from a mission control standpoint. I let out a breath I didn't realize I'd been holding.

Jamie must've been starting to relax as well because she said, "Do we go to the right or left at the top of the stairs to get to our hotel?"

Before I could answer, the man sped up around the mother and child. The move startled me. I didn't like sudden movement. Then I saw it as a good thing.

Get away from us.

Once suspicious guy was a few steps ahead of the mother and child, he suddenly turned and shouted something in Arabic. Now he was facing toward us. The woman stopped walking. We all stopped so fast, I almost bumped into her.

I saw a silver flash.

A knife!

My reaction was instinctive. Quick. Immediate. Curly would've been proud of me.

Except... the angle was wrong. The woman was between me and the attacker.

The knife was already speeding toward the woman. She was holding her child's hand with her right hand. She put her left arm up in the air and cowered back as she saw what I was seeing. The attacker plunged the knife into the side of her opened and vulnerable chest. Just under her raised arm. Near her heart.

She fell backwards into me.

I either had to sidestep her and deal with the threat and push her off of me or catch her.

One of my hands was carrying my laptop. I reached out with my left hand to steady her. My hand stopped her momentum as she slumped to the ground.

The attacker was only a few steps away from me, but it was far enough away that I couldn't reach him. He was still facing us, almost frozen in place. Our eyes met for a second time. He gave me a steely stare of satisfaction. Like it was for my benefit. The bloody blade was still in his right hand.

I looked over at Jamie. Her angle was even worse to act. She was behind the young boy, who'd been dragged down to the ground with his mother who still clutched his hand. Jamie reached out and blunted his fall.

I was torn. Should I tend to the mother or go after the attacker.

Blood was already gurgling from her mouth. I knew that sound.

Not good.

The attacker started running for the exit. That motivated me to move. I was on one knee. I gently laid the mother all the way to the ground and stood. He had a head start and was already on the stairs. I bolted after him. Made more difficult by the throng of people who were coming down the stairs and the ones exiting up the stairs.

When I reached the top of the stairway, I looked in each direction. The attacker was running. A block or so ahead to the left. He disappeared into an alley. I wasn't prepared to chase him. I didn't even think to do any preplanned reconnaissance. Normally, I would memorize the layouts of the streets.

Why would that be necessary on my honeymoon? At this point, chasing him would be a waste of time and energy. I went back to see about Jamie and the woman.

Jamie was sitting on the platform. The woman's head laying in her lap. She was stroking the woman's hair with one hand. Jamie's hand and clothes were soaked in blood. The little boy sat next to his mother crying. Jamie had one arm around him, trying to console him. A crowd had gathered around them. A couple of people were on the phone, presumably to call the authorities.

I knelt next to the mother. Her eyes were fixed straight ahead on the ceiling. A blank stare of unbelief enveloped her face.

Then she coughed. More blood trickled from her mouth.

She closed her eyes and quit breathing.

4

Iran

As far as Pok was concerned, the plan couldn't have gone better. Commander Niazi's man timed his attack on the woman perfectly. Right in front of Halee and his bride. As an added bonus, the man escaped. Pok never expected that to happen in a million years. He knew of Halee's skills. The odds of the man pulling off the attack without Halee stopping it had been less than fifty percent in his mind.

Niazi seemed equally pleased. "I knew my man could do it," he said, clapping his hands together.

"A major success. I hope your man eludes capture," Pok said.

"He'll disappear into one of our neighborhoods. The police won't chase him there. He'll wait for things to die down and then strike again at a later date when needed."

"Excellent," Pok said, as they continued to watch the scene unfold in the subway. A crowd had gathered around the woman, and the police hadn't yet arrived. They could see Halee sitting on top of her doing chest compressions. That must mean she was near death. Hopefully.

Pok wouldn't allow himself to celebrate long. He knew they wouldn't all be this easy. Getting the man onto the same subway car at the same time as Halee wasn't that hard to do. Knowing the flight arrival time and anticipating the time it took to get through customs was also easy. Tracking Halee around London and coordinating a man to get close to Halee again would be more difficult now that Halee would be on high alert.

"I have another man in the vicinity ready to go if you want to launch another attack," Niazi said. "They have to exit through the stairway. We can hit someone while Halee is walking to the hotel."

"Not this soon," Pok replied. "Halee must think these attacks are random. If we hit him again, he'll know something's up. If he gets suspicious, he'll go underground. We'll never find him. He's too good."

"My men are better," Niazi said. "We could've killed Halee right then and there."

Pok knew that wasn't true. He watched Halee closely as he got off the subway car. It seemed like he was suspicious of the man. The attacker got lucky. The woman was between Halee and him. Had she not been, Niazi's man would've met a different outcome.

He'd take this time to regroup. Halee would be tied up in questioning for a while. Then they'd go back to the hotel. Pok was unsure if they'd go out again or would go right to bed. He figured they'd go to bed. When they went out a few hours from now, probably at dinnertime, he'd be ready and would try another attack, even though it would be risky.

He was torn. Should they risk another attack so soon after the last one? Originally, he had planned three. That seemed like overkill now. The last thing he needed was for Halee to realize he was behind the attacks and then go on the offensive. Right now, Halee had no clue. So, Pok had the advantage. Maybe for the first time ever. He might not get an opportunity like this again.

Sometimes, the prudent thing to do was to cut your losses. In this case, the prudent thing to do might be to accept his winnings before there were any losses. He'd have to think about it carefully. If Halee and his wife went out again, he'd play it by ear. If they could get a man close enough, they'd go for it. Otherwise, they'd wait until tomorrow to launch an acid attack.

Those attacks would be easier. A man with a knife had to get in close proximity to his target. Acid could be thrown. Niazi's men only had to be in the general area of Halee. Day three, the attacks were suicide vest bombings. Even easier to coordinate. Those people only had to be in the vicinity.

Day four were car bombings. Those just needed to be on the same block as Halee. When the dirty bomb went off on day five, all of downtown London would be affected. Halee would be at the royal wedding. In the blast radius.

Maybe taking another knife attack off the table was the prudent thing to do.

Pok didn't think he could help himself. If the opportunity arose again, he was going to have to take it.

* * *

The woman needed CPR. No breathing. No pulse. And no movement. The three signs that drastic measures were needed to save her life.

"Lay her head on the ground," I said to Jamie, who still had the woman's head in her lap. She needed to be flat on her back. I got on my knees next to her.

After taking several deep breaths of my own, I tilted the woman's head back, held her nose, and blew two breaths into her. Then put my ear to her mouth to listen for any signs of breathing.

Nothing.

People were crowding in. I shouted for them to back away and give me some space. A quick glance around the platform confirmed that the paramedics hadn't yet arrived.

The woman was bleeding from the side of her chest. That told me the wound had possibly penetrated her heart. I found the wound. That caused me to pause. Performing chest compressions on a person with a chest injury could make things worse.

The general rule was to do CPR anyway. The person was dying. If I did nothing, she would die for sure.

I couldn't afford to wait. I put my hands in position and pushed down gently but firmly so I went down at least two inches into her chest.

Blood came squirting out of the wound right onto my clothes. The wound had penetrated her heart. I stopped doing compressions immediately. In my backpack was a spare shirt. A passerby was standing over us, and I told him to press the shirt against the wound. I showed him how to do it.

"Press hard," I said strongly. "We have to stop the bleeding."

Where are the EMTs?

I sat on top of her chest so the man could get a good angle on the knife wound. In these situations, I had to calm my adrenaline. My strength was such that I could press on her chest so hard I might break her ribs or sternum. I took another deep breath to calm my nerves.

Jamie was still tending to the boy trying to shield his eyes from the horrific scene playing out in front of all of us.

For a good three minutes, I alternated between rescue breaths and chest compressions. Two breaths, then compressions at a rate of 100 per minute for thirty seconds. Then repeated the process.

My heart was racing. The mother was unresponsive.

"Come on," I said to her. "Don't die on me."

Finally, the EMTs arrived and took over. By that time, I had blood all over my hands and clothes. Without thinking, I wiped them on my shirt and shorts, soiling them further. I rubbed the sweat from my brow, smearing blood on my face. The extra shirt the guy had been holding against the side of her chest was soaked in blood.

Jamie's hands, shirt, and shorts were red stained as well from where she had been comforting the woman in her lap.

"Does anyone know what her injuries are?" one of the EMTs asked.

"She has a stab wound to the side of her chest," I said.

He raised her arm and I showed him where the knife had entered.

"She's been unresponsive for at least four minutes," I added.

By that time, the British Transport Police had arrived and began cordoning off the scene. We were pushed back and away, behind a line of police officers.

The boy was still clutching Jamie's leg. She picked him up and held him close to her. Keeping her hand on his head so he couldn't look at what the authorities were doing with his mother.

I approached one of the officers.

"That's his mother," I whispered, pointing at the boy.

He nodded as if he understood and got on the radio. Within five minutes a woman had arrived to take charge of the boy. About the same time, his mother was loaded onto a stretcher. The EMTs were still performing CPR as they took her away.

I retrieved my backpack and laptop, then took Jamie in my arms, and we stood there in shock for nearly a minute. Not sure what to do. Should we leave? We were witnesses. We could provide a description of the suspect. At the same time, we were both mentally and physically exhausted.

A man approached us in a suit and tie. He looked like a detective. Probably chose us to question because we were still there and covered in blood.

"My name's Mick Weaver. I'm a counterintelligence officer with MI5. Did you see what happened here?"

"A man attacked the woman with a knife," I said. "We were right behind her. I saw the whole thing."

"Can you describe the man?"

This was right in our wheelhouse. Jamie and I were both trained to remember every detail of a crisis situation. What details I didn't remember, Jamie did. By the time we were finished, Agent Weaver had a complete description of the man down to the color of his eyes. By the look on his face, Weaver seemed impressed. Maybe confused. That normal tourists wouldn't be that thorough in their descriptions.

That reminded me that we should dial it down some. Even though we were on our honeymoon, we were to maintain our cover with the CIA. No one could know who we were or our relationship with the CIA. The goal of AJAX was for us to be able to travel around the world undetected. Able to operate undercover without being on the radar of other intelligence services. Brad would not like it if we were drawn into a terrorism investigation.

"Can I get your number in case I have any other questions?" Weaver asked.

I gave him my cell phone number.

"Where are you staying?"

"At the Palace hotel."

"I'll be in touch if I need anything," Weaver said. "I doubt I will. It should all be on tape." He pointed to a security camera.

"I hope you catch the guy," I said.

"You have a good rest of your trip," Weaver added.

How are we supposed to do that now?

5

The Palace Hotel

The eyes of the lady behind the hotel counter were as big as British teacup saucers. I suddenly realized how strange we must've looked to her. Checking into a five-star hotel covered in blood. She was so shaken she left the counter and went in the back. When she returned, a man, presumably the manager, was with her.

"Have you been in a row?" he asked sincerely in a very British accident. I assumed he meant fight.

"There was a knife attack on the subway system," Jamie answered.

For some reason, I was still badly shaken. My knees felt weak and holding my hands steady took all my effort as I took my passport out of my backpack.

"Were you hurt? Do I need to call an ambulance for you?"

"We're okay," Jamie said. "We helped the woman who was injured."

"I'm sorry we look like this," I said. "We need to get to our rooms so we can get a shower and change."

"Of course," he said. "Please come with me."

He opened a door beside the counter and stood to the side to let us go in first. We were taken to an office in the back where we were given our keys after we showed him our passports and he confirmed our reservation. I was relieved the reservation was correct. At least we got something related to our wedding right.

"I've upgraded you to a suite," the manager said. "If there's anything my staff or I can do for you, please don't hesitate to ask. Thank you for being a, what do you call it... Good Samaritan."

"Thank you for the kind words," Jamie said. "Mostly, we need to get some rest. It's been a long flight and not a good start to our honeymoon."

"So, you're on your honeymoon! Perhaps I could have some champagne sent to your room?"

"Not right now," I answered. "Can we take a raincheck? I think we just want to get a shower and some rest." Celebrating with champagne wasn't something I felt like doing at that moment.

"We would like to take tea later this afternoon," Jamie said. "Is there someplace you would recommend?"

It startled me to hear Jamie talking in a semi-British accent. Had I been in the mood, a smile probably would've come on my face.

"Afternoon tea at Kensington Palace is delightful," the manager said twisting his mustache with one hand. "It's a lovely walk from here."

"That would be fine. Please make a reservation for two. Under our names."

"Brilliant. Anything else?"

"Where can we go to buy clothes?" Jamie asked.

"There's Oxford Street and Camden Market. Either would have what you would be looking for."

"How do we get there?" Jamie asked.

He took out a map and showed Jamie the directions. "You can take a carriage or the underground," he said.

Jamie looked at me. I shook my head no. "I don't believe we'll be getting on the underground again today."

"Of course. I understand. A carriage will take you right to the shopping. You can even walk if you're up for a bit of a hike."

I didn't want to ride in a carriage either. Jamie must've seen my confusion because she mouthed the word, taxi.

"We can decide later how we'll get there," Jamie said to the manager. "Thank you. You've been very helpful."

The whole conversation was mostly a blur. My mind was still on that subway platform. The woman's eyes staring at me were seared into my psyche.

The manager personally escorted us to the service elevator and took us to our room. I could tell he was concerned about other guests seeing us. The entire time he was fidgeting and nervously looking around. We probably should've changed our clothes in the subway restrooms. I didn't really think about it. Jamie was right, though. We needed clothes. I only brought two pairs of shorts and four shirts. One pair of shorts and two of my shirts were ruined.

Our room was on the top floor. Along with all the other suites, the manager explained.

Jamie let out some oohs and aahs when we walked into our room. At least one good thing had come out of our ordeal. This would be an ideal place to stay on our honeymoon.

"I hope this room meets your satisfaction," the manager said, obviously pleased with himself and proud of the property he managed.

The room was a luxurious upgrade. Beyond what we could've expected.

"This is lovely," Jamie said. I remembered Jamie had a mission in London when she first joined the CIA. That must be why she could turn on the British accent and dialect so easily and speak their language. Her wide range of skills never ceased to amaze me.

"This will be fine," I said, tersely in my most American voice, as I escorted the manager to the door and put the *Do Not Disturb* sign on the doorknob as he walked out.

"Thank you for all your help," I added, so as not to seem too rude. He had been helpful.

As soon as he was gone, I set my backpack on the desk and turned on the television. Then sat in front of it on the edge of the bed. The blood was dried on my clothes now, so I wasn't concerned about staining the lush bedspread. I probably should've been more careful, but my focus was on the television screen.

"What are you doing?" Jamie asked.

"I want to see if the attack is on the news."

The screen flickered and there it was. Pictures of the familiar scene. Now empty. Just police tape and a big blood stain on the platform. I looked down at my hands and pulled my shirt out to look at it. The same blood was on me. Fighting back tears took all of my strength. The memories of the afternoon started flooding back in my mind.

"One woman has been taken to a local hospital," the reporter said. "No word yet on her condition."

I knew her condition as well as anyone. If she survived, it'd be a miracle. I mouthed a quick prayer for her. Jamie sat on the bed next to me with one arm on my shoulder and her left hand clutching mine.

"I pray she's okay," I said.

"Me too. I'm going to jump in the shower," Jamie said, although I barely heard her. My focus was glued on the screen.

For some reason, Jamie didn't get up right away.

"You need to get out of your clothes," she said as she stood in front of me, blocking my view of the television.

"Alex," she said, shaking my shoulder.

I felt completely numb. I could hear her words, but they weren't registering.

"Alex," she said gently. "We need to get you out of your clothes."

She helped me pull off the shirt. Then my shorts. Jamie walked into the bathroom and returned with a robe. She put it around me.

"Do you want to take a shower first?" she asked.

"No. You go ahead. I want to watch the news."

"Are you okay?" she asked hesitantly, like she wasn't sure if she should leave me alone.

"I'll be fine," I replied. I shook my head and shrugged my shoulders, really tightly, to try and loosen them up.

"I'm okay," I repeated. "Go get your shower. That'll feel good."

Jamie was gone for at least twenty minutes. When she returned, I was still in my funk, not feeling better at all. Worse, if that were possible. The news reports kept saying the same thing over and over again, so I turned down the sound and just stared at the screen. I kept reliving the events. Playing it over and over again like a movie in my head. Trying to figure out what I should've done differently.

Jamie came back in the room and sat next to me.

"Any more news?" she asked.

"No. They haven't updated the condition of the woman."

"There's nothing you could've done, Alex. You did everything you could to save her life." Jamie said the words kindly, and I appreciated them, but they weren't true.

"You and I both know that's not true," I said roughly, speaking aloud what was in my head. "I should've listened to you. You knew the man was a terrorist, and I ignored it."

"I didn't know for sure. The man seemed strange to me, that's all."

"If I'd listened to you, that woman wouldn't be in the hospital, near death."

"Like you said, we're not on a mission. We can't be expected to spend our time seeking out threats. I could've confronted him too."

"We're always on a mission. God's given us a gift. You knew that guy was bad news. That's your discernment. We're trained to spot threats and take them out. We were the only people on that subway who could've stopped him. And we didn't. Now I have to live with that."

"What would you have done?"

"Confronted him! Made him show me his hands."

"Then what?"

"Made him show me what was in his pocket."

"So... he shows you a knife. That's not a crime."

She had a point. I didn't have the right to go around searching people because they looked suspicious to me. If I'm working a mission thread, that's different. We're authorized to take down anyone we deem a threat to the mission. As an ordinary citizen, Brad would've never wanted me to confront that man.

Neither of us said anything for a good minute. Jamie kept alternating between rubbing my shoulder and stroking my hair. I could feel the difference in our relationship. Even though we'd only been married a little over a day, we were closer. More one flesh, like the Bible says, even though we hadn't yet consummated things. Something I hadn't thought about since the event happened.

"I suppose you're right," I said. "But... why does this feel so different?"

"What do you mean?"

I turned to face her. "We see innocent people hurt and killed all the time. It comes with the job. This time it feels different."

"It feels the same to me."

"I don't know. I've always been good at compartmentalizing my feelings. All the bad stuff gets locked in a vault. I guess... since we weren't on a mission, this is affecting me like it would if I were a normal citizen. I don't think I'm making any sense."

"No. You are. I get that. For me, it always affects me the same way. I'll never get used to the evil in the world. That there are people who would attack an innocent woman with a small child like that. It's so senseless."

"Despicable."

"That's why we put ourselves through this. For them. The problem is that we can't save everyone. Every victim is hard for me too. Even now, I want to go out and knock some heads together and save somebody. All over London there are girls in sex slavery. Right this very minute. And where am I? I'm in a five-star hotel, with my new husband, who

I'm dying to make love to. Those girls are going through hell. Why am I so lucky? I have a great life with you."

The mention of her wanting to make love to me, sent a wave of desire through my body. I tamped it down. It didn't seem like the right time.

"The grace of God, I guess."

"For sure."

"I'm going to take a shower. That'll make me feel better."

"I'll be waiting," Jamie said, with a glimmer in her eye.

I knew what she meant.

That didn't make me go any faster. The hot shower felt so good I didn't want to get out. The water soothed some of the pain I was feeling. The luxury shower had several different pulsating features. It felt like I was standing up in a jacuzzi.

Even then, it couldn't take away all the pain. The soap scrubbed off the blood on the outside but couldn't fully erase the sorrow I felt on the inside. That would take time, I decided. Being with my wife for the first time would go a long way to helping me recover.

While I felt refreshed somewhat, I was still exhausted. The hot water had relaxed me to the point that I was suddenly sleepy. It had been nearly thirty hours since I had closed my eyes and slept.

Once I was dry, I slipped the bathrobe back on. When I stepped out of the bathroom, I stopped in my tracks.

Jamie had tears running down her cheeks.

"What's wrong?" I asked.

She pointed to the television screen. The sound was on. The headline on the screen in bold red letters blared in my head like an ambulance siren.

ONE PERSON DEAD FROM KNIFE ATTACK ON LONDON TUBE.

6

"I'm so sorry, Alex," Jamie said.

She stood from the edge of the bed and was now next to me, her arm wrapped around mine as she tried to comfort me. I'd just learned that the woman on the subway platform had died.

It felt like a knife had been thrust deep into my heart as well. I didn't remember feeling such pain.

When I tasted blood, I realized I was biting my lip. My lame attempt at fighting back the tears so Jamie wouldn't see me cry. Why I thought that was necessary, I hadn't a clue. Jamie knew what I was feeling as much as I did. I'm sure she felt it herself.

Remorse. Anger. Sadness. Guilt. Rage.

I wanted to kill the man who did this.

Jamie must've sensed what I was thinking. "We have to let it go," she said gently. "If we don't, this will consume our honeymoon."

"I want to find him," I said, as I pulled my arm away from her and began pacing the room. "If I could get hold of the security footage, I might be able to hunt him down."

"You know as well as I do that he's disappeared. He'll blend into the Muslim community and won't come out for weeks. If he's still in the country."

"We have to do something."

"Let the authorities handle it. Like you said, we're not on a mission. We just happened upon that attack."

Jamie stood next to me again. She stopped me from pacing. She held my arms still.

"Listen to me," she said firmly. "That man was going to knife somebody."

"I could've stopped it."

"What if we had gotten on a different subway car? The attack would've taken place anyway. It's not our fault."

What she said was true. I hadn't even thought about that. The man would've attacked someone whether we were there or not. If I let it, I could become obsessed with finding him and ruin our honeymoon.

Her words eased my tension somewhat. I pulled her closer to me. This was where our marriage was so meaningful. In our line of work, we saw the highest highs and lowest lows imaginable. We saw evil and destruction at its most heinous levels. Death was a way of life for us. Most people dealt with life and death matters a few times in their lifetimes. We dealt with it on almost every mission. Most of the time, there was no time to grieve any loss of life. We felt lucky we weren't the ones killed. We knew that in a few days we had to face the same death and danger all over again.

Curly always said we shouldn't get emotionally involved in the victims. He drilled in us to stay emotionally unattached to whatever happened. The truth was that had we been on a different subway car, we'd see the news reports of a subway knife attack and be unemotional about it. Maybe slightly angry and sad, but not devastated. Like how I felt now.

What happened was a matter of chance. Bad luck had us on the same car as the assailant and the woman with the child. Maybe God put us there to stop it and we failed. Whether chance or divine providence, I couldn't do anything about it now.

Curly also said, *everyone dies eventually, but not everyone really lives.* Meaning don't spend one second on things you can't control. I was usually good about tamping down my feelings. For some reason, this death was hitting me hard.

I can't let it affect our honeymoon. That's not fair to Jamie.

"What do you want to do?" I asked her.

"There's nothing we can do. I don't think we should go hunting for the attacker."

"That's not what I meant. I agree with you. What do you want to do now?"

"I think we should get some sleep," she said. "I'm exhausted. I know you are too."

"I don't think I can sleep. But you go ahead."

"I'm going to stay up with you."

"I'm okay."

"I'm worried about you," she said.

"I'll be okay," I said more strongly. "It's just going to take a few minutes to get over the shock of it."

The remote to the television was on the bed, and I picked it up and roughly turned off the set. All the news was doing was reminding me of something I now had to forget. And quickly.

Easier said than done.

Much easier if it wasn't staring me in the face. I felt better when the screen went dark. Another thing I learned from Curly. Don't obsessively replay the scenes again and again in your mind. Do your analysis, learn from it, and move on. The subway car analysis was easy. I should've confronted the man and made him show me his hands.

Nothing I could do about that now. Close the file. It was as simple as that. I wouldn't make that same mistake again.

Rehashing it again in my mind was a waste of energy. Jamie was right, I needed to focus on her and our honeymoon. What I really wanted to do was to be close to her and make love, but it didn't seem right.

"If we're not going to sleep," I said, "then let's get dressed, go shopping, go to the tea at Kensington Palace, and get this honeymoon started. That'll take our mind off of things."

"That sounds like a plan," Jamie said excitedly as she bolted into action and began going through her backpack to get out a change of clothes.

"Let's stop by the gift shop and get some energy drinks," I said. "I'm going to need something to keep me going."

Jamie walked over and planted a big kiss on my lips. "There's you some energy," she said.

A jolt of adrenaline shot through me like a B-12 shot.

"There's more of that for you later," she said with a sly grin.

At that moment, I had enough energy in me that I felt like I could run a marathon.

* * *

Iran

Pok panicked.

He hadn't expected Alex and his wife to exit the hotel so quickly. His team wasn't prepared. He was kicking himself for relaxing. If he had blinked, he would've missed them leaving. By chance, he saw them walk out and get into a cab.

A lapse in judgment. Pok was busy gloating about the success of the first mission. Now, he was beside himself for fear that they wouldn't be able to pull off another knife attack. He desperately wanted to duplicate the success of the subway attack.

"Where did they go?" Pok shouted to his room full of observers.

No one responded.

"Which cab did they get in?" he asked urgently.

"Does anyone have eyes on them?"

No matter how many times he repeated the question, no one could answer. Pok picked up a notebook and threw it across the room.

"I want you to find them. And find them now!"

He knew how difficult that would be.

They could be anywhere.

* * *

Kensington Palace Pavilion
Kensington Gardens
Orangery Tea Room

After shopping, we went back to the hotel and changed into nicer clothes. Then we rushed over to Kensington Palace so we could take the tour of the castle before our reservation at three for afternoon tea. A nagging ache in my heart reminded me of the earlier day's events, but I was feeling better. Jamie had a way of doing that to me.

Security was tight at the Palace. Not only was it a tourist attraction, but it was also the personal residence of the Prince of Wales. His niece was getting married that weekend and the Palace grounds were bustling with activity.

Jamie and I acted like a couple of school kids. Joking. Laughing. Kidding. Acting silly even.

"The rest of the day, we're only allowed to speak in a British accent," Jamie had said earlier while we were shopping.

Jamie was good at it. I couldn't tell the difference between her and the real Brits. Me... I was horrible. Jamie said my accent was a cross between an Irish brogue, an Australian, and a Hungarian gypsy.

She changed the rules of the game. "Don't let anyone else hear you but me," she insisted right before we entered the tearoom. "You sound funny."

"I'm glad I amuse you," I said.

Seeing her smile and laugh released the tension deep inside of me. "I'm going to try my accent on the waitress and see what she thinks," I said after we were led to our table.

"Don't you dare!" Jamie retorted. "You let me do the talking."

"I think I sound like Sean Connery. You know James Bond."

A little teacup was on our table. I held it up, "I would like a little shot of tea," I said in my mutt of an accent.

"That doesn't sound like Sean Connery. It sounds more like Sean Penn."

We were so tired, we were giggling.

"Let me do the ordering," Jamie said, laughing so hard she was almost crying.

I know I had a mischievous grin on my face, by the way she refused to make eye contact with me. Every time she'd see me, she'd burst into laughter. So, she kept her head to the side, only glancing at me out of the corner of one eye.

When the waitress approached, Jamie put on a friendly but serious face giving me one last glare which meant not to say anything.

"We'll have the afternoon tea sandwiches," she said. Not in a British accent, but in a formal, elegant way. "We'll also have the scones with welsh butter. And the ones filled with cream and jam."

"We also have a selection of afternoon tea cakes," the waitress said.

"That would be splendid," I chimed in, unable to keep from laughing.

Jamie shushed me.

The waitress seemed to be humoring me. "Would you like tea or coffee, sir?"

"Yes, please!" I almost sprayed water from my nose as I had just taken a sip and tried to contain my laughter.

She's going to think we're drunk.

"She meant do you want either or?" Jamie asked like a mother would say to her child.

"I'll take either." For some reason that seemed funny to me, and I started giggling again.

"You need to choose one or the other," the waitress said with a grin.

"This is afternoon tea, so I must have tea," I said in my most serious British, whatever it was, voice.

I felt punch drunk. Like I was so tired, I wasn't tired anymore. All the caffeine from the energy drinks had worn off, and I was going on adrenaline again. Coffee didn't seem like a good idea.

"I'll have a glass of sparkling wine," Jamie said.

"Can I get a martini, shaken not stirred?" I said in my fake Sean Connery voice.

Jamie rolled her eyes.

"Ignore him," Jamie said to the waitress. "Just bring him some tea to start."

When the waitress left, I said, "I think she liked my British accent."

"I think she thought you were ridiculous."

"That's rubbish!"

"Don't embarrass me, Alex."

I pulled out my phone and pulled up a search engine.

"What are you doing?" Jamie asked.

"Looking up British slang words."

"This should be good," Jamie said sarcastically. "By the way. Take your elbows off the table. This is not a local diner. You're at Kensington Palace."

Jamie leaned toward me and said slightly above a whisper. "Pretend you're having tea with the Queen. Act like you belong here. I don't want people thinking I'm married to a Neanderthal."

I ignored the comment and found a list.

"Chirpse means a flirt," I blurted out.

"You certainly are a chirpse."

"Tosspot is a fool. Tool is an idiot."

"Three for three. Are you sure these aren't slang words for you?"

This time I rolled my eyes.

"Sussed means to discover someone's true nature."

"I can relate to that," Jamie said this time laughing out loud. "I'm learning something new about my husband by the minute."

"You're bashy," I said.

"What does that mean?"

"Nice to look at."

"Thank you, kind sir."

"You're also a Yats."

"Okay. I'll play your game. What's a Yats?"

"A female."

"I'm definitely that as well."

The lady brought our tea about that time and Jamie's glass of wine.

"You're also trollied," I said, after the waitress left. Jamie seemed to be tiring of the game.

"Haven't we had enough of British slang words?" she asked.

"You're also knackered."

"Alex!"

"Knackered means you're tired."

"I am that. I can barely keep my eyes open. Even with all the caffeine."

"Trollied means you're drunk."

"I'm not drunk! She just brought my wine. I haven't had my first sip." Jamie took a big sip for emphasis. "Now I have," she said, and then burst out laughing like she'd already had a couple of drinks.

She shushed me. We were making a scene.

A few minutes later, the waitress approached with a tiered tray full of bite sized sandwiches and sweets. My face was still buried in the phone looking up British slang words.

"Don't you think my wife is dog's bollocks and bee's knees?" I asked the waitress.

A huge grin came on her face. Jamie's eyes widened in surprise like she couldn't believe the words that had just come out of my mouth.

"What did he just call me?" Jamie asked the waitress.

"He said you were awesome," she replied, grinning.

"Bob's your uncle," I added.

Jamie looked at me with her mouth twisted into a confused look. Then she looked at the waitress. "What did he say?"

"There you go!" she replied.

I scanned the phone for more words. The waitress decided to join in.

"He's lost the plot," the waitress said to Jamie.

I started scrolling through the terms.

"He's a bit wonky," she added.

"Hey!" I said, amused that she was blurting out names before I had time to look them up.

"I remember that one," Jamie said. "Wonky means you're crazy."

"Crazy about you," I said.

"What does 'lost the plot' mean?" Jamie asked the waitress.

"It means that he's crazy. Same as wonky."

"That he is," Jamie agreed.

"You two make a cute couple," the waitress replied.

"We're on our honeymoon!" I said with a huge grin on my face.

"That explains it. Congratulations."

The waitress walked away, and I was totally satisfied with the exchange. A little levity was exactly what we needed.

Jamie took another sip of her sparkling wine. She looked so pretty it almost took my breath away. I couldn't help myself. I reached across the table and kissed her. She smelled sweet. And tasted like the wine.

"Do you think you can just steal a kiss anytime you want, Mr. Halee?"

I reached over and gave her another one.

She motioned for me to move in closer. Then she whispered in my ear. "After we finish eating, would you like to go back to the hotel and steal my virginity?"

"Absobloodylootely!"

I had read that on the list.

"I'll take that as a yes."

I suddenly didn't feel so tired.

* * *

Iran

"We found Halee!" one of Pok's men said almost breathlessly, as he rushed into Pok's office.

A bolt of excitement went through Pok like an electric current.

They'd been searching for nearly four hours for Halee and hadn't had any luck. The couple had left the hotel several hours before, and Pok's men had lost them in a maze of taxis. Pok was about to abandon the search and try again tomorrow. He hadn't expected it to be this difficult.

"Where are they?" Pok said excitedly.

"They're at the Kensington Palace. In the tearoom. They went in about an hour ago."

"Good work. That means they're about done with dinner. We're going to have to hurry."

Pok sprang into action. He found Niazi. "Do you have a man near Kensington Palace?"

Pok pointed to a spot on a London map.

"I can have someone there in ten minutes."

"Halee's in the tearoom. Right here. By the gardens. They should be exiting anytime."

"I'm on it," Niazi said as he got on his phone.

Pok heard him barking instructions.

When Niazi hung up, Pok said, "Even if they leave the tearoom before your man gets there, he can intercept them anywhere along the way. They'll probably walk back to their hotel. Along this path." Pok drew a line on the map.

"I have a man within a few blocks from there," Niazi said. "He has a radio. I'll be in direct communication with him. You tell me when you want him to act."

"We have cameras all along the route. Same as before. Have your man locate a target behind Halee. Then attack him or her with a knife. Hopefully, your man can get away again and we'll have the same outcome as earlier."

"Inshallah."

Pok could hardly contain his excitement. Twice in one day.

And Halee doesn't suspect a thing.

7

Kensington Gardens
London

When finished with afternoon tea, Jamie and I took a stroll in the beautiful Kensington Gardens. Even though the sandwiches and desserts were bite sized, I felt like I'd eaten a full meal. The sugar rush from all the sweets gave me a temporary burst of energy. It seemed to have had the opposite effect on Jamie. She couldn't quit yawning. Probably from the glass of wine.

It did feel good to finally relax from the traumatic events of the day. Not wanting to discuss them, I brought up a different subject.

"Have you thought about who you want to hire at AJAX?" I asked. AJAX was our new corporation we'd be running our covert operations out of.

"I have thought about it. Do you think it's really going to happen?"

"The first ten million dollars was wired into our business account today. I meant to tell you. I forgot. You know... with everything that happened."

Thinking of the woman caused a sharp pain to shoot through my heart and felt like a deep jab of a knife. Then went away as quickly as it came. Either I tamped it down, or I was doing better at dealing with it. Curly always said the residue of a gunfight didn't go away completely until the next one. That probably applied to a knife fight as well. The problem was that I didn't know when our next mission would be or when I could get back in the action and shake this nagging feeling.

Jamie had a way of snapping me back to reality.

"We have ten million dollars in our account, and you were complaining about the bill at the tearoom?" she said with emphasis.

"It cost a hundred and forty dollars!" I retorted. "For some tea and little sandwiches."

"And worth every penny! I loved it. How often do you get a chance to have tea at Kensington Palace?"

Jamie was back to talking in her British accent.

"You're one to talk," I said. "Why didn't you buy that shirt at the women's clothing store?"

"It was a hundred and sixty-five dollars! And it wasn't a shirt. It was a blouse."

"Why didn't you get it?"

"I'm not spending a hundred and sixty-five dollars on any blouse. Unless it has diamonds all over it. Don't you like what I'm wearing?"

Jamie backed away and pulled on her shirt.

"Buy one get one half off," she added. "I only paid sixty for both." Jamie said the words smugly and dripping with satisfaction.

"I do like it. In fact, I like it as much if not more than the more expensive one." I meant it. Jamie had always had good taste in clothes and an eye for bargains.

"That's probably why they trust us with so much money," I continued. "Speaking of saving money, you know... one thing we haven't talked about is where we're going to live when we get home. I think you should move in with me."

"Because you're the man?" she asked strongly.

"No. Because my condo is bigger and has a pool."

"Those are two very good reasons."

"We'll save money not having two places."

"Yes, we will," Jamie said, letting out a big yawn.

"Are you sure you're not too tired to make love?" I was suddenly concerned that Jamie was going to be too exhausted to follow through on our plan. That thought sent me into a mini panic.

"No way! I can't wait!" she said, trying to sound convincing, but she was clearly trying to stifle back another yawn.

"What time is it?" she asked.

"Four thirty."

"After we do stuff... We'll be asleep by six. We can sleep for twelve hours if we want. There's nothing on the agenda for the morning. No place we have to be. We can catch up on our sleep. Like Curly always says."

"Sleep when you're dead," we said in unison.

"Sounds like a good plan." I was glad the "stuff" was still on. Apparently, that was going to be our word for sex.

My heart raced at the anticipation. Feelings of love and desire pulsed through me with every heartbeat.

Jamie snuggled in even closer as we continued to walk through the garden. It felt good and even intensified the feelings of love I had for her at that moment.

"Back to your original question," she said, interrupting my thoughts with her businesslike voice. "I'd like to bring Josh into AJAX," she said. "You know the guy that parachuted into Cuba with me."

"I know who he is," I said tersely.

Jamie slapped me on the arm. Josh and Jamie had weathered a hurricane huddled up together attached to a pole. Josh being there might've saved Jamie's life. That didn't keep me from razzing her about it.

"Josh is a colonel," Jamie explained. "He led many missions in Afghanistan, Syria, and Iraq. He's proficient with a gun. A natural born leader. And fearless. I think he'd be a good tactician to have on the team. I don't know if he'd be interested, but he was the first person I thought of."

Josh led a team of hurricane trackers who flew into hurricanes and gathered vital information for the Air Force. I didn't know if he were obligated to his position or if he could make a career move. He also took out four bad guys while having Jamie's back on a mission. They rescued four teenage girls who'd been kidnapped and forced into sex slavery by a Cuban oligarch. I agreed that he'd be a good addition if we could get him.

I didn't say anything for a good minute, thinking about other possible candidates. Jamie interpreted my silence as jealousy.

"You don't have any reason to be jealous of Josh," she said. "He's married and twenty-five years older than me."

"I know. I've just been *joshing* you. Pun intended," I said as I poked her in the ribs and smiled wide.

Jamie let out a groan.

I kept jabbing her with my fingers.

"Josh... Do you get it? Did you see what I did there?"

Jamie pulled her arm away from mine, stopped walking, and contorted her face into a grimace. "There are two things you're not allowed to do in this marriage, Alex Halee."

"What's that?" I said with a chuckle.

"Talk in a British accent and make corny jokes."

"We've only been married for two days, and you're already telling me what to do."

"Better get used to it."

Jamie suddenly quickened her step. I matched hers, but it startled me.

"Let's get going," she said. "I want to go back to the hotel and show you what you have to look forward to for the next fifty years."

"There you go, telling me what to do again," I said jokingly even though the excitement in me intensified even more. If that was possible.

Jamie was no longer on my arm. She was walking faster. It took several large strides to catch back up.

I was in as big a hurry for the "stuff" as she was.

* * *

I saw the man before Jamie did.

Coming toward us. We were on the walkway that led out of Kensington park.

Middle eastern.

Scruffy beard.

Shifty eyes.

Wearing a jacket. Right hand in the right pocket of his jacket.

My entire body tensed as I was now on full alert. Sirens were going off in my head warning me of the danger and cutting through the fog of the sugar high.

The man was still thirty yards ahead of us, but the gap was closing quickly. We made eye contact. I saw the hate. Same look the other man had.

Between us was a woman walking with a child. A little girl this time. The scene brought back an eerie feeling in me.

Could it be happening again?

Jamie and I were holding hands. I jerked my hand away, startling her. There was not enough time to explain.

I had to hurry. The man was getting close to the woman and young girl.

I nearly sprinted past them. The man pulled his hand out of his jacket.

A knife!

In his right hand. I was headed straight toward him.

Normally, in that situation, I'd change my angle and go to my left. His right. So we'd be perpendicular, and he'd have to slash the knife in an awkward direction. In this instance, I wanted to stay between him and the woman and child.

He wasn't holding the knife like he was going to thrust it forward. His arm was back, like he was going to make a wide sweeping arc.

A mistake.

He would expect me to jump away. Instead, I bolted forward. Closer to him. The last thing he would expect. I turned my body sideways, so I was at a ninety-degree angle to him. Another move that would confuse him.

He tried to adjust the trajectory of the knife, but it was too late. I caught his wrist with my left hand. With one twist, downward, clockwise, his arm became hyperextended. He let out a cry. Almost a shriek. In one motion, I brought my right elbow down right into the back of the joint. The elbow dislocated and every tendon, cartilage and muscle made a crunching sound as they were torn from their normal position.

His entire arm went limp and the knife fell harmlessly away.

I heard the woman scream and out of the corner of my eye, I saw her grab her child.

I wasn't done dealing with the threat. The man's wrist was now limp in my left hand as the arm had no strength to resist. The man balled his fist and made a feeble and reflexive attempt to hit me with his left hand in the back of my head. I intended to reload my elbow and smash it across the side of his head, first.

Before I could, Jamie was at the man's left side doing the same thing I'd done, but in an opposite manner. She grabbed his left wrist with her left hand. She twisted his wrist counter-clockwise, hyperextending the arm in an unnatural position. Then she brought the palm of her right hand directly into the elbow joint with devastating force. The sound of bone cracking and tendons and cartilage exploding in the man's elbow was even louder than it had been when I hit him.

The man cried out in excruciating pain.

Simultaneously, as if we were of one mind, we both swept the man's legs out from under him. Because we were still holding on to his wrists, he fell face first, flat on the pavement. His skull cracked against the concrete, making a horrendous sound. To me, it was music to my ears.

He was out.

I jumped on his back and placed my knee in the middle and began pressing down.

"Alex, don't!" Jamie said. "You'll kill him."

With all my weight on my knee, I had cut off his ability to inflate his lungs with air. He would die within a minute if I didn't release the pressure.

The lowlife would've killed the woman if I hadn't been there. No doubt in my mind. He deserved to die. But Jamie was right. The man was disarmed and no longer a threat. I released my knee. His breathing was still labored.

He'd probably lose both arms. That brought me the satisfaction I needed at the moment.

I noticed the bulge in the back of his pants. The man had a gun. No one was looking. I glanced around to find the location of the security cameras. I put my body between the camera and the man.

I slipped the gun out of the back of his pants and into the front of mine, without anyone seeing.

Then I stepped back to take a couple of deep breaths and assess the scene.

A bicycle policeman arrived almost immediately. Then an ambulance. More police.

Then Mick Weaver. Agent Weaver. MI5 counter-intelligence terrorism unit. The same man who was at the first scene on the subway platform.

He took one look at us and his eyes narrowed, and his brow furrowed.

I shrugged my shoulders knowing what he must've been thinking.

The assailant was loaded into an ambulance. Weaver walked over and looked at the knife. He stooped down and moved it around on the ground with a pen.

"What happened here?" he asked us.

"The man had a knife," I said. "He was going after a woman and her child. Same as before. We took him down before he could do anything."

Weaver pointed toward the beat cop. "The police officer said the man's injured pretty badly."

"He got what he deserved. I didn't want to give him a chance to hurt anyone."

"Where did you learn how to do that?"

"My buddy owns a gym. Back in the states. He teaches self-defense classes."

"Here's what I don't understand," Weaver said, moving in closer to us so only we would hear his words. "There've been two knife attacks in London today. What are the odds that the two of you were at both of them?"

I shrugged my shoulders again.

"Bad luck, I guess. I don't know. I can't explain it."

"Bad luck for the bad guy, it looks like."

"I suppose. Good for the woman. She gets to live. The other one wasn't so lucky. She died."

"I know. I heard. The two of you are going to have to come with me," Weaver said.

"Where are we going?"

"Down to headquarters. I want to ask you some more questions. Look at the security tape. Sort out what happened here today."

I let out a groan.

"I told you what happened."

Jamie added, "Do we have to? We're on our honeymoon. We're also really tired. We were just on our way to our hotel to go to bed and get some sleep."

"Sorry. But yes, you have to. I'll have you out of there in two or three hours. Tops."

Two or three hours!

8

Iran

P ok was furious.

He'd watch the whole debacle play out on screen as Halee and his wife obliterated Niazi's man. The only thing good about it was that he now knew Halee's wife was a CIA officer as well. Had to be in order to pull off the moves he'd seen her make. Watching the man have his arms shattered by his arch enemy was unsettling. Even more so because Niazi's man hadn't followed the plan.

"Your man was supposed to come in from behind," Pok said accusingly to Niazi. "So Halee wouldn't see him." Even though he wanted to make his point, he had to be careful. Niazi wasn't a man to be threatened or disparaged. He was powerful enough to make Pok disappear off the face of the earth if he so chose.

"That's what he was going to do. Walk past him. Then turn and attack the first person behind Halee. But you saw what happened. Halee jumped him. My guy was defenseless, two against one."

"Well, at least one of our attacks was successful," Pok said, talking about the one earlier that ended in the death of the woman. "We've at least gotten Halee's attention now. You now know that Halee is not to be underestimated."

"*I'm* not to be underestimated!" Niazi bellowed. "Tomorrow are the acid attacks. Halee will rue the day he attacked one of my men."

"Remember, you're not supposed to kill Halee yet. I need him to complete my plan. Halee needs to live until Sunday."

"What about the girl? The one with Halee."

Pok paused for a moment to think about the ramifications of attacking Halee's wife. He didn't see a downside. Seeing her face splashed with acid, would bring almost as much satisfaction as seeing Halee killed. Niazi had shown Pok pictures of what acid will do to a person's face. The skin was literally peeled off and the person was permanently disfigured if they even survived it.

"Do whatever you want to her," Pok said. "I don't care. Take her out tomorrow if you want."

I wouldn't want to be that girl.

* * *

Thames House
MI5 Headquarters
Westminster, England

Weaver had kept us waiting for more than two hours. He'd said we'd be out of there in two to three hours.

I wasn't sure what our rights were. Could we walk out if they weren't going to charge us with a crime? In America, they couldn't detain you without a reason. Everything I did was in self-defense. Surely, there was no reason for them to treat us this way.

Jamie had her head on the table resting on her folded arms. She was fading fast.

I felt great. Curly was right. All I needed to get out of my funk was to maim a bad guy. The residue from the morning event had been replaced by the afternoon's confrontation. The emotional complexity of what we did for a living was difficult to explain. Perhaps it was the only way we could keep our sanity. Which sounded strange. Killing or hurting another person, a bad guy, was the way to get over seeing an innocent victim die. Most people wouldn't understand. I wasn't even sure I understood it. Facing people who want to kill you over and over again, unless you kill them first, wasn't something the average person could comprehend.

Video games and action movies tried to simulate the feelings, but they couldn't. Having a man swing a knife at you, and then live to tell about it, left a person with emotions that could never be duplicated without the real danger involved. That's why more than ninety percent of the people in Curly's training program washed out in the first month. Only half of the rest made it to the end. Very few lasted more than a few years in the field.

Curly said Jamie and I were the best of the best. Two of only a dozen who had "it." "What is "it"?" I had asked him.

"I don't know," he replied. "It's like a good woman in bed. You don't know what makes her good. She just is."

I heard footsteps in the hall for the hundredth time. Each time before, they always passed by, and no one came into the room. I'd memorized how many steps before they would fade away to the other end of the hall, and I couldn't hear them anymore. That's how bored I was.

This time, the footsteps stopped right in front of our door. I could hear breathing on the other side.

Weaver walked in. Jamie lifted her head up from the table. Her eyes were sagging, and she rubbed them roughly to try and wake up.

"Sorry to keep you waiting," he said. "I had trouble getting all the security footage together."

"If you have the security footage, why do you need us?" I asked. "You can see what happened."

"I can see it, but I don't understand it. Perhaps you can shed some light on it."

"What's not to understand? Two people with a knife. From news reports it seems like it's happening more and more frequently in London."

"Is it possible you two were the target?" he asked.

"No!" we both said in unison.

"How do you know for sure? It's a pretty big coincidence that the two of you were in direct proximity to both attacks. I don't believe in coincidences."

We didn't either. Curly drilled in us that there were no such thing as coincidences. In the two hours we'd been sitting there, I'd been racking my brain trying to make a connection between us and the two Muslim attackers. I even tried to connect them to the weird occurrences surrounding our wedding. Nothing came to mind that made sense.

I even wondered if somehow Pok was involved.

"If we were the target, why didn't the knifer attack us?" I asked what I thought was the obvious question. "Why did he attack someone next to us?"

"I don't know. You're right. It doesn't make sense."

"We don't even know that the second guy was going to attack someone near us," Jamie said groggily.

"She's right. I saw the guy from a distance and confronted him. He didn't pull the knife until he saw me coming. If I hadn't come after him, maybe he would've kept on walking. So really, the second attack is not like the first one. The first one was a random act of violence. We just happened to be in the wrong place at the wrong time. Because of the first one, I overreacted to the second guy."

"I'm not so sure," Weaver said almost to himself. "I want to show you some footage from our security cameras."

I hoped it wasn't of the woman getting killed on the subway platform. Those images were starting to fade. Seeing them again might cause all the emotions to come flooding back. According to Curly's theory, they might be there until the next fight. Who knew when that would be?

At least now I knew how to get rid of them. Put myself in another dangerous situation. If I had to, I'd go to a bar and start a fight. Or go to a bad area of town and put a sign on my shirt saying, "Please attack me." My thoughts were amusing me. I tried not to let it show on my face.

Not only that, I had a gun now. I'd hidden it outside the MI5 head-quarters in some bushes. A gunfight might be just what the doctor ordered. The psychiatrist ordered as it were.

I'm so weird.

It took all of my energy to keep from smiling. Given the solemnity of the footage we were about to watch, I didn't think that was a good look for Inspector Weaver to see. Was he an agent or inspector? I wasn't sure.

Weaver brought a laptop in with him. He turned it so it faced us. Then stood to the side. A laptop was another thing that helped my mental well-being. I could immerse myself for hours into hacking into a highly secure website. That made me oblivious to everything else around me. Including my feelings. Probably a better cure for my malaise than a gunfight.

Fortunately, the footage was from the London airport. Where we first boarded the Tube. I turned my focus on the footage. The man who killed the woman was on the subway platform. Weaver was narrating as the video rolled.

"That's the man," Jamie said pointing to the computer screen.

"Yes, it is," Weaver confirmed. "That's our assailant. Notice a train comes, and he doesn't get on."

"Is that train going to central London?" I asked to get a sense of where I thought he was heading with this line of thought.

"No. But the next one is. Watch this."

We watched another train stop at the platform. And leave. The man made no move to board. He was nervously pacing back and forth on the platform. Several more trains came and went.

The video skips ahead. I see us enter the platform and walk toward the car. The woman and child were not in the footage. I seemed to remember that they were already on the subway when we boarded.

Suspicious guy followed us on.

Weaver asked, "Why did he skip the one train to central London and wait to get on the same one as you?"

"Maybe he was trying to build up the courage," I said. "He seemed nervous to me."

Jamie wasn't speaking up and adding something to the conversation which surprised me. She must've been really tired. When it came to missions, the operational aspect was what she loved the most. If she could, she'd watch footage of both attacks and analyze them ad nauseum. Her way of getting better. Learning from them. Evaluating what she could've done better.

When I was in college, I played quarterback for Stanford University. Our team lost the National Championship game to Alabama on a last second touchdown. I've never seen a replay of the game, even though it was my best game as a collegian. For me, the past was the past, and I didn't want to relive it.

"That would make sense," Weaver said. "But watch this."

He rewound the footage. Then hit play. Then froze it.

"Look at his face," Weaver said. "His demeanor changed when he saw you."

I had to admit that I saw the man's eyes widen, and his whole body tense up. Something I wasn't going to admit to Weaver. There was something else on the tape that Weaver hadn't noticed. My demeanor changed as well, as soon as I saw the man. I hadn't realized it at the time. Looking back at the tape, I could see my reaction. I knew immediately that the man was a threat.

Guilt came rolling into me like a flood. The whole thing was my fault. If I'd been on a mission, I'd have acted on my recognition of the potential danger. It's instinctive in us to always be alert. Curly drilled that in us. We were to always be on the lookout for threats to our mission. Every day, even at home, I took precautions. Sat with my back to the wall at a restaurant. So that no one could sneak up on me. I'm always aware of my surroundings. Looking for anything suspicious. It's second nature to me. Sometimes I don't even know I'm doing it.

In this instance, I was clearly distracted. Being on my honeymoon was the only excuse I could think of. That and looking forward to getting back to the hotel and being alone with my wife which only made me feel guiltier.

Clearly, I saw the man when we boarded. I knew he was bad news and ignored it. Something I'd have to live with. Even if it was in my subconscious.

"Can you explain that?" Weaver asked, shaking me back into reality as I suddenly realized I hadn't responded the first time he pointed it out.

"The guy was looking for someone to attack," Jamie answered. "He probably saw me and thought I might be a potential victim. Once he got on the train and saw that I was with my husband, he thought better of it and went after the easier target. The woman with a small child. It makes perfect sense to me."

Weaver closed the laptop. His mouth twisted to the side and his eyebrows furrowed like he was considering Jamie's analysis of the situation. The guy was targeting us. I'd felt it on the subway at the time, I suddenly remembered. While I wouldn't admit to Weaver, it had sent my mind scurrying in all different directions, trying to process the why and how.

How did the man know we were in London?

Who sent him?

Why didn't he attack me if I was the target?

Weaver's next question jolted me to the core of my being. "Are you with the CIA?" he asked.

"No!" Jamie and I both answered again in unison.

The truth.

Technically, we were no longer with the CIA. Brad fired us the day before our wedding. Now we worked for AJAX. I wouldn't even know how to describe our relationship with the CIA now. I made a mental note to ask Brad. What do we say if we're asked? The day he fired us, Brad said the CIA would deny even knowing us if we got in a jam. I assumed that was the case if Weaver called them now. Maybe he already had.

"Are you on a mission?" Weaver asked accusingly. "If so, you're supposed to check in with MI6 first. You need their permission before you operate on British soil."

"I have no idea what you're talking about. We're just a couple on our honeymoon," I said.

"And can we go now?" Jamie asked in her most whiny voice. "I haven't slept in two days. I'm exhausted."

"Yes, you can go. But... be warned," Weaver said sternly. "If I find out you're on a mission and you're lying to me, I'll arrest you on the spot. Then your honeymoon will be ruined. That's if you're even married. That might all be a ruse."

I wanted to make a joke about the fact that it had yet to feel like a honeymoon. But I bit my lip to keep from smiling. Jamie wouldn't have been amused either.

Weaver escorted us out of the building. "I'm watching you," he said as we left.

"I'm sure you have better things to do than watch us," I retorted. "We're extremely boring people. Tomorrow, we're going sightseeing. I can assure you, sir, that following us is a waste of your time and resources. Go catch the man who killed that woman."

That seemed to satisfy him, and he walked away. I made a mental note to watch for tails tomorrow. Tonight, I was too tired to bother.

"What do you think about all that?" Jamie asked as she let out another yawn.

"I don't know."

"Do you think Pok could be behind it?"

"I was thinking that might be a possibility."

But how?

9

By the time Jamie and I got back to our hotel shortly after ten o'clock, I'd convinced myself that Pok wasn't involved with all the weirdness surrounding our wedding or the terrorist attacks in London.

Jamie wasn't so sure.

"Pok's a hacker," I argued. "He's not an operator. He doesn't have the capability of coordinating terrorist attacks in the field. Besides, the attackers are middle-eastern."

"That's true, Alex," she said. "But isn't Pok in Iran?"

"I think so. But how would he know we're in London?"

"You can't underestimate Pok. How do you know he's in Iran? A good hacker can find anyone these days. Cell phone records. Travel records. Even social media pages. I bet you could find anyone if you searched long enough for them."

"How would he know we were at Kensington Palace?" I asked.

"I don't know," Jamie said, her eyes furrowed as she was deep in thought. "He couldn't possibly know. Unless he had someone tailing us."

"I haven't sensed any tails. Not that I've been looking for one."

"Me neither."

Tails were something we were trained to spot even if we weren't looking for one. Most countries weren't good at it. Iranian tails were laughable in their incompetence to carry one out. North Korea didn't conduct spy operations outside their region. Those two facts ruled out Pok. He didn't have access to any other spy agencies.

Russians were better trained but could generally be spotted with some evasive maneuvers. We could rule them out. They didn't carry out these types of terrorist attacks. While they wouldn't be opposed to helping Pok under the right circumstances, they wouldn't waste their time on something as small as a couple of knife attacks.

Mossad agents were the best. The Israelis had the techniques down to a science. They could be detected, but it could take hours of evasion before you could discover them. Of course, they weren't involved. They were on our side.

We could rule out being followed.

"Not only that, but the tail would have to know we were coming to London to intercept us at the airport. How could they know?"

Our passports and travel plans were under the names Alex and Jamie Steele. We never traveled under our real names, even if the trip was personal. In this instance, keeping the first names made sense, just to make it easier for us to remember. We only came up with the last name a couple of weeks ago and had never traveled under those names before. No one could possibly have known about our plans to come to London.

That ruled out the first guy having a connection to us.

"The second guy has me baffled," I said to Jamie. "Curly always said there's no such thing as a coincidence."

"While I don't believe in coincidences as a general rule, they do happen," Jamie retorted. "But we don't *know* that the second guy was targeting us. Or anyone else for that matter. You moved on him before he could show his hand, so to speak."

"He was up to something," I said. "I could see it in his eyes. Same as the first guy. I didn't want to make the same mistake twice. I couldn't live with myself if I let another woman die right in front of us."

"You did the right thing. He had a knife. But... that's not what I'm saying. How many middle easterners are there in London?"

"Thousands. Probably tens of thousands."

"Exactly. How many of them are trained terrorists?"

"Probably thousands. What's your point?"

"The point is that the odds are pretty high that we'd run into one on the street. Given our training, we'd spot them in a second. After what happened on the subway platform, you were probably scrutinizing every middle eastern guy you saw. That man might've just been walking somewhere. The odds are he had nothing to do with us."

"First guy was definitely planning something."

"No doubt. And he carried it out. We both sensed it on the train. But that doesn't mean he was targeting us."

The conversation was going nowhere. We were both too tired to be thinking clearly. And we had other things on our minds. At least I did.

"I suppose you're right," I said, wanting to change the subject. I walked over to Jamie and took her in my arms and tried to give her a seductive kiss.

She pushed me away which startled me.

"Hey!"

"You stink," she said, lifting her arm and smelling herself. We had been out in the hot and humid London heat for most of the afternoon and then were stuck in a dank MI5 interrogation room for the better part of three hours.

"So do I," Jamie said. "I'm taking a shower. You can take one after me."

Before I knew it, she was in the bathroom and the shower was running. That gave me time to continue to think about Pok. I hated it when those nagging feelings consumed me. More often than not, they were right. If I ignored them, I usually regretted it. I had to keep reminding myself that we were on our honeymoon and not on a mission.

More than likely, I was just being paranoid.

Who could blame me after what I saw happen on that subway car?

But... my job wasn't to protect all of London from terrorist attacks. They had tens of thousands of intelligence agents, police officers, and operatives who could take on that job. Mick Weaver seemed capable. That brought a smile to my face. The man was good. He knew right away we were CIA. Denying it didn't fool him. He might even put a tail on us tomorrow. British tails weren't always easy to spot unless we took evasive measures. If we did, Weaver would know for sure we were operatives.

Former operatives.

What were we? I couldn't get used to the fact that we were no longer with the CIA.

It didn't matter. Tomorrow was going to be an uneventful day. I had convinced myself that the events of the day were coincidences.

Tomorrow, we'd go sightseeing. Get this honeymoon started.

No! Not tomorrow. Starting tonight!

I didn't hear the water running. Five minutes later, Jamie walked out of the bathroom in a silky white nightgown.

"Do you like it?" she said.

"No," I replied, standing from the bed and walking toward her. "I don't like it. I love it!"

"I bought it special. For our wedding night. It's a surprise for you. I hope you do love it."

I did. When I got to her, I intended to show her how much I loved it.

"Don't touch me!" she said as she put her hand on my chest and pushed me away. "I just took a shower. I put on perfume just for you. Don't ruin it."

She did smell good. Some kind of flowery fragrance was filling the room.

"I won't be long," I said excitedly as I rushed into the bathroom.

I saw Jamie yawn as I took one more look at her before I closed the door.

This'll be the fastest shower I've ever taken.

* * *

It wasn't the fastest shower I'd ever taken.

The hot pulsating water felt too good to just get in and out. Plus, halfway through the shower, the thought hit me like a semi-truck. What if Pok somehow hacked into London's security camera system? What if he was following us on the cameras?

My imagination began to run wild like a stallion let loose on a range in Wyoming.

The code started appearing in my mind. Numbers and characters were forming into concise and orderly patterns. I was trying to figure out how I would hack into the London camera system.

Is it possible?

No!

Why not?

Jamie said that there were over six-hundred-thousand cameras in London. Did Jamie say that? I suddenly couldn't remember if she said it or if I'd read it somewhere. Didn't matter. The point was that there were cameras everywhere. If Pok was in Iran, he could coordinate these attacks with Iranian sleeper cells.

The airport! Our plane reservation.

Did Pok change it? If so, he'd know when we were arriving. He'd guess we were taking the tube to central London. He might even know our hotel reservation.

How? He wouldn't know our last name. As far as I knew, he didn't know Jamie was my fiancé.

And my email was secure. My firewalls were impenetrable. That was a ridiculous thought. No code made by man was foolproof. Of course, anything could be hacked into. Just because we haven't done it, doesn't mean it can't be done. Same with the security cameras. I'm sure London has taken extreme precautions. Still... a man like Pok might be able to penetrate them.

I scrubbed my head with shampoo.

Didn't I already wash my hair?

My mind was a jumbled mess. I had too many things going at once. The questions were hitting me faster than machine-gun fire.

How did Pok hack into my cell phone and find out our wedding plans?

Was he behind changing the florist? The limo?

Did he hack into Curly's cell phone and change the date? That seemed possible. Curly's phone was from the dark ages.

How did Pok hack into my phone and change the text to Curly? When I looked at the thread, my text to Curly said Wednesday. I would swear on a stack of Bibles in a court of law I texted him Tuesday as the day of our wedding.

A panic rushed through me as fast as the pulsating jets which were pounding my body.

How did Pok hack into London's security camera system?

Jamie is waiting for me!

Am I imagining the whole thing?

How long have I been in the shower?

Judging by my hands, which were starting to wrinkle, I'd been in the shower too long. Jamie wouldn't be happy.

I rinsed one last time and turned off the water. After toweling off, I brushed my teeth. Jamie didn't like for me to wear cologne, so I didn't put any on. The robe with the word *His* on it hung on a hook on the door. Jamie had obviously done that for my benefit.

Suddenly, thoughts of Pok and hacking were a distant memory.

Finally, I was going to get to be with my wife. I had to make sure I was in the right frame of mind. Part of me wanted to pull out my laptop and start seeing if hacking into the London camera system was even possible. The other half thought I was crazy. The most beautiful girl in the world to me was waiting on the other side of the door.

I took a deep breath. Two of them. Suddenly, I felt nervous. My hand shook. My heart raced. I couldn't remember ever being this nervous. I looked at myself in the mirror. *You got this!*

I flipped off the bathroom light and walked into the bedroom area of our luxurious suite. What a perfect setting for our first time. The lights were dimmed. Jamie was under the covers.

"Honey," I said gently as I got into bed next to her.

No response. She was sound asleep!

10

Day Two

The next morning

The first night sleeping in a bed with my new bride had not gone at all like I'd envisioned it. The next morning, I woke up about thirty seconds before Jamie did. When I opened my eyes, we were facing each other, our heads twelve to fourteen inches apart. Her being the first thing I saw that morning brought a flood of joy into my heart. I lifted my head slightly to see the time.

8:26.

We'd slept nearly ten hours. Much needed rest. While we still hadn't "slept" together in the Hollywood sense, or "laid" together in the biblical sense, I still felt intimate with her. We slept together in the same bed for the first time, and it felt good to wake up next to her.

Jamie must've felt the movement because she slowly opened her eyes. She smiled when she saw me.

What happened next shouldn't have been a surprise. How movies and television depict couples waking up in bed together were not at all realistic and bordered on the absurd. After a long night of sleep, the first thing they often did was start kissing passionately and ravaging each other with lovemaking.

Within seconds of Jamie seeing me, both of us, at the exact same moment, put our hands over our mouths, jerked our bodies away from each other so we had our backs to each other and then bolted out of bed. The last thing I wanted was for my new bride to smell the foul odor coming from my mouth. A broken garbage disposal wouldn't smell worse.

She must've been thinking the same thing because she was across the room as far away as possible from me. Her hand was no longer on her mouth but was in her hair, straightening it.

Horrified, I made a bee line for that bathroom and beat her to it. After brushing my teeth vigorously, I gargled twice with mouthwash. My hair was also mussed, and I straightened it. Grungy sleep gunk had crusted on my eyelids. I brushed them off.

Only then did I surrender the bathroom.

Jamie went right in after me and was in there for a good five minutes. When she came out, she looked more like herself. I came up to her to give her the first kiss of the day. She pushed me away.

"I haven't brushed my teeth yet. Trust me. You don't want to kiss me."

"You were in there for five minutes. I figured you were brushing your teeth."

"I don't like to until I've had my coffee."

The room had a coffee maker, Jamie walked over to it and was looking through the various brands.

"Decaf!" she said with disgust. "I'm not having that. I need caffeine." She found what she was looking for and put it in the coffee maker.

"How come you don't want to brush your teeth before you have coffee?" I asked.

"The mint in the toothpaste ruins the taste."

Something I didn't know about her. I suddenly realized my fantasy of a lifetime of morning sex was dashed on the first day. It also didn't take long to realize Jamie was also not a morning person. I knew that, but not to this extent. When I woke up, I was raring to go. Jamie was groggy. Almost punch drunk. She got back into bed, laid her head down on the pillow and closed her eyes.

Not until the beep of the coffeemaker, did I see signs of life in her again. With each sip, her eyes opened a little wider, and her speech got a little more coherent. By the end of the first cup, she was almost back to her old self. After a second cup, she was ready to take on the world.

"I'm famished!" she said.

I suddenly felt it too. My stomach growled. We hadn't eaten since afternoon tea at Kensington Palace.

Jamie disappeared into the bathroom again. This time when she came out, she was dressed for breakfast. Her teeth were brushed, and she laid a big kiss on me, sending a wave of desire through my body like I'd been hit by a lightning bolt. I kissed her harder.

"I'm so sorry I fell asleep on you last night," she said. "I feel really bad. It was supposed to be our wedding night."

"It's not your fault," I said. "The day certainly didn't go like we'd planned.

"Let's go have some breakfast," she said excitedly. "Then we can come back to the room. It'll be fun." She winked at me as she said it.

"I thought you wanted our first time to be at night."

"It's nighttime somewhere."

I wasn't going to argue with that logic.

* * *

The breakfast buffet at the Palace Hotel was spectacular. The hostess explained the intricacies of it.

"A full English breakfast is called a 'fry-up,'" she explained. "In Ireland it's sometimes called a chub."

Jamie and I looked at each other with the same fascination.

"We have a hot and a cold breakfast. Hot includes eggs and meats. We have baked beans, bubble and squeaks."

She must've seen the look of confusion on our faces because she said, "potatoes and cabbage."

Then it became like a game to her as she clearly found amusement in throwing out names we didn't know.

Black pudding was sausage. Sausage could also be called bangers or hog's pudding.

Tattie scones were potatoes. Haggis and oatcakes were also on the menu. Soda bread. An Irish bread, she explained.

We learned that a traditional English breakfast consisted of more than forty interchangeable items. Eggy bread, crumpets, jolly boys, which she explained were pancakes. Crempog—Welsh pancakes. Every kind of imaginable bread was included.

"Do you have English muffins?" I asked jokingly in my fake British accent, much to Jamie's chagrin based on the groan she let out. The waitress didn't seem to mind.

"Of course," she said. "Complete with every possible compliment."

I assumed compliments were jams, jellies, butter, and cream cheese. Among other things.

"The buffet also had a variety of fish dishes," the lady continued. "Including kippers, which are herring, arbroath smokies or smoked haddock, kedgeree, a curried fish dish, and deviled kidneys."

I didn't ask what deviled kidneys were, and didn't want to know, since I planned on avoiding all of the fish dishes. "Everything sounds good and all, but just give me a plateful of eggs, sausage, and hash browns."

"You're such a man," Jamie said. "I want to try one of everything."

Before I knew it, she was at the huge presentation, going from each section to look at all of the delicacies.

"Look, they have caviar! And champagne! I'm going to need more than one plate."

"Pace yourself," I said. "You can always come back for more."

They had more different things on the buffet than I could eat in a week. I remembered thinking that it was a good thing we were going to be there for five days. The breakfast buffet might be one of the memorable highlights of our trip.

How were we going to make love for the first time after stuffing ourselves with so much food? What we'd really need to do was go for a five-mile run to burn it off.

When I was halfway through my third plateful, I saw them.

A couple.

American.

Walking into the restaurant.

The spitting image of us.

He was tall, muscular, with sandy blond hair. Clearly a football player either now or in his college days. Looked like a California beach dude. She was drop-dead-model gorgeous. Tall as well. Thin. Perfect features. Blondish hair. When she walked, she glided across the room like a swan moving effortless across a pond.

Since I'd known Jamie, there were only a handful of times when she wasn't the prettiest girl in the room. This was one of those times, although I wouldn't say that to her face.

"Look over toward the door," I said to Jamie. "Discreetly."

She turned her head slightly. We were trained how to notice things without being noticed. She must've been thinking the same thing because she let out a wow.

"That couple looks familiar," I said.

"She's a famous model. What's her name? I know it. It's not a name. It's an initial. Q. W. T. Oh! It's on the tip of my tongue."

Everyone in the entire restaurant was staring at the woman, so I didn't feel out of place doing the same. A couple of young girls, maybe ten or eleven years old. went up to the lady and asked for her autograph. She graciously provided them one. Then a selfie. A small crowd gathered around her. She greeted every one of them and gave an autograph until the last person left satisfied.

Her smile was mesmerizing. Not the least bit pretentious. The man stood dutifully to the side. Like he was used to it.

They went through the buffet. As they entered the eating area with the tables, they walked straight toward ours. That startled me for a moment. If the man hadn't had a huge grin on his face, I might've wondered if something was up. Out of habit, we were sitting at a table with our backs against the wall. Typical CIA protocol.

"Is your name Alex Halee?" he asked.

How did he know my name? We were traveling under the names Alex and Jamie Steele.

Before I could answer he said, "My name is Tad Gentry." He sat his plate down on the table and extended his hand. I wiped mine on a napkin and then shook it.

"Do I know you?" I asked.

"I played football at UCLA. You were starting quarterback for Stanford. I played against you. Well, not really. I was a freshman. You were a senior. I got in for a few plays."

"Okay," I said hesitantly but in a more friendly manner. With everything that had happened, my threat radar was on ten. It didn't take long to realize he was probably who he said he was. A tourist on vacation. Jamie confirmed it even more in my mind when she confirmed the identity of the girl.

"You're a famous model," Jamie said. "I've seen you on the cover of magazines."

"My name's Gina Garth," she said humbly and meekly. "Well, Gina Garth Gentry, now."

"G! That's the initial." Jamie smacked the palm of her hand on her forehead. "I was trying to remember your name."

"That's right. But my friends call me Gigi."

"Would you like to join us?" Jamie asked.

That sent a groan through my head. I wished she'd asked me first. The plan had been to finish breakfast and go back to the room. My heartbeat slowed down considerably when they sat down.

"What brings you to London?" Jamie asked.

Gigi flashed her humongous wedding ring. "Honeymoon. We're new-lyweds. Can you tell? We just got married." She snuggled up next to him with a hug then started to move food around on her plate. The contrast was startling. His plate was piled with food like mine. Hers was barely covered with only a few items. Unlike Jamie's plate which was more like mine and Tad's. Filled to overflowing.

"When did you get into town?" Jamie asked.

My bride was outgoing and friendly when she wanted to be. She could carry the conversation if she had to. If I didn't curb it at some point, she'd spend two hours or more talking to them. People fascinated Jamie. She loved meeting new people. I had to admit that these two were more interesting than most.

"We've been here for two days," Gigi said in a sweet and silky voice that matched her pleasant smile. She really was stunning.

"Have you seen any good sights that you would recommend?" I asked.

Gigi looked at Tad with an embarrassed look. His was more of a sat-isfied smile. Almost a mischievous grin as his lips contorted and his eyes shifted back and forth.

"We haven't really left our room much," Tad said almost embarrass-ingly. "If you know what I mean."

I did know and I was jealous! Actually... I didn't know what that was like.

"We're newlyweds as well," Jamie said displaying her ring for Gigi to look at. Gigi took Jamie's hand and looked at it admiringly. Although Jamie's ring was nothing like hers. Jamie seemed proud anyway.

My thoughts were on what Tad had said. I wanted to shout at the top of my lungs, "We're newlyweds, but we haven't had sex yet! At this rate, I'm not sure we ever will!"

I refrained and settled in.

The conversation seemed like it was going to go on for a while.

11

The conversation with the Gentrys continued even longer than I'd expected. For more than an hour. Tad and I talked football, and the girls talked fashion, modeling, runways, hair, makeup, and any number of topics I had no idea Jamie was so interested in.

The Gentry's were good conversationalists and easy to talk to. I had to admit that I genuinely liked them. A really good thing came out of the conversation when Tad asked, "What do the two of you do for a living?"

"Exports," I blurted out.

"Imports," Jamie said at the exact same moment.

We looked at each other.

"Imports and exports," I hurriedly said. Truthfully, we hadn't talked about the cover for our new corporation. What did AJAX do? Brad, our handler, said that was for us to figure out. The cover was important because we would use it as the ruse to travel into foreign countries. For the right business reason, we could even go into middle eastern countries, soviet bloc, or Asian theatres and be welcomed with little to no questions. A perfectly planned cover would open all kinds of opportunities for us to conduct covert operations in those countries.

Humanitarian was the logical choice, but it was overdone. Countries were more skeptical and on the lookout for covert operations under the guise of a charity. We needed a solid business reason for AJAX to exist. One that wouldn't invite scrutiny. Neither of us were prepared to answer the obvious next question.

"What do you import and export?" Tad asked.

I said the first thing that popped into my head. "Art!"

Jamie tilted her head in disbelief.

"We buy and sell fine art," I said like it was true.

A broad smile came on Jamie's face. I knew that'd make her happy.

"That's right," she said. "We travel the world in search of artwork to collect."

"That's so fascinating," Gigi said. Tad didn't seem the least bit interested.

I wasn't interested in art either, except for that it was the perfect cover. Jamie loved art. Her minor in college was Art History. On the few times we traveled to a foreign country together, she always wanted to go to the local art museum. That wasn't always possible considering the nature of our operations. When we did, she was like a kid at the zoo. She could spend hours in a museum. I wanted to leave after ten minutes. Something that would have to change now that we were in the art business. Apparently.

"Have you been to the National Gallery?" Gigi asked.

"No!" Jamie said. "But that's the first thing on our list. Have you been there?"

I remembered Jamie mentioning that the National Gallery was the biggest art gallery in all of England. A must see on our list of tourist attractions.

"We're going there now," Tad said. "You guys should come with us."

"We sort of had plans," Jamie said reluctantly.

I could see the disappointment written all over her face. Her shoulders had drooped, and her smile was fake.

"It's okay. We can do that later," I said kind of roughly. "Let's go to the museum with them."

"Are you sure?" Jamie asked me.

"I'm sure." I said it with mixed emotions. Disappointment was mostly what I felt. Then I warmed to the idea. Spending the day with the Gentry's would be fun. Maybe things would be better if our wedding night were actually at night. This time, nothing was going to ruin it. We'd enjoy the day and come back to the room early. It was all planned out in my mind.

"It's settled then," Tad said.

"We'll meet you down in the lobby in ten minutes," I said.

On the way back to the room, Jamie was apologetic. For the second time that morning. "Are you sure you're okay with us going to the art gallery? We could've said no."

"I'm sure," I said sarcastically and for effect even though I really was fine with it. "I'm kidding. Really. It's okay. It'll be fun."

Jamie was clearly excited, and that made me excited. The main thing was we were married, and we were together. That fact warmed my heart.

"I'll make it up to you," Jamie said. "I promise. We'll go to the museum. Then catch some other tourist sights and come back to the room and make love. It's going to be a great day."

"I hope there aren't any more incidents," I said, thinking about the events of the previous day.

"There won't be. I think you're right. Those were isolated and not related to us at all."

At breakfast, Jamie and I had talked about it at length before Tad and Gigi showed up. My angst from the night before had dissipated. I didn't see any way Pok could orchestrate such an extensive operation. It wasn't his style. He was a cybercriminal. He got his kicks stealing money. I'd never known him to be involved in any type of violence.

"Do you want to bring the gun just in case?" Jamie asked.

The gun was carefully hidden in the room.

"I don't think I could get in the National Gallery with it. I'm guessing they have metal detectors."

"You're probably right. Besides, someone with a knife couldn't get in either."

"They wouldn't attack a tourist area. I don't think, anyway. Besides, Tad looks like he could handle himself as well. Between the two of us, no one's going to mess with our girls."

Tad played safety in college at UCLA. Second team All American his senior year. I knew from experience that safeties were tough guys. We called them headhunters. They sat back in the secondary waiting for someone to come into their area. Then they laid the wood on them and took their heads off if given the chance. Receivers hated hard hitting safeties like Tad. So did quarterbacks. Many times, after I escaped the pocket and was running for my life, a safety had made me see stars.

"Thank you for doing this," Jamie said sincerely as we were about to leave the room. She hugged me tightly.

By that point, I didn't mind. Seeing her this happy, made me happy.

* * *

Iran

Pok was almost nauseated. Niazi had just shown him more pictures of people who'd been attacked with acid. The images of the victims were horrifying.

Niazi had been almost gleeful in describing how his men would pull off the acid attacks today. This was what trained killers like him lived for. Inflicting as much pain and terror on innocent civilians as possible.

Pok was more comfortable behind a computer, figuring out how to steal people's money. This kind of extreme violence was new to him. And he liked it.

"Torture in a bottle," was what Niazi called it.

When Pok's assistant mentioned innocent people being hurt, Niazi exploded.

"There are no innocent people in the west. They support their leaders who start endless wars against my people. They put economic sanctions on our government, so our people barely have enough to live on. It's a war. Everyone is fair game in war."

Pok had to search his soul to see if he agreed. While Alex Halee wasn't innocent, his wife was. Did she deserve to be maimed and disfigured for the rest of her life simply because she was married to the lowlife scum? The plan was to attack her with the acid today. Right in front of Halee. At first, he had been elated. Now he wasn't so sure.

Of course, if his plan came to fruition, she'd be a widow in a few days anyway, Pok realized. That was his main goal. Kill Halee. End the threat to his enterprise. The dirty bomb was to kill thousands of people. What did Pok care if Halee's wife got what Alex deserved?

At this point, Pok could do nothing about it. The genie was out of the bottle, so to speak. He was so far into it nothing was going to stop Niazi from carrying out the plan. Pok couldn't stop it even if he wanted to. Which he didn't. Even if it did make him queasy. He just wished Niazi would quit talking about the acid.

"Most of the time we use sulfuric acid," Niazi explained even though Pok had not asked. Niazi loved talking about the weapons of his warfare.

"Occasionally nitric acid is used," he continued. "Actually, you can use any number of things. Even household products. Hydrochloric acid can be used, but it's not as damaging to skin. Even things like bleach and rust remover can do a tremendous amount of damage. Hydroxyzine peroxide is a good substance. Ammonia. Chlorine. Even a pool cleaner will blind a person if thrown right into the eyes. Sulfuric acid is the best, though. That's what my men are using today."

"How do they make it and carry it without harming themselves?" Pok asked reluctantly, not sure he even wanted to know.

"They mix it at their house and put it into a squirt bottle. That way they can direct a stream directly onto a person without getting any on themselves."

"What are the effects of the acid?"

"Sulfuric acid will peel the skin right off the body. Normally, it's not fatal. That's the beauty of it. It causes excruciating pain. I've seen it firsthand. We tested different chemicals on numerous prisoners. It took many attempts, but we eventually perfected it. Sulfuric acid will make a person suffer from the burns for the rest of their lives. They'll need a dozen or more surgeries. Skin grafts will be necessary. Most of the time, it'll cause permanent blindness if it comes in contact with the eyes. Which is the goal. Our men are trained to spray it right into the face of the person. The fumes from the acid will burn their lungs and cause breathing problems for the rest of their lives."

Pok shuddered.

"Acid is so much better than knife attacks," Niazi continued. "Knives are fine to hurt or kill a person. But acid terrorizes people. That's what we want. Strike fear in the hearts of our enemies."

Pok made himself overcome any reservations. His Supreme Leader in North Korea would be proud of him. He took several deep breaths to strengthen his resolve. Drawing on his hatred for Halee helped.

Now was not the time for cold feet. It was a time for bold action. These people weren't innocent, Niazi had argued. The west must be fought with every weapon available to them. Halee would not hesitate to kill him. That's what he needed to remember.

Nothing would make Halee suffer more than seeing his new wife lying on the ground, writhing in pain, disfigured for life. Pok needed to focus. They had a lot of work to do before this mission was considered a success. Halee was certainly capable of stopping an attack. It must be planned and timed perfectly.

Pok went back to his office to go over the plan again.

Several minutes later, his assistant burst in without knocking.

"Halee's on the move," he said excitedly.

"Where?"

"He just left the hotel."

"Don't lose him."

Pok pulled the hotel up on his screen. Then rewound until he saw Halee and Jamie walk out of the hotel with another couple. He had to do a double take.

The other couple looked just like Alex and Jamie.

12

National Gallery
Trafalgar Square
London

Going to the National Art Gallery in London with Jamie was like having our own private tour guide. I had no idea she knew so much about art. Tad and Gigi seemed impressed as well, as Jamie's knowledge of painters, paintings, styles of art, and obscure art trivia was on full display.

Had it not been for her, I would've been bored. The plan was to spend two hours at the gallery and then go to the Tower of London. Gigi wanted to see the Crown Jewels displayed there. Jamie wanted to see the weapons armory and dungeon. What a contradiction in personality. Here at the gallery, my bride was totally into the arts. There, it was swords, knives, and weapons of warfare over jewelry.

As it turned out, we were at the National Gallery for nearly four hours, and that wasn't long enough to see everything. I expected it to be torture but was pleasantly surprised. Observing Jamie in her element was as pleasurable as viewing the paintings. Although I enjoyed those as well.

If this was going to be our new business, I'd better learn to appreciate it.

That's what Jamie said after I had blurted out art collecting at breakfast. She was totally into the idea.

"That was brilliant," she said. "We can buy and sell art. I love it."

I was warming to the idea as well. The gallery was giving me a new perspective on the arts. Particularly the Artemisia Gentileschi exhibition.

When we came to that exhibit, Jamie was as excited as a puppy about to be fed a treat. I couldn't even pronounce the artist's name, much less tell who she was.

Jamie knew everything about her.

"Artemisia was an Italian baroque painter of the seventeenth century."

"I thought baroque was a type of musical instrument," I said.

Jamie gave me a glare as if to say, just keep quiet so you don't show your ignorance.

"It's also a style of painting," she explained. "More of a movement than anything else. There's baroque architecture as well. And musical instruments as Alex pointed out."

If Jamie noticed my purposeful smug look, she didn't acknowledge it. She barely took a breath between sentences.

"Artemisia is best known for her biblical paintings," she said.

That explained why Jamie loved her so much. Jamie loved everything Bible.

"According to the exhibition handout, this is the largest collection of Gentileschi paintings ever assembled," Jamie continued.

She then took us through the exhibit pointing out each painting. She barely referred to the guidebook. Most of the paintings she recognized and knew by heart.

Mary Magdalene. Joseph and Potiphar. Lot and his daughters.

"She's particularly known for painting the story of David and Bathsheba. Here's a famous painting called Bathing Bathsheba."

We all crowded in together around it. "You can see David off in the distance, watching."

Fascinating.

We spent more than an hour in that room. After the exhibit, we split up for the last hour. Jamie and Gigi went off on their own, and Tad and

I went to get a snack and a drink. We spent the better part of the hour talking about football, which was more in my element.

We were interrupted by an urgent text from Jamie.

You have to see this. Meet us in Room 4.

No mention of what she wanted us to see. It took several minutes to find Room Four. The Gallery was so huge it would be easy to get lost, and Jamie had the map.

When we found her, the hallway outside the room was buzzing with activity. People were milling around. A table was set up just outside the main doors. A sign above and behind the table said *Art Auction*.

Jamie's face was lit up like a billboard on Times Square. She had something in her hand with the number 87 on it.

"What are we doing?" I asked.

"They're having an art auction. I registered us."

"What's in your hand?"

"An auction paddle. It's for bidding. We're not going to bid, but you can't go in without one."

"Okay," I said hesitantly. This might be fun. "Are you guys into it?" I asked Tad and Gigi.

They seemed like they genuinely were.

After the first painting was auctioned off for more than eleven million pounds, I was into it as well. That amounted to roughly fifteen million dollars! It felt like my mouth was permanently agape in disbelief at what I was witnessing.

The atmosphere was invigorating. The room was abuzz. This is the type of excitement I felt when I played football in a full stadium. The auctioneer was skilled at keeping the auction moving while enticing the crowd to bid. As the price of a piece went higher, so did the intensity. When two people got in a bidding war, the crowd went into a frenzy. As an auction neared the end, the tension was as thick as a San Francisco fog.

TERRY TOLER

I had no idea an art auction could be so much fun.

The room was filled with people of considerable means. We seemed out of place in our shorts and tee shirts. Most were there in suits and ties and fancy dresses. They let us in anyway, so I decided not to feel embarrassed. All the chairs were taken, so we stood in the back. I didn't mind. We had a better view from there anyway. Watching the people and their reactions was the best part.

More than a hundred pieces of artwork were to be auctioned. Jamie had the list and was whispering information about the paintings as they came up in order. Some only went for four or five hundred thousand pounds, but most brought seven figures. I had no idea people paid that much for artwork.

When one piece, a Manet, went for twenty-seven million pounds, I almost fell over. A deafening cheer went up in the room. Jamie was right there with them. Hooting and hollering. Whistling. Clapping enthusiastically. It felt good to see her so happy. I was glad we decided to go to the museum and really glad she found the auction.

"Next is a Degas," Jamie said excitedly.

"What's a Degas?" I asked.

"Not what," she said, "Who? Edgar Degas is the artist. A French Impressionist painter. He lived in the late 1800s early 1900s. He painted dancers."

The painting was smaller than some of the others. We had to strain to see it from our vantage point. It looked like a painting of a ballerina in a tutu.

"I love this painting," Jamie said.

"How much do you think it'll go for?" I asked.

The four of us made a game of it. Each one would guess how much a painting would go for and then see who was closest. Jamie won hands down. Her estimates were almost always the closest. My guesses were way off. The ones I thought would go for a lot went for the least amounts. The ones I thought for sure were worth less, sold for the most.

88

"At least six million," she answered.

The auctioneer started his rhythmic cadence which I was getting used to.

"Who'll start at a million?"

No response.

"Do I hear five hundred thousand?"

That wasn't unusual. Several times, people waited to bid. Probably not wanting to be the first one. Or waiting to see how high it was going to go before they dipped their toe in the water.

"I can't believe no one's bidding on it," Jamie said as the crowd was still sitting on their hands.

"They may have already spent all their money. Or Degas isn't as popular as you think. I'm going to change my guess to a hundred thousand," I said as Jamie rolled her eyes.

Finally, the auctioneer coaxed a bid of three hundred thousand. I was wrong again.

"That's a steal," Jamie said.

Then he got a second bid. Three fifty.

"Do I hear four hundred?"

"Four," I heard a shout.

"Give me five!"

"Yep."

"How 'bout seven?"

The painting was gaining momentum. Before we knew it, the price was over a million. The auctioneer barked out words faster than a carnival dog. The idea was clearly to get people bidding on impulse. Before they had time to realize what they were doing.

Then a number of bidders got involved.

One million two fifty.

Then a million five.

Six.

Two million.

The excitement was building in the room.

It went to two million five hundred thousand almost immediately.

Then it slowed down.

Jamie's eyes were fixed on the auctioneer. I could see the excitement in her face as her eyes were widened and her mouth gaped open. Her shoulders were tensed. She was leaning forward. I loved watching her so excited.

"Do I hear two million six hundred thousand?"

A paddle went into the air.

"Two million seven fifty?"

"Yep!"

A lady was standing to the side with a phone in her hand, talking to someone. I presumed someone was bidding on the phone.

Only two bidders were left now. The one in the room bid two million eight hundred thousand. The person on the phone raised it to two million nine hundred thousand.

"Will you give me three?"

The man in the room, shook his head no and sat back in his chair.

"Are you crazy?" Jamie said to no one in particular. "It's worth twice that."

The woman on the phone was shaking it like she'd lost the connection. The person bidding in the room apparently didn't see it. I could from my vantage point. All the man in the room had to do was raise it to three and he would probably get it.

"Do I hear three million?" the auctioneer asked.

"Anybody? Last call. Three million? Anyone? Don't let this gem get away," he urged the crowd.

No one responded.

"Going once! Going twice!"

Suddenly, without notice the auctioneer shouted, "We have three million. A new bidder in the back of the room."

Oohs and ahs went up throughout the whole room as people turned in their seats to look.

I looked around as well to see who the new bidder was.

Jamie had her paddle high in the air!

"Three million. Going once! Going twice! Sold to the pretty lady in the back."

What in the world just happened?

13

Jamie was so excited she hugged all three of us. Tad and Gigi seemed as stunned as I was. I wished I shared Jamie's enthusiasm. We'd just purchased a painting at auction for three million pounds. If I did my math right, that added up to more than four million dollars.

Has Jamie lost her mind?

My second thought was, *is there a way out of this?*

"Can you excuse us?" Jamie said to Tad and Gigi. "Alex and I have to go and pay for the painting." She said it like she was going to pay for a fifty-dollar dress at a women's clothing store.

Jamie grabbed my hand and almost dragged me out of the room. Then I realized it was a good thing. We needed to talk about what just happened. In private. Away from Tad and Gigi.

"What did you just do?" I said roughly, once we were alone in the hallway.

"I know! Can you believe it? We got a Degas for only three million pounds."

"I don't think we should've spent four million dollars on a picture."

A hurt look came on Jamie's face as her lower lip contorted.

"First of all, it's not a picture. It's a painting. A work of art. From a master. Second of all, it's a steal at that price. We can flip it and double our money in no time."

"How can you be so sure?" I said in a stern tone, so she'd know I wasn't happy.

"Why are you upset? You're the one who had the idea to buy and sell artwork. I thought we agreed to that."

"We didn't talk about buying a four-million-dollar picture right off the bat."

"If you call it a picture again, I'm going to slap you across the side of your head. If you're going to be a connoisseur of the arts, you've got to learn the lingo."

"That's just it. I'm not a connoisseur of the arts. But I am a co-owner of the business. You should've talked to me first."

"There wasn't time. I had to make a split-second decision. You need to trust me. I know more about art than you do. Besides, you said we had ten million dollars in our account. That's what it's for. To run our business."

"It's so we can run our operations. Not buy expensive pictu... paintings."

"The business is the cover for our operations. This purchase will put AJAX on the map as an art dealer."

"Couldn't we have started smaller? Get our feet wet before diving into the deep end?"

"We did start small. Three million pounds is not a lot for a master-piece. If we want to make a splash in the art world, we have to spend money. What is it you're always saying? Go big or go home. We're going big."

Jamie kissed me on the side of my lips as if that would change my mind. I thought I had a valid point. We should make those decisions together.

"How am I going to explain it to Brad?" I argued.

"I didn't know you had to. He said it was our money. We risked our lives to get it."

That was true. Jamie had infiltrated a sex trafficking ring run by a noted terrorist in Belarus. She agreed to meet him in a hotel room, alone, at considerable risk under the guise that she was going to have sex with him. It turned out for the best but only because of Jamie's considerable skills. We kidnapped him. Stole his two billion dollars. Commandeered his luxury corporate jet and lived to tell about it. The CIA didn't know what to do with the money and the jet, so they put it in our new corporation.

Jamie had a point. We had two billion dollars at our disposal. Three million pounds was a drop in the bucket. I had to consider whether I was upset about the money or my ego took a hit because I wasn't involved in the decision.

Nothing I could do about it now anyway. Sometime, when we weren't on our honeymoon, I might bring it up again. For now, I'd try and be supportive. The one thing Curly always taught us in an operation was to have each other's backs. I surmised that would be even more important for a married couple.

"Where do we go to pay?" I asked with intended resignation in my voice, so she'd know I was still displeased.

"Main desk."

The auction was over, and people were filing out. Several came up and congratulated us on our purchase. We pretended like we did this all the time. A number of people gave us their cards. They had paintings to sell or a wish list of what they were looking to buy if we came across it. At least a half dozen people asked for one of our cards. I told them we were out and made a mental note to get some made as soon as we were back home.

Suddenly I felt important. Like an art celebrity. What was the word Jamie had used? *An art connoisseur.* I liked the sound of that.

When the crowd started to thin out, we went to the desk to give the lady our banking information. I couldn't believe I was authorizing a purchase of more than four million dollars. That made me feel even more important.

Until I thought about the conversation I'd have to have with Brad.

I'd wait and tell him after the money was already out of the account. As Curly always said, better to ask forgiveness than permission.

"Can you hold it for us?" Jamie asked the lady in charge at the desk. "We're on our honeymoon and won't be home until next week."

"Of course," she said.

"I'll call you with a shipping address when we get back to the States."

Jamie was thinking ahead. The last thing we wanted was a four-million-dollar painting left on our condo doorstep. I almost wondered if we should take it with us. That didn't make sense. How would we carry it on the plane? What would we do with it when we weren't in our hotel room? We couldn't carry it around London. Then I thought of something to ask.

"Will it still be covered under your insurance while it's in your care."

"Yes, sir."

"Excellent. We'll need to notify our insurance company to put it on our policy. That might take a day or two." Like we even had an insurance company. I didn't even know who insured paintings of this value. Lloyds of London maybe. I might check it out while we were in London.

After our business was settled, we went to find Gigi and Tad. A crowd had gathered around her, and she was dutifully giving out autographs and having her picture taken with fans. We stood to the side, waiting. She smiled and gave us a slight wave. Tad stood by with a smile on his face.

A woman approached us. I recognized her as the one on the phone with the bidder.

"Congratulations on the Degas," she said.

"Thank you," Jamie replied. "I'm thrilled."

"May I ask if you purchased it for personal or professional reasons?"

Jamie answered. "Professional. Although, Degas is my favorite painter. We own a business that buys and sells fine art. The AJAX corporation. Perhaps you've heard of it?"

My wife's response made me smile. What we were doing came naturally to Jamie and to me. Almost every mission with the CIA was covert. And we always had a cover. Sometimes I was an architect. An engineer. A salesman. I was even a doctor once. Jamie and I posed as a married couple for three months back when we first started dating. Lying was second nature to us.

In this instance, we weren't really lying, but the cover was new. We had to act like we'd been buying and selling artwork for years.

The woman hesitated. She wanted to say something.

"Why do you ask?" I said, not giving her any more time.

"Another person was bidding on the painting. I was on the phone with him. He really wants it. The purchase was to be a surprise for his wife's thirtieth birthday next week." She leaned in to whisper. "He's sixty-five. Need I say more. And filthy rich."

The woman was trying to suppress a laugh. She clearly enjoyed sharing that bit of gossip. The filthy rich part got my attention. Maybe he was still interested in buying it.

"Anywho... He was prepared to continue bidding on it, but we lost the connection. He's an oilman from Texas. He was out in an oil field somewhere while the auction was going on. I tried to get him back on the phone, but the auctioneer closed the auction before I could."

"His loss, our gain, I guess," Jamie said.

Where was she going with this? Maybe we could sell it right away and make a couple hundred thousand dollars on it. My mind raced with possibilities.

"Everything is always for sale," I blurted. "For the right price. If he's still interested."

Jamie glared at me. We'd only been married for a day and a half, but I could read her mind. She was telling me not to seem too anxious.

"Splendid. My client's prepared to offer you four million pounds for the painting."

My jaw almost hit the floor.

"I think we'll pass," Jamie said.

I think my jaw did hit the floor when she said that.

Could Jamie read my mind as well? If she could, she'd know I was screaming at her at the top of my lungs. *Take the money! That's more than a million dollars profit.*

"What would you sell it for?" the lady asked.

"The painting is worth six million dollars," Jamie said. "We have a number of buyers in the United States who would pay that or more."

No! I wanted to say. This was too good an opportunity to pass up. There were no buyers in the states. I don't even know where we'd find one.

"I'll have to ask my buyer. I'm not authorized to go that high. Will you be here for a few more minutes?"

A crowd was still milling around Gigi. We weren't going anywhere anytime soon. I would wait all afternoon if I had to if it meant selling the painting.

"We can wait for you," I said. "Go talk to your buyer and get back with us."

When the lady was gone, I bit my lip. It was all I could do to not lash out at Jamie for turning down a million-dollar profit. I decided to keep quiet. But questions remained.

Was Jamie bluffing? Or has she lost her ever-lovin' mind?

* * *

Ten minutes later, the woman approached us again. "My buyer had a question. Is the price six million dollars or six million pounds?"

"Pounds," Jamie said.

That made a difference of over a million dollars.

The woman let out a sigh. "He'll agree to the price. Six million pounds. Do we have a deal?"

"Not yet," Jamie said, much to my consternation.

What now?

"We need to discuss your fee," Jamie said. "It should be cut in half."

I wanted to glare at Jamie, but she was purposefully avoiding making eye contact with me.

"Why should I cut my fee?"

"Because you sold the painting twice in less than an hour."

"Yes. But I got you a buyer for six million pounds."

"But you're selling the painting for twice as much. So, you're making the same amount as you did on the first sale. I think that's fair. We doubled our money and so did you. That's a win/win in my book."

My heart did a couple of somersaults when the lady agreed. All my trepidation turned to euphoria in a matter of seconds. I had no idea my wife was such a shrewd businesswoman.

"I'll go draw up the bill of sale," the lady said. "The money is already in our escrow account. We'll wire it into your account this afternoon. Thank you. You've made my buyer very happy."

When the lady was out of earshot, Jamie squealed like a schoolgirl.

"I'm so proud of you," I said. "Remind me to never doubt you again."

"Oh, I *will* remind you. Everyday. For the rest of our lives."

About that time, Tad and Gigi walked up.

"What are the two of you so excited about?" Gigi asked.

"We just sold the painting."

"You did?"

"For six million pounds."

This time both of the girls squealed like a couple teenagers. Gigi hugged Jamie tightly with effusive congratulations. Tad shook my hand, and we bumped shoulders in sort of a man hug. We'd only know them for a few short hours, but it felt like we were becoming good friends. The plan was for us to leave the Gallery and go to The Tower of London. That was going to be delayed.

Jamie said, "Change of plans. We have to sign the paperwork and take care of all the details. You guys go on without us. We'll meet you there."

"That's fine," Gigi replied. "We can catch a cab over."

One last hug and they were gone.

"We'll text you when we get there," Jamie shouted to them as they walked away.

The plan was set. What I really wanted to do was go back to the room and celebrate. Obviously, that was going to be delayed for a few more hours. Jamie was really happy, though. I had a feeling making more than four million dollars in one day was going to make our time even more exciting.

If that was even possible.

* * *

Iran

Pok was having an early dinner away from the television monitors in the employee cafeteria.

A welcomed break. His eyes had been glued to the screens the entire day. Not much had happened. Halee and his wife and the other couple went to the National Gallery. They'd been in there for hours.

When his stomach started growling, he decided to grab a bite to eat. He gave specific instructions to his assistant to come and get him if Halee and his wife left the Gallery. Niazi had a man armed with acid outside waiting to attack. While Pok didn't want to miss it, he had to eat something. He could always play it back on tape should something happen while he was gone.

When he finished his last bite, his assistant came running into the eating area, "Halee and his wife left the Gallery. About ten minutes ago."

"Did our man launch the attack?"

"No. He didn't have a chance. They got into a cab and left."

"Where'd they go?"

"The cab dropped them off at the Tower of London."

"Were they alone or was the other couple with them?"

"It was just the two of them."

"Excellent."

The problem Pok foresaw at the Gallery was space to launch an attack. Trafalgar Square was always crowded and patrolled by British Police. As he remembered, the Tower of London had a big courtyard area. That would be a perfect place to attack. That would give Niazi time to move his man into position.

Pok's heart started racing at the thought of success.

He immediately stood and didn't even bother cleaning up the dishes. He had to get in front of the television screen as soon as possible.

I can't wait to see the man throw acid in Jamie's face.

14

Jamie and I signed the bill of sale for the painting and left the National Gallery for the Tower of London. On the way, Brad, our CIA handler called. I knew what it was about. He'd probably seen the transaction for the money coming out of the account but wouldn't have seen the money coming in, since we just closed on it.

Time to have some fun with him.

"Is there something you want to tell me?" Brad asked me after I answered.

"No. I don't think so." He couldn't see the smug look on my face.

"Something about a four-million-dollar transaction on your AJAX account?"

"Oh that. We bought some artwork. A painting. Degas. Have you ever heard of him?"

"Why would you buy a four-million-dollar painting?" Brad was clearly not amused at my sarcasm.

"Jamie and I decided that the cover for AJAX is buying and selling artwork. We thought we'd get started on it."

"While I like the idea of artwork as a cover, you should've run it by me first."

I suddenly felt guilty. That's probably how I sounded to Jamie when I went off on her.

"Why should I run it by you?" I argued, raising the intensity of my words. "I thought this was our company and our money to run as we see fit. I distinctly remember you saying we were off the books and that our budget was a hundred million dollars the first year. This money is a drop in the bucket compared to how much we have."

I suddenly realized I was using the same arguments Jamie had used with me.

"That's what I said, but—"

"But nothing. You said you trusted us with the money. That's what you should do. We wouldn't have bought the painting if we didn't think it was a good idea. I don't want to have to run every expenditure by you."

"That doesn't mean you aren't accountable to me for what you spend," he said, matching my intensity.

Now I was getting annoyed. I'm sure it's how Jamie must've felt.

"We brought that money in. It's not even the CIA money. We're going to buy a lot of paintings over the years. Don't micromanage us. The last thing I need is you looking over our shoulders."

I could tell he was about to say something.

"Besides," I continued, "we already sold the painting. You'll see an eight-million-dollar wire in our account later this afternoon."

Eight million, two hundred thirty-six thousand, and two hundred dollars to be exact.

I had memorized the number for posterity. Our first transaction for AJAX and our first purchase as a married couple.

I repeated myself for emphasis.

"Like I said, don't micromanage us. We know what we're doing."

I hung up on him.

Jamie laughed out loud.

"I guess that put him in his place," she said.

"That felt good," I replied. We'd both wanted to tell Brad off a thousand times over the years. While I often pushed back on him, it had never gone as far as hanging up on him.

Then the guilt returned when I thought about how I had handled it with Jamie. We were in the backseat of the taxi. I turned so I was facing her.

"I'm sorry I was rude about the painting," I said. "I should've trusted you."

Her eyes softened as she seemed genuinely appreciative of my words.

"And I should've talked to you about it first," Jamie admitted. "I got caught up in the moment. Anyway... apology accepted."

No more words were necessary. They would've only ruined the moment. We kissed a little. Actually, a lot. Both of us were oblivious to the taxi driver.

Anticipation was building. I could feel it. Jamie must have felt it as well as she suddenly became breathless and pulled out of the kiss.

"We won't stay long at the Tower of London," she said, her face red.

"I wish we could go back to the room now," I said.

"We can't stand them up."

"We could, but it'd be rude. You're right. I don't want to do that to them. I really like Gigi and Tad," I said.

"I love them," Jamie said effusively. "I hope we can stay friends."

She texted them and said we were on our way. Gigi responded that they signed up for a tour that was about halfway over. They were on their way to see the Crown Jewels. We made an agreement to meet them in the courtyard in an hour.

That would give us time to visit the Royal Armory. A separate wing at the attraction with a large collection of weapons and instruments of torture. Jamie had read about it before we ever left home. It was the one thing she insisted on seeing. That and the art gallery. We were going to knock them both out on the same day.

* * *

Pok had his eyes transfixed on the courtyard at The Tower of London. The camera shot was from a distance, so he wasn't able to see their faces. Definitely them though. The big guy had to be Alex. The blonde had to be Jamie, his wife. They were walking from building to building with a group of people. Probably on a tour.

Niazi's man was already in position with a bottle of acid hidden in his coat. The man wandered around the courtyard. He came in and out of the picture.

Biding his time. It wouldn't be long now.

* * *

The White Tower, as it was called, housed more than weapons of war. It had various types of guns, including those used for sport by sovereigns through the years. The first room we entered was called the Tournament Room where instruments for jousting were displayed including armor and the lances used for the contests.

"This is boring," Jamie said. "I wanted to see the torture room."

We learned from the handout that an entire room was devoted to weapons of torture used in the Spanish Armada. The walls were lined with glass cases filled with various weapons including knives, spears, lances, and swords. Along with several instruments of torture, diabolically designed to create maximum pain.

The room gave me the creeps. Some of the devices were downright sadistic in their design. They rang too close to home. I'd never been tortured, but I'd come close. The worst of it had been Curly's training. For a good four days, he simulated what we might experience should we be captured in the field in a soviet bloc or third-world country. We were waterboarded, sleep deprived, called every name in the book, and forced to go without food and water for long periods of time.

We were never physically abused, which was against training regulations, but no rules applied to the mental and emotional abuse we were put through. I was glad when that part of our training was over. I'd never allow myself to be tortured in the field. Whoever wanted to harm me would have to kill me first. That's assuming I didn't kill him before he had a chance.

Jamie and I went to two different sides of the room. She spent more time looking at the weapons display. I focused on the armor. The "Line of Kings" collection displayed armor worn by royals throughout the centuries. Called the Tudor Room, the exhibit was started by King Henry VIII. A fascinating king who beheaded a number of his wives, if I remembered my history lessons correctly.

Jamie said the courtyard where we were to meet Gigi and Tad was where people were tortured and executed, including Anne Boleyn. That reminded me that Tad and Gigi were probably in the courtyard by now.

The top floor of the White Tower had windows that overlooked the area between the buildings. The windows were opened, allowing a gentle breeze to flow through the exhibit hall. I could see a group gathered in the far-right corner of the courtyard, standing on a slight incline. Tad and Gigi weren't hard to spot. They towered over the others.

I wasn't more than fifty yards from them. I shouted to get their attention. They looked up at me. When they saw me they waved enthusiastically.

A movement out of the corner of my eye, startled me.

Out of place.

Someone was running. Shouting.

My mind took too long to process it.

A middle eastern man was running toward the group with something in his hand. Shouting "Allahu Akbar." I recognized those words as a war cry.

Tad and Gigi were still looking at me. I tried to warn them of the threat but couldn't. They saw the man after it was too late.

The terrorist came upon the group. For whatever reason, he went straight to Gigi. She instinctively took a step back. The man squeezed the bottle in his hand and a stream of liquid spewed out right into Gigi's face.

I shouted, "No!"

Not sure why, it's just what came out of my mouth.

Gigi let out a horrifying scream that even echoed in our building. Getting Jamie's attention. Within seconds Jamie was next to me looking out the window.

Gigi grabbed her face and fell backwards into the ground. Tad reacted. Like the football player he was, he lowered his shoulder and tackled the man. They rolled to the ground. Tad was on top of him.

The bottle was still in the man's right hand. He squirted some of the liquid on Tad's back. I heard him cry out in pain and roll off the terrorist. To my horror, Tad was flapping on the ground like a fish suddenly out of water.

Jamie bolted toward the steps.

I took off after her.

When we exited the building, the terrorist was running across the courtyard, back toward the front of the area in the direction of the exit. Jamie veered to her left. Toward the man.

I followed. Only a few steps behind. The courtyard was filled with the screams of agony coming from the area where the group was attacked.

Two security guards were in pursuit of the man with their guns already drawn. They opened fire, hitting him several times. He fell to the ground. Jamie changed direction and veered to her right toward where the victims were.

I was still headed in the direction of the terrorist, but then changed course as well. The officers had the man subdued. Maybe he was dead.

Tad and Gigi were laying on the ground along with several others in the group. Jamie went to Gigi first. She knelt down next to her.

Suddenly, without warning, Jamie cried out in pain. A bone chilling scream. She rolled onto her back and was clutching her legs.

What just happened? My mind tried to process the scene. Now Jamie was in trouble. Before, I was headed to help Tad. I changed direction and went right to Jamie.

"My legs are on fire," she said as I arrived next to her.

Her legs were bright red. Blisters were already forming.

Apparently, when she knelt next to Gigi, she had gotten acid on her knees. I glanced over and saw a small pool next to Gigi.

Jamie's hands were bright red as well from touching her knees trying to brush the acid off of them.

"It hurts so bad!" Jamie said, her face contorted into a grimace.

"Don't touch your face or eyes," I warned her.

I had a bottle of water in my backpack. I took it out and began spraying Jamie's kneecaps. Then her hands. That seemed to calm her some.

"Go check on Gigi and Tad," she had the presence of mind to say.

Tad was still on the ground several yards away from his bride. Writhing in pain. Almost delirious. He kept trying to reach his back. At least he was moving.

Gigi seemed to be in worse shape. She lay on the ground, totally still. An eerie moan was all I could hear from her. She was obviously in shock. Except for her form and the clothes she was wearing, which I recognized from earlier, I never would've known it was her.

The once-gorgeous model was now disfigured beyond belief. I wanted to turn my head away but forced myself to look at her. I tried to remember my training. We were taught what to do in case of a chemical attack on the battlefield.

Water.

I was out. I'd used all mine on Jamie.

I looked around. Others were coming to help. I didn't see anyone with water. We needed a water hose or a bucket.

I felt helpless.

The only thing I could do for Gigi or for Tad was to pray.

The whole scene overwhelmed my senses. My friends laid on the ground in agony, which was killing me inside. The smell of chemicals and burning flesh almost caused me to become nauseous. The chemicals in the air burned my eyes. Still lingering, even though it was several seconds after the attack.

Who would do something so heinous?

I looked over at the terrorist in utter contempt. He wasn't moving. I hoped he was dead.

There was nothing more I could do. Just go back to Jamie and comfort her.

"Is Gigi okay?" she asked.

"I don't know," I said.

I purposefully put my body between hers and Gigi's to block her view.

In all my years in the CIA, I'd seen some horrific things. This was the worst thing I'd ever seen. By far.

15

Royal London Hospital

The senseless acid attack of American supermodel Gina Garth Gentry had created an international incident. The outcry and denunciations from governments across the globe were swift and severe. London authorities were to blame for not cracking down on terrorists and their policy of open borders that allowed them to come in undetected to carry out such heinous crimes.

I still couldn't believe it happened right in front of my own eyes.

Even Londoners were demonstrating against the violence. The Queen called for a moment of silence and a day of prayer.

Gigi was taken to Queen Victoria hospital which was world renowned for handling burn victims. The nonstop news reports said she was in critical condition. Her road to recovery, if she survived, would be long and arduous. Jamie's injuries were less severe. The main concern was possible infection. She was given a powerful antibiotic and a painkiller.

I glanced over at her when she let out a slight moan. She'd been asleep for the last hour. At first, she resisted taking the painkillers. When she finally asked for it, I knew the pain had to be severe. Jamie had as high a pain tolerance as anyone I knew. If she wanted the medication, then she was really hurting.

Her hands were wrapped in heavy gauze. It looked like she had two oven mitts over them. Her left knee was heavily bandaged as well and was elevated.

She looked much worse than she actually was. The doctor said she could be released tomorrow if everything went well. Within a couple days, she should be close to normal. Thank God. I couldn't imagine what Tad was going through at that moment. I know how I would've felt if it had been Jamie and not Gigi.

Tears welled up in my eyes. I brushed them roughly away. Then I cleared my throat. I took out my phone and dialed the last number on the list of recent calls.

Brad answered on the first ring.

"Did you call to hang up on me again?" he asked jokingly.

"Jamie's in the hospital," I said, ignoring the jab which was deserved under any other circumstance.

"What happened?" he asked. The concern obvious in his voice.

"Did you hear about the acid attack in London?"

"Yes. It's all over the news."

I figured he had. Not many things happened in the world related to terrorism that Brad didn't know about it.

"Jamie and I were there. We witnessed it."

"How did Jamie get caught up in it?"

"Trying to help. She got some acid on her. It burned her knee and hands, but she'll be okay. We knew the victim. The model."

"Such a tragedy. Her career is obviously over. Hopefully, she'll survive."

"Sounds like it's touch and go."

"The President is putting a lot of pressure on the Prime Minister and the Queen. People are calling for a boycott of London over it. They've got to do something about the attacks or it's going to affect tourism. We've been warning them. Unfortunately, it might take something like this to get their attention."

"We've been here two days and we've already seen three attacks."

Silence on the other end told me' Brad was processing that information. I knew that would send up a red flag in his analytical mind. We all tended to disregard the possibility of coincidences in our line of work. The odds of randomly witnessing three terrorist attacks in a forty-eight-hour period of time, defied logic.

That's why I was calling him. I didn't see how they were connected to us. Maybe he would. Then he asked the obvious question.

"Is it possible you were the target of the attack? Or Jamie?"

"I've thought about it, but who would be behind it? And why?"

I told him the details of the other attacks.

"Those are pretty big coincidences," Brad said.

"Nothing makes sense."

"I saw pictures of the model. She kind of looks like Jamie. Could Jamie be the target and not you?"

"I thought it was Pok, but how could he pull something like this off? What about Jamie? Does anyone come to mind who might be after her?"

"She has plenty of enemies. A lot of people would like to see her dead. But they all operate locally in their own regions. They don't have ties to Iranian terrorists. You're the most likely target."

"How are they tracking me?"

"Have you sensed any tails?"

"No. That's the thing. We've been all over London. Jamie and I were at the National Gallery. We left. Got in a cab and went to the Tower of London. They would need more than one tail to keep up with us."

"They'd need eyes everywhere."

"What did you just say?"

"I said they'd need eyes everywhere to follow you that closely and pull off something like this in a planned operation."

Security cameras. They did have eyes everywhere.

"I gotta go."

I hung up the phone abruptly for the second time today.

I gathered up my things.

"Jamie," I said from the side of her bed. "I'm going, but I'll be back soon."

Her eyes twitched open. She was still out of it.

"Don't go," she said. "We're supposed to make love tonight."

She reached out to me with her two huge bear claws. It would be at least two more days before she'd be in any condition to make love. If then.

"Go back to sleep," I said. "I'll be back in a little bit."

I doubted she heard me. Or if she did, that she'd remember it.

As I walked out the door, I almost ran into Weaver who had his hand in the air like he was about to knock on Jamie's door.

"Not now, Weaver," I said roughly. "I was just on my way out."

"How's your wife?" he asked.

"How did you know she was here?"

"She's on the victim's list."

"She'll be alright. Just some slight burns on her knees and hands."

"That's good to know. I need to ask you some questions."

"I was on my way out. I really have to run."

A plan was forming in my mind. I needed to know if I was being followed by the security cameras.

"We can do it here, or down at headquarters. Your choice."

The last thing I wanted was to go back to the headquarters and get tied up for hours. There were about four more hours until sunset. Enough time to carry out my plan if I hurried.

"Hurry up. I really have to go. Can you ask me your questions as we're walking? I don't have anything to tell you that you don't already know."

"Can you explain how you happened to be present for another attack?"

"We weren't present. We were in the White Tower. The attack happened in the courtyard. We just ran down to help. That's how Jamie got acid on her."

"But you knew the victim. The model. Witnesses saw you together earlier that day. At the National Gallery."

That confused me. Weaver didn't have time to interview witnesses at the Gallery. That told me he had been following us on the cameras. Or at least someone on his staff was and had informed him of what we did today and who we did it with.

"We're staying at the same hotel," I answered. "Then we went to the art gallery together. Which apparently you already knew. Like I said, I doubt I can tell you anything you don't already know."

We got into the elevator and pushed the lobby floor. I didn't mention we were meeting them at the Tower of London. He wouldn't know that unless he was listening in on our conversations. I highly doubted that was the case.

"Any chance you were the target?" he asked as the elevator sped toward the first floor.

"Why would we be the target?" I asked.

"If you're with the CIA, you might be a target."

"I'm not with the CIA. Do you know why we were at the National Gallery?"

He had a blank look on his face.

"I didn't think so. If you did, you'd probably know we purchased a painting for three million pounds."

By the widened eyes, it was clear he didn't know that piece of information. Telling him almost brought a smile to my face, but I had to maintain our cover.

"I told you, we buy and sell paintings."

I hadn't actually told him that information, since we just came up with it that morning. The bill of sale was still in my pocket. I reached in and pulled it out and handed it to him.

He studied it carefully.

"Would the CIA let me buy a painting for three million pounds?"

The art business was going to be a good cover for operations. That argument would win the day every time. If anyone were ever suspicious of us, that would satisfy them. Under any other circumstances, Brad would never authorize that kind of money to be used for a cover.

Weaver was clearly confused as his eyebrows were furrowed, and all the lines on his face were showing at once. His whole theory had just been blown out of the water.

"Listen," I said. "I really have to go. I'd say go find the killer. But I heard he's dead."

He died on route to the hospital, according to reports. Weaver pulled out his card and handed it to me. He probably forgot that he had given me one earlier at the subway station.

"If you think of anything, please call me," he said, as we exited the building together.

"I do have a question," I said. "Were there security cameras in the courtyard where the acid attack happened?"

"Yes. I've already seen them."

"Are those private cameras?"

"They are, but all private cameras, at least those on the street and in public spaces, feed into our central location."

"Thank you. That's what I wondered."

"Why do you ask?"

"Just curious. I wondered how you know where we are all the time."

"I could follow you around the entire city if I wanted to."

"Then you already know that we're on our honeymoon and not on some mission with the CIA."

He nodded his head. Maybe he was agreeing with me, but I could still tell that he was skeptical.

"I hope your wife gets better," he said sincerely.

"Thank you. Me too."

I felt bad lying to him, but it was part of the business. He really was a decent guy and a good detective. He'd put pieces of the puzzle together better than I had. He simply couldn't connect the dots. Neither could I. Maybe there weren't any dots to connect. I was determined to find out and had a plan I thought would work.

Weaver didn't know it, but what I was planning would help him. If I found a group plotting terrorist attacks across London, I wouldn't hesitate to share that information with him. With Brad's approval.

I hailed the first cab in line. On the way back to the hotel, I stopped and bought three burner phones and cut the cab loose. Then I walked the rest of the way to our hotel and changed clothes. I got the gun out of its hiding place and put it in the front of my pants. The clothes I was wearing were perfect for concealing a weapon.

After exiting the hotel, I walked quickly to Trafalgar Square. Keeping my eyes peeled for threats but trying to not make it look obvious. I didn't make any evasive maneuvers to lose a tail. If there was one, I wanted them to follow me.

Trafalgar Square was a large plaza right in front of the National Gallery. A huge tourist spot, large crowds gathered there for pictures, and the location was a transfer point for buses and cabs. The acre of concrete also had cameras set up everywhere. The spot I chose for maximum visibility was next to the Lion fountain. I made sure my face could be seen from any number of angles.

At the same time, I looked for another location away from the cameras. Someplace where I couldn't be seen and could get to quickly if necessary.

Then I waited.

* * *

Iran

"What are you up to, Alex Halee?" Pok said to himself.

He'd seen Halee leave the hospital and catch a cab back to his hotel. While he was disappointed that Halee's wife hadn't been the victim of the attack, she was still injured which brought him some satisfaction. And the attack couldn't be traced back to him. The Iranians had already put out disinformation that a radical group from Somalia was behind the attack. That would keep the London authorities busy chasing a rabbit hole.

Niazi was ecstatic. His man had performed admirably. So much so, that he was thirsty for another attack. His men were prepared to launch again at his command. He continued to compliment Pok on the brilliance of his plan.

When Halee went back to the hotel, Pok wasn't sure what that meant. At first, he was concerned that Halee would be tied up at the hotel for the rest of the night. When he left the hotel and started walking on the street, Pok was optimistic that another attack was possible.

Now Halee was in Trafalgar Square. In plain view. By the lions. For no reason.

That made Pok suspicious. Was Halee on to him? Should he lay low? Niazi's man was just out of sight of Halee's location.

So far, everything was going as planned. At some point, he needed for Halee to figure out that he was behind the attacks. It wouldn't be hard for him to surmise that Pok had tapped into the security cameras. It was the only feasible explanation. He needed him to come looking for him. Then the trap would be set.

He sensed that Halee was already suspicious. Perhaps he needed a little more coaxing. More proof. He'd give it to him. An acid attack in a busy London square would be the confirmation Halee needed. The London investigators would piece it together as well. Why was Halee present at every attack? This would confuse them. Did Halee set them up himself, so he could be the hero?

Pok lived for creating confusion in his enemies. He felt like a puppet master controlling Halee with a set of strings of his own design.

He gave Niazi the go ahead.

"Send your man in. Launch another acid attack near Halee. Tell your man to wait until he has Halee in sight. Then go for the first target he sees."

Pok settled in his chair and stared at the screen. Halee was clearly visible. Leaning against one of the statues.

This should be good.

16

Trafalgar Square
London

I saw him before he saw me.

A good thing, considering the risk I was taking. Luring a terrorist with a bottle full of acid into a crowd of people bordered on reckless. But I had to know. Was I the target? Were the knife attacks and the acid attack on Gigi related? Was I being surveilled by a terrorist group through the London security camera system?

Was Pok involved?

The fact that within twenty minutes of showing my face in Trafalgar Square, a terrorist showed up, was all the proof I needed. Now I had to make sure no more innocent people were injured.

Trafalgar Square consisted of two fountains and one big obelisk in the center surrounded by four large lion statues at each corner. Behind one of the statues was a dark area. Meaning the cameras didn't capture that spot. Upon seeing the terrorist, I walked around the lion into the dark area, careful to stay out of the terrorist's view.

The shirt I was wearing was bright red, by design. I wanted to be seen. Red was the color most easily spotted. For instance, red cars statistically got the most speeding tickets because they were the most noticeable. In my current dress, I stuck out like a clown in a rodeo.

Once out of the view of the camera, I slipped the red shirt off and left it on the ground. Underneath the red shirt was a grey one. A color that would blend into the environment and wasn't as easy to see. In my back pocket was a baseball cap. In my right front pocket, a pair of dark sunglasses. Within seconds, I had a totally different look.

That would allow me to walk around the square and not be spotted. Or at least that was my hope. My height might be the only thing that might give me away. Hopefully, the terrorist wasn't smart enough to connect me to the man in the red shirt. I turned my face slightly away from the cameras in case they used face-recognition software. Whoever monitored the cameras would probably be scrambling right about then searching frantically for me.

My plan worked, evidenced by the fact that the terrorist looked confused. He walked to the spot where I'd been standing. Another clue I was being monitored on the cameras. How else would he know where to find me?

The monitors probably knew I'd left that spot, but I was counting on a delay in communications. While they could relay my location to the terrorist in real time, they had to find me first. That allowed me to get within a few feet of him without being spotted. In my disguise, I'd be able to walk right by him. Close enough to where I could smell the acid. Another confirmation he was a terrorist, and I was the target. Or at least the unsuspecting tourists around me were.

Since he hadn't recognized me, I was able to linger near enough to him to take him out if he made any move to remove the acid from his jacket. That sent my heart racing even faster if that was possible as images of Gigi flooded my mind. The memory of how destructive the acid was sent fear through my spine.

The only competing emotion to the fear was anger. This man intended to kill more innocent people. Throw acid in someone's face and ruin his or her life like his lowlife friend had done to Gigi. It made me even angrier when I considered that maybe Jamie had been the target all along.

Either way, seeing the man was fueling my rage like a poker stirs a fire. My original intention was to let him enter the square and then leave. If he made any attempt to act, my hand was within inches of my gun and I'd shoot him down. That would blow my cover, but at least innocent lives would be saved. Weaver would understand.

If the man didn't act, I'd intended to leave him alone. Let him walk away since I'd gathered the intel I needed. Now that I'd seen the man and was close enough to kill him, my will wouldn't let him walk away. He'd just regroup and launch an attack on some other unsuspecting innocent at a later time. Maybe even me.

Not going to happen.

I'd act as his judge and jury. Guilty. He needed to be taken off the face of the earth. I sentenced him to death right on the spot. Not on the spot exactly. I had a plan to do it in private. The hunter was now the hunted. Death was about to be his fate.

I just had to lure him away from the cameras.

* * *

MI5 Headquarters

"Where's Alex?" Weaver asked his control monitor with a sense of urgency in his voice.

He was in MI5 headquarters watching Alex Steele's every move. He'd followed him from the hospital to his hotel. Then watched him leave the hotel and walk to Trafalgar Square. Not hard to spot, Alex was wearing a red shirt and shorts. For whatever reason, he was hanging out at the Lion statues in Trafalgar.

Why?

Something about Alex was suspicious, Weaver didn't know what it was but was determined to find out. A few phone calls to MI6, the foreign intelligence side of the British security services, had led to dead ends. They didn't know who he was. The CIA didn't know him either. No operative by the name Alex Steele was operating in Britain at that time. If the CIA had a man operating in a mission on British soil, MI6 was supposed to be notified first. No one was naïve enough to believe that the CIA didn't sometimes engage in undercover operations without following normal protocols, but Alex Steele was moving around London in plain sight. Posing as a man on his honeymoon. Nothing undercover about his actions.

Weaver didn't buy the honeymoon ruse for a second. Steele was acting like an operative. Watching him in Trafalgar was raising even more alarm bells.

Then suddenly, totally out of the blue, Steele disappeared from camera view. One minute he was standing next to the lion, a second later he was gone. Weaver kept changing camera angles trying to find him. Even more proof the man was a trained spy. The average person couldn't escape his surveillance cameras which were the best in the world.

Then he saw him.

A suspicious man.

Wearing a jacket. Middle eastern. His hand in his right pocket.

He fit the profile of the other attackers. Was it a knife or acid?

Weaver watched him walk to the exact spot where Alex had been standing.

What's going on?

Was that what spooked Steele?

Weaver had a SWAT team a block away. Just in case something went down. He hesitated. Should he send them in? Or just watch to see what happened?

Better safe than sorry. The worst that would happen would be the man wasn't a terrorist and was clean. Actually, the best thing. The man might be upset for being profiled, but Weaver could live with that when it came to terrorism. Brits didn't attack other Brits with acid. That wasn't entirely true. Some British gangs were involved in acid attacks with rival gangs, but not in tourist areas. Not on the subway platforms or inside The Tower of London. The middle easterners were the ones who attacked innocent civilians with knives, acid, and suicide bombs. Usually not inside tourist attractions either, but these were perilous times. He wouldn't put anything past anyone.

He had to err on the side of caution.

"Send in the SWAT team," he said to his assistant. "Stat."

* * *

Iran

"Where's Halee?" Pok shouted. "We lost him. He was right there, standing beside the statue of the lion. He disappeared. Like a deleted keystroke on the computer."

Pok panned through each camera angle. Nothing. Alex was gone.

"What do you want me to do?" Niazi said.

"Abort," Pok said.

"My man's in place. He can launch an attack. There are a lot of people around."

"No! Halee must be nearby. He must witness the attack. That's the plan."

Pok wondered if he'd been tricked. Maybe Alex showed his face and then disappeared on purpose. Why else would he be in the square and not at the hospital with his injured wife? Pok surmised that Alex was setting a trap to see if the camera system was following him.

That brought a smile to Pok's face. Alex must've known he was being watched. That didn't mean he knew by whom or how. Pok expected Halee to figure it out by day four of the plan. Perhaps, he was smarter than Pok had given him credit for and started piecing things together two days sooner.

Either way, he didn't want to take any chances by having an attack not tied to Halee. He needed the British authorities to connect the attacks to Halee. That wouldn't happen if even one attack happened and Alex wasn't there.

"Tell your man to get out," Pok said. "Abort now."

Fortunately, Niazi didn't argue further. He got on the radio and shouted out instructions to his man on the ground.

"Tomorrow's a new day," Pok said to Niazi after he gave the order to abort. "Things are going very well."

Niazi agreed, although he was clearly disappointed that he couldn't pull off this attack. Pok went back to the screen and searched for Halee again. He saw Niazi's man walk out of the square. Rather than follow him, he continued to search the plaza, curious as to where Alex had gone.

He wasn't as disappointed as Niazi. The success of the first two day's attacks were gratifying. Better to not get greedy. Halee might've avoided a second attack today, but he wouldn't be able to avoid one to-morrow. If Alex tried the same maneuver with a suicide bomber, the outcome would be different. All Niazi's man had to do was walk in the same area as Halee. As long as Pok had eyes on him, Halee could do nothing to stop it.

Niazi had explained how the bombs worked. A detonation switch was in the bomber's hand at all times. In fact, the button was activated when the bomber pushed the button. It didn't detonate until the but-ton was released. The purpose of that was in case the bomber got cold feet. After all, a lot of people had the courage to blow themselves up when they were talking about it. A different scenario often came into play once they were actually attached to a bomb and were seconds from ending their life. Many a mission in the past had failed when the bomber chickened out.

The button design fixed that problem. Once the bomber pushed the button, he had to continue to hold it down or he would be blown up. He would eventually anyway. It was only a matter of time as to when.

Pok could hardly wait.

Today had been a good day. Tomorrow would be even better.

* * *

London

The terrorist walked out of the square, and I followed a few paces behind. He was headed back in the direction he'd come. Before entering the square, I'd done a quick surveillance of the surrounding streets. I'd memorized each block and could picture them in my mind. I also knew where the security cameras were and was careful to keep my head turned so they wouldn't capture my face.

Two blocks ahead on the right was an alley. The alley had no cameras. That's where I would make my move.

The man's hands were no longer in his pocket. He'd obviously been told to stand down. I had my right hand in my right pocket, fingering a knife. I pictured in my mind how I'd attack him. I'd come up from behind with catlike speed. My left forearm would wrap around his neck. He'd instinctively move his left arm up to his neck. My right hand would grab his right wrist and twist his arm behind him.

I was bigger and stronger and could easily drag him into the alley. Once there, I'd take out the knife and plunge it under his right arm, into his heart. Just like his fellow low life did to the woman on the subway.

I could taste the vengeance. For all the victims. The woman in the subway. Her son who no longer had a mother. Gigi. Tad.

Jamie.

While killing the man couldn't undo all the hurt these attacks had caused, they would at least clear them out of my mind. I'd gained some self-awareness. The next attack helped to get rid of the emotional fallout from the last one. I'd get tremendous satisfaction once the man ahead of me was dead.

We were coming up on the alley.

I quickened my pace. My heartbeat matched my steps.

I heard screeching of tires.

A flash of movement on the street. Coming from behind me.

A vehicle came to a halt right in front of us.

The man stopped walking. I slipped into the doorway of a store and ducked my head to hide my face.

The men were shouting. At the terrorist.

"On your knees!" they ordered.

Five men had submachine guns pointed at him.

The man fell to his knees. Two heavily armed men surrounded him and threw him to the ground.

I turned and walked away, careful to keep my face off the cameras. Not daring to look back.

At the next road, I took a left, then another right, then got into a cab.

"Take me to the Palace Hotel," I said.

Then I took a deep breath and let it out. My heart pounded so hard in my chest I could feel it in my ears.

The reality of my situation came into focus.

Two people were watching me on the security cameras.

Weaver and someone else.

17

The Palace Hotel

It felt like a cement truck had run a stop sign and broadsided me in a compact car. I'd been in difficult situations before. This one seemed impossible.

So, I called Brad.

"I'm the target." My voice cracked as I said it.

"How do you know?"

"There have been four terrorist attacks since I've been in London. They all happened right around me. What are the odds?"

"If you're the target, how come you haven't been hit."

Rather than answer, I wanted to get some things off my chest.

"I'm on my honeymoon! My wife's in the stupid hospital! A woman is dead. A friend of mine is permanently disfigured. I can't leave my hotel room, man. I'm not on a mission. What am I supposed to do?"

"Just calm down and tell me what's going on."

"Someone's tracking my every move on the London security cameras. As soon as I go anywhere, a terrorist shows up. What do I do when Jamie gets out of the hospital? We can't go anywhere or do anything. If I leave the hotel, I'm putting someone's life in danger."

I was in my hotel room pacing around like a tiger in a zoo.

"Take a deep breath, Alex. Let's talk about this. What happened?"

"I went to Trafalgar. The only thing that made sense to me was that I was being followed by the security cameras. So, I showed my face. Within twenty minutes a terrorist showed up. With acid. Looking for me."

Even though I was getting it off my chest, I didn't feel better. The frustration was mounting. Inside, I felt like how a howler monkey must feel when he's swinging around the cage acting like an idiot. I just wanted to scream at the top of my lungs like I'd seen them do.

"Did anyone get hurt?"

"No! Thank God. But someone could've. MI5 showed up and arrested the terrorist. I was following him and was about to take him out. They got to him before I could. That means they're following me too. They were obviously tracking me and saw the man on the cameras. That's how they knew he was there. Because they're tailing me."

"MI6 called today asking questions about you."

"They think I'm involved somehow. This guy Weaver, with MI5, keeps questioning me. Why wouldn't he? If I were him, I'd do the same thing. Every time there's a terrorist attack, I'm there. It looks suspicious."

"They wanted to know if you're one of us."

"What did you tell them?"

"That we don't know who you are."

"That's just great! You could've backed my story. I told them I'm on my honeymoon. That I'm not on a mission with the CIA. I don't know why these attacks are happening, but they're not my fault."

"We told them the truth. You aren't part of the CIA anymore. I told you that if you ran into trouble, we would say we didn't know you."

"This was not trouble of my own making. I didn't ask for this."

"Is Pok behind it?"

"Who else would it be? No one else has the ability to hack into London security cameras. He's obviously playing some kind of sick game. What's strange is that he could take me out anytime he wants. Those cameras are everywhere. I can't walk anywhere without Pok knowing it. That makes me a sitting duck. And Jamie's a target just because she's with me. I'm not so sure she wasn't the target of the acid attack at the Tower of London. The terrorist might've gone after the wrong person."

"Assuming it's Pok, what's his endgame?"

"How would I know? He's probably just messing with me."

"I don't think he'd go to all this trouble for a couple of small attacks just to mess with your mind."

"Well, I don't know, and I'm not hanging around to find out. As soon as Jamie's released from the hospital, I'm getting out of here. We're coming home."

"What about your honeymoon?"

"There hasn't been a honeymoon! We haven't even had sex yet."

"Too much information."

"Can you imagine that? We've been married for three days and haven't even had a chance to do it. Every time we start to do something, a terrorist shows up. I thought for a week, we'd just be a normal couple. We're starting our new life together. Instead, I'm in the middle of a huge mess. This was supposed to be the best week of our lives. Instead, Jamie's lying in a hospital bed, and I'm chasing a terrorist with acid in his coat. Gigi's fighting for her life. Her career's over. It's not fair, man."

I could barely fight back the tears of anger.

"They say the girl's going to make it. You know. The model. Gigi. She's in for a long recovery, though. At least she's going to live."

"That's good. I hadn't heard that."

That settled my emotions. Temporarily.

"That's another thing," I said more calmly. "I'd like to go by the hospital and see her and her husband. I can't. A terrorist might show up. Who knows what might happen? I can't keep putting innocent people in harm's way. I've got to get out of here."

"You can't come home. I need you to stay in London."

"What are you talking about? Did you not hear me? People are dying because I'm here."

"Let me finish. We've been picking up chatter. Something about a dirty bomb at the royal wedding. MI6 knows about it too. That's probably why the British authorities are looking at you so hard. They're scrambling and under a lot of pressure to find the bomb. It seems like the small attacks are just a precursor for a bigger one. You're their only lead."

"I'm not a lead. I don't know what's going on."

"Yes, you do. You're the closest person to the problem. You know Pok inside and out. How he thinks. What he might be planning. I need you to work the problem."

"I don't work for you anymore, remember," I said roughly. "I'm not with the CIA."

My words dripped with sarcasm. Brad ignored them and continued in his businesslike, monotone voice.

"I was scrambling to put a team together. You were the logical choice, but you're on your honeymoon. But... since you're already there. You and Jamie are right in the thick of it. You need to find out what Pok's planning and stop it."

"How do you suggest I do that?"

"I have confidence in you that you'll figure it out. Remember though, you're off the books. I'm not authorizing you to run a mission in London. This has nothing to do with the CIA. But I'm telling you, in no uncertain terms, find Pok and find him now! Whatever it takes."

These were obviously the new rules of engagement. I was running a mission for the CIA, but I wasn't. He was authorizing me to do whatever it took but would disavow any knowledge of it. In other words, my neck was the one sticking out a mile. With a wink, he was telling me to hack into the cameras myself. That's really what he was saying. Something he could never tell me to do if I was officially with the CIA.

That's when it began to make perfect sense to me. AJAX. My role with the CIA. I knew what to do. Hack into the security system and trace it backward until I found Pok and his location. Even if I were still with the CIA, that's what I would have done. It didn't matter if I was with the CIA or not. Brad knew I'd do that very thing with or without his permission.

What he was doing was giving me his blessing. An order even. In no uncertain terms. But not directly, where it could blow back on him. If it ever came up, he'd deny we even had this conversation. That's why I wasn't officially with the CIA anymore.

Brad had actually done me a favor. He had taken off my restraints. In my new-found freedom were risks. But I would've taken those risks anyway. I always did whatever I had to do to save lives and complete a mission. This way I could do them with his blessing, so to speak.

This might be my honeymoon, but I was now on a mission. The only way to find out what Pok was up to, was to find Pok.

"What happens when I find him?" I asked. "Actually, I already know where he is. He's in Iran. Which would explain the coordination with the Iranian terrorists in London."

"Get me a specific location."

"Then what?"

"Let's just say, there's a cruise missile with his name on it. Two warships and a nuclear submarine are going through the Strait of Hormuz as we speak."

"That could start a war."

"We don't care. If he's about to set off a dirty bomb in London, and Iran's helping him, then all bets are off. That's an act of war. They started it. You have to bring me proof Pok's behind it and that Iran is helping him. You also have to find the bomb before it goes off at the wedding."

"That's a big lift."

"You're a big guy. With big shoulders. Plus, Jamie's with you. You probably couldn't do it on your own. But with her there... She'll figure it out if you can't. Is she up for it?"

He was joking, but not really.

"You know Jamie. She'd crawl out of bed and around London on her hands and knees if she had too. Plus, Gigi was her friend. It's personal now. She'll be fine."

"Get back to me and let me know what's happening. The wedding is in three days."

"I already know what's happening. Pok hacked into the London cameras. He's coordinating with the Iranians to launch attacks near me. The attacks are getting bigger and more brazen every day. Leading up to the big attack Sunday at the wedding."

"That makes sense to me. Now go prove it."

"The only thing I don't know is why he's conducting the attacks around me."

"For MI5 and MI6's benefit. He wants to implicate you in some way."

"What do I do about it?"

"Save the Queen, and you'll be a hero in Britain."

"I'll try."

"One other thing," Brad said.

"What's that?"

"Don't get arrested. I can't help you."

"Easier said than done," I said, letting out a deep sigh.

The cameras were everywhere. Weaver could arrest me anytime he wanted.

18

Royal London Hospital

I made the decision to go dark. Meaning undercover, operationally. The only time Pok and Weaver would see my face on a security camera was when I wanted them to. A week of our training at The Farm, the CIA training facility for new recruits, was spent on counter surveillance. Curly drilled in us how to stay off the radar and avoid detection. Skills I was putting to good use now.

The only flaw to my plan was Jamie. Both Pok and Weaver knew that eventually I'd end up at the hospital. That didn't mean they got to watch me get there. Both were probably surprised when I showed up at the entrance and smiled at the front entrance camera for their benefit. If Weaver didn't already know I was an operative of some kind, he knew now. A normal person wouldn't know the techniques I was now deploying.

It didn't matter. From this point on, I was in control. They'd know what I wanted them to know when I wanted them to know it. While my avoidance techniques were defensive, by morning, I planned on going on the offensive. I'd take the battle to Pok. A plan was already formulating in my mind. First, I had to prove he was behind the hack into the security cameras. Jamie's hospital room would be a perfect place to do that.

The lady at the nurse's station said she was still asleep. She did wake up for a couple minutes and wanted a drink, took another pain pill, and then went back to sleep. Perfect. As much as I wanted to be with her,

I needed at least eight hours of uninterrupted time to hack into London's security camera systems.

Turns out I didn't need that much time.

Finding out how Pok did it wasn't that difficult. Pok and I were probably the only two people alive who could actually do it, and I knew exactly where to look. Security camera systems were the most vulnerable of all electronic equipment. For whatever reason, equipment providers lagged behind other industries in providing security from hacking. Which was ironic considering the entire purpose of cameras and systems was to provide security to the end user.

The entire industry received a wake-up call a few years back when a company called Triple Safe Security was proven not so safe. The company provided home security systems to millions of customers around the world. They were vulnerable, and the company didn't even know it. Their camera systems were being commandeered by malicious actors through a backdoor password reset flaw. Brazen hackers even posted on the internet, the step-by-step process on how to exploit the system. With the information, even low-level amateurs could hack into the home security camera systems of unsuspecting customers. Once commandeered, they were even able to talk to the homeowners through the system.

A famous video released on the net showed a woman at home alone. A man started talking to her through the system, making lewd comments and threats. She'd purchased the system a few weeks before to keep track of her dog while she was away. The security camera system was supposedly state-of-the-art. Or at least, she thought so based on how much she paid for it.

It had night vision capabilities, HD video, and two-way talk feature. Turns out those were the same features the hacker accessed with chilling consequences. The pervert had been watching her for days and even recorded her, releasing the video on the internet much to her horror. The night vision capabilities allowed him to even watch her at night.

Needless to say, the incident drew worldwide attention, and the company was embarrassed. Its stock price fell by more than fifty percent. and they quickly reached an out-of-court, seven-figure settlement with the woman. A class action suit followed, and eventually the company filed for bankruptcy.

The good thing was that the incident increased overall awareness of the problem. While strides had been made, exploitable remote vulnerabilities still exist. Remote, meaning from a third-party location. Other companies filled the void, and while their systems were better, they weren't foolproof either. Nothing really was with thousands of hackers working day and night trying to find a vulnerability. Every system had a way in if you just knew where to look.

I did.

The London security camera system had many more safeguards than a home security system for obvious reasons. However, tens of thousands of private security cameras were accessed into their system. Each with a different username and login password. These were often nothing more than the default passwords set by the factory. In other instances, users used predictable passwords such as *12345*, or *ABCDE*, or the current year. Such things as birthdays and anniversaries were commonplace. Pets names. Things that were easy to predict. Software was available that could try literally thousands of passwords every few seconds until it came upon the right one.

Armed with that basic knowledge, Pok could access individual cameras in the system with little trouble. That didn't get him into the overall system, but it was a start. He could gain access to thousands of cameras by simply exploiting the username and password vulnerabilities. However, what Pok wanted was administrative access. That's what he needed to track me around London like a dog tracked a coon by its smell. A coon's scent went with the animal everywhere it went. In my case, my face couldn't escape being on the cameras unless I was making a concerted effort to conceal it.

Pok found a backdoor command line of code that granted administrative access. The code was temporary, and part of the system used
during the testing phase when the system was first developed. It
should've been removed at launch but was overlooked for whatever
reason. A minor mistake, but one that Pok used to gain access to the
entire system.

Once Pok was in as an administrator, he was able to maneuver
around the system undetected. He couldn't manipulate the cameras or
the system without getting caught, but that wasn't his goal. All he
wanted to do was follow me around. As long as he could see the camera
feed in real-time, he could coordinate with the terrorists to get in close
proximity to me.

Once I confirmed that the system had been hacked, I paused to consider my next move.

I could lock Pok out easily enough by fixing the code. I could create
a patch that would make it nearly impossible for him to get back in.
That seemed like the easiest solution and the safest for me. That would
all but eliminate the threat to Jamie and me. But we wouldn't know
where Pok was. This was a unique opportunity for me to find him.

What I had to do was figure out how to reverse the process. Turn the
tables. Spy on him. Was that possible? For more than an hour, I sat on
the sofa in Jamie's hospital room staring off into space. Thinking. How
could I do it without him knowing?

It was possible.

The feed from the cameras went through multiple links to get back
to his computer system. If the images could get there, so could I. I just
had to follow the links. A bolt of excitement went through me when
I realized his computers and televisions would have cameras and microphones. Not only could I find his physical location, but I might also be
able to surveille him in real time. Watch his every move like he'd been
watching me.

If he was careless, I might overhear or see where they intended to place the bomb. I could feed that information to Weaver and thwart the attack. If I simply shut Pok down now, I'd never gain access to that information.

Who knew when I might get another chance?

The risk—he would still be able to see me on the streets. For that matter, he could see everything happening in London in real-time. That would make my movements harder. Any hope of a normal honeymoon was out the window. How would Jamie feel about that? I had no doubts she'd jump into the mission headfirst.

But we had to be careful. We avoided one acid attack. There'd be another. I needed a plan to eliminate the potential of innocents getting hurt or killed.

Starting tomorrow morning.

A two-fold plan.

One that would destroy Pok. Another that would show Weaver that I was one of the good guys.

Now I needed some rest. I looked over at Jamie. She was resting peacefully. The doctor said she'd be able to go home tomorrow morning. The bandages could come off in the early afternoon. She'd be back to normal a day or two after that. With some soreness and tenderness, but, knowing her, she'd probably be back to her sassy self before that.

I looked forward to it.

I missed her.

* * *

I bolted awake. I looked at the time and realized I'd been asleep for a couple hours. Somehow, I'd been thinking about how to find Pok in my sleep, because when I woke up, I knew just what to do.

Jamie was still asleep. I powered up my laptop. By following the feed through multiple links, I found him within an hour. Confirmed when

I saw his ugly mug on the screen. Rage filled me to the point I wanted to hit something. Hit him.

I should've killed him when I had the chance in North Korea.

At least now I knew where he was. I also had the proof Brad needed. As a bonus, I had access to all of his cameras and microphones. The hunted coon was now the hunter. The best part was that he had no clue.

Once I accessed the microphones, I could hear Persian. He was definitely in Iran. Hundreds of people were at computer screens. Dozens of televisions were watching the streets of London real time. There wasn't much of a sense of urgency. Probably because they all knew I was at the hospital. The real action would begin when I walked out. Of course, they had no idea when that would be.

I wasn't going to make it easy for them.

What I needed to do then was gain intelligence. I scanned every available camera angle. Finding the exact latitude and longitude of the cyberwarfare lab would take time, so I didn't focus on that. Brad would need that before he launched an attack. I'd get to that later. Jamie was starting to stir. She'd have a lot of questions I'd have to answer.

Jamie raised her head, looked around, and then laid back down on the bed. That medicine had really wiped her out. Which bought me some more time.

An Iranian man looked like he was in charge. Revolutionary Guard was my guess. He had that hardened look of a fighter who'd seen many battles. He was probably coordinating the attacks. Right now, he was sitting back in a chair drinking a beverage. Probably a cup of coffee.

Pok had a whiteboard behind him with writing on it. The words weren't clear. I strained to see what they were. Pok was standing in front of it. Staring it at. When he stepped aside, I could see that the words were out of focus anyway. I took a screenshot of it.

Then I zoomed into the words.

My heart started beating faster.

The grogginess from my lack of sleep was overrun by adrenaline. The words were chilling.

Day One: Knife attacks.

Day Two: Acid attacks.

Day Three: Suicide Vest bombings.

Day Four: Car bombings.

Day Five: Dirty Bomb at Royal Wedding.

Today was day three! Vest bombings.

They intended to send suicide bombers into my path today.

I had to go back to the drawing board. My plan wouldn't work. A vest bomber could kill dozens of people. Maybe hundreds.

What should I do?

Should I tell Weaver?

I should call Brad.

"Hi. Honey. How long have I been asleep? What time is it?"

The voice I'd been dying to hear.

Jamie was awake.

19

Day Three

Agent Mick Weaver walked into the MI6 headquarters looking for answers. He was certain he had a CIA officer operating in his midst and was armed with videos to prove it. While he often worked closely with his counterparts in the foreign intelligence services, he could count on one hand how many times he'd actually been inside the main building. The feeling of awe felt the same as the first time.

"Legoland" as the iconic building was often referred to, fit its name. It looked like it had been put together by a resourceful kid with a large amount of Legos at his disposal. He seemed to remember the architect had won a number of awards. Once inside, it looked like any other office building except for the mystery and intrigue which no doubt happened between the walls in secret.

Weaver felt a little out of place. He dealt with local crimes. Important, but nothing like the international ramifications of the things that were investigated inside MI6.

He looked down at his watch. As was his strict custom, he was fifteen minutes early. Now the time was fifteen minutes after the scheduled appointment, and he was fuming. His time was as important as the foreign intelligence officers', even if they didn't think so. He checked in at the front security counter, and they told him to wait. Thirty minutes ago.

Waiting caused his blood pressure to rise and made him antsy. That and he expected more attacks today which also had him on edge. He expected his phone to ring at any time with his assistant conveying another deadly attack in downtown London. One in which Alex Steele was somehow connected. He really wanted to be in front of the security cameras to see it as it happened.

But he needed to talk to an officer at MI6 and get his take on the problem. While he was convinced Alex Steele was on a CIA mission, it didn't make sense to him. That's what he hoped his appointment, foreign intelligence service officer Bond Digby, could shed some light on. The man's name brought a smile to his face, releasing the tension somewhat. How ironic to be a spy with the name of Bond, even if it was his first name.

Digby finally arrived. "There's always a fire to put out somewhere in the world," he said.

There's a fire right here in London, Weaver wanted to quip but held his tongue. No use starting the meeting off on the wrong foot.

Digby led Weaver into his office. It had a conference table in the corner and Weaver had video to show him and suggested the table would be better suited for both of them to be able to view his footage.

"Let me get right to the point," Weaver said. "A man named Alex Steele arrived in London on Wednesday morning from the States. With a woman. He claims they're on their honeymoon. As soon as they got off the Tube, they witnessed a knife attack on a woman also getting off the train. Unfortunately, the woman was killed, and the terrorist got away. Steele chased the man up the subway stairs but lost him. He came back and performed CPR on the woman. But as I said, she didn't survive."

Weaver was a fact freak. He intended to lay out all his information in a methodical manner. Digby seemed bored already. So, Weaver jumped over his memorized presentation and got right to the purpose of the meeting.

"I think Alex Steele is working with the CIA."

"I called them, and they said he wasn't." Digby leaned back in his chair.

"Do you believe them?" Weaver asked.

"I don't have any reason not to."

Rather than argue the point, Weaver moved on to the next set of compelling facts. "Later that day, another attack occurred. Outside Kensington Palace. Steele and his so-called wife were present for that attack as well. This time they disarmed the attacker who had a knife."

"Sounds like the man did you a favor. What's the problem?"

"The next day, there was an acid attack at the Tower of London. Steele was there. So was his wife."

"I heard about that attack. Such a tragedy. The woman was a beautiful model. I hope she makes it. Either way, her life will never be the same again. You say Steele was there?"

"Yes," Weaver said with incredulity. "That's my point. Why is he always present at these attacks? There was another acid attack in Trafalgar Square later that afternoon. Again, Steele was there. Actually, the attack never happened. I sent a SWAT team in and they took the terrorist into custody before he could launch his attack. I have Steele on video stalking the guy. He was about to take him down, but my men arrived first. Steele got away."

"How does Steele know when the attacks are about to take place?"

"I don't know. That's what has me baffled. Is he conducting a CIA intelligence gathering mission on British soil?"

"Not supposed to be. He would've checked in with us first. And that would be very reckless. A beautiful woman was disfigured for life. If he knew that attack was about to happen and didn't notify us, I'd have a huge problem with that."

"Apparently, he feels the need to stop these attacks on his own. I don't know why. I hoped you could shed some light on it."

Digby shrugged his shoulders then pointed to the laptop which was opened on the table.

"I assume you have something you want me to see?" he said, in the form of a question.

"I have video footage of the attacks. I thought if you saw the man, you might recognize him or at least confirm from his actions that he is an operative."

The video of the subway attack came up first. Digby leaned in to get a close look at the screen.

"Rewind that," he said before it even got to the attack.

Weaver hit a key on the computer and went back to the beginning, which started when the woman exited the subway car with her child.

"Stop it right there." Digby said.

Steele had not yet gotten off the subway car. The video was frozen on his wife.

"I know that girl," Digby said. "Her name's Emily. I don't remember her last name."

"Steele says that's his wife, Jamie Steele."

"I don't know if she's his wife, but she's definitely with the CIA. I worked with her a couple years ago on a case. She's with the sex-trafficking division. It's not uncommon for them to use fake names."

Weaver's heart did a somersault in his chest. If the wife was with the CIA, so was the man. His suspicions were confirmed.

"What do you know about her?" Weaver asked.

"That she's the best damn field officer I've ever worked with. She saved my life."

"How so?"

"A long story but here's the short version. She uncovered a sex trafficking ring at local massage parlors in Soho. No shocker there. Everybody knows they exist, but she was determined to bring them down. She followed protocol and brought us in before she acted. Obviously, being a woman, she couldn't just walk into the place, but I could. So, I went in, got into one of the back rooms on the guise that I was a john. The prostitute gave me her price. I paid her and then told her that I just wanted to talk. My purpose for being there was intelligence gathering. I wanted to know how many women were employed there and if they were free to leave."

Digby took a deep breath and looked up at the ceiling.

"Anyway, the woman was uncooperative at first. She kept insisting that she didn't know anything. I got the sense that she was afraid to talk. All of a sudden, she said she had to go to the bathroom, and she left the room. I sensed something wasn't right and told Emily through the radio. Next thing I knew, some Asian guys were in the room with guns pointed at my head. I thought they were going to kill me. Anyway, Emily barged in with her guns drawn. She took on three men, and disarmed them. They were writhing on the floor faster than I could blink an eye. I didn't even have time to help her."

"Sounds like you were lucky."

"I owe her one. If she hadn't come along, I'd be a dead man."

"That confirms what I saw. Steele and his wife are obviously professionals."

Weaver showed him the footage of the second knife attack. It showed the woman and Alex disarming the terrorist. "Look at what they did to the attacker," Weaver said, pointing at the screen.

Digby winced when he saw it.

"The man lost both his arms," Weaver added.

Digby nodded. "That's what I mean. Her skills are off the charts. Those two were definitely trained by Curly."

"Curly?"

"He's a trainer at the Farm. That's where the CIA trains their officers. Our people go there sometimes for joint training. Curly's the best there is. I saw him not that long ago. He told me that Emily, or whatever her name is, was the best he'd ever trained."

143

Weaver showed him the acid attack. Digby studied it closely.

"Looks to me like Emily, the wife, heads straight for the attacker."

"She would've taken him out, but the guards shot him down first."

Digby clearly saw Alex running right behind her.

"That's strange," Digby said. "That they'd be at all three attacks. It's like they knew they were going to happen ahead of time."

"There was a fourth one. Later that day. Like I said, Steele was at that one."

"Steele is definitely former CIA. I can tell by his actions. I don't think he's currently with them, though, or they would've told me."

"Here's something strange. Steele bought a painting at the National Gallery for more than three million pounds. Where does a CIA man get that kind of money?"

Digby leaned back in his chair again and clasped his hands behind his head.

"The CIA wouldn't authorize that kind of money for a cover. That's for sure. Steele had to do that on his own. But where did he get that much money?"

"That's why I'm here. I have a theory, but it's just that, a theory."

"Did you bring Steele in for questioning?" Digby asked.

"I've talked to him three times."

"And what does he say?"

"That's he not with the CIA. He and the girl are on their honeymoon. The fact they are at the attacks is purely a coincidence."

"I don't buy that."

"Me either."

"The money also has me baffled. Steele is right. He's not with the CIA anymore. But what happened?"

"Any ideas?" Weaver asked.

"He could've stolen the money. That might be why he was cut loose. A guy this good wouldn't be let go for no reason."

"Wouldn't he have been arrested?"

"Only if they could prove it. Which is hard to do. Guys in the field only make a drop in the bucket compared to the risk taken. The temptation is strong. Steele could've come across a drug dealer, or arms dealer, took the money and justified it by convincing himself he did the world a favor. The money was better off in his hands than some terrorists. I'm not justifying it. I'm just saying that might've been what he was thinking."

"Why the attacks though?" Weaver said. "If Steele knew about them, why didn't he try to stop them?"

"Apparently, he did try. But on two occasions, he wasn't able to. The man with the acid threw it on the girl before Steele could stop him. It's almost like Steele knows about the attacks in advance, wants to stop them, but isn't always successful. Or maybe he doesn't want to be successful all the time so it doesn't draw suspicion on him. Very strange. Why would he risk people getting hurt?"

"Steele's wife got acid on her and she's in the hospital."

"I'd bet a year's salary she doesn't know anything about it," Bond said. "That girl is diamonds. I just don't see her being involved for any amount of money."

"Do you have a theory?" Weaver asked, anxiously waiting for the answer.

"I do, but it's pretty far-fetched."

"Hey. I'm at the end of my rope. I can't figure it out."

Digby leaned back again and contorted his lips like he didn't want to say what he was about to say.

"Munchausen."

"The syndrome?" Weaver had heard of it. Munchausen Syndrome was when mothers hurt their kids to gain attention.

Digby explained. "Hear me out. What if Steele is a Munchausen spy. Follow the logic. He's on the outs with the CIA. He got fired for whatever reason. Probably for stealing money. That's how he can throw money around like he's a big shot. No CIA officer I know can buy a painting for three million pounds. Anyway, he learns about the attacks. He shows up to stop them. He becomes a hero again with the CIA. Maybe he gets his job back."

Digby paused, leaving an eerie silence in the room for the better part of thirty seconds.

Then continued. "Or maybe Steele just misses the action. Some guys can't live without it. When you're used to killing people for a living, it gets in your blood. It's hard to go back to being normal. Anyway, Steele is doing it for attention. Obviously. That's my theory."

"What should I do about it?"

"Arrest him."

"On what charge?"

"Accessory. Conspiracy. Whatever. I don't think the CIA is going to have his back. Worry about proving it later. If you put enough pressure on him, maybe he'll tell you how he knows about the attacks ahead of time. Hell. Charge him with obstruction of justice. Anyway. Get him off the street. We've got the wedding coming up this weekend, and there's talk about a dirty bomb."

"I read about it in this morning's briefing."

"The last thing you need is to be chasing Steele around town. We've all got better things to do than that. You might not be able to make the charges stick, but you can lock him in a cell for a few days. At least until after the wedding."

Weaver's phone rang. His assistant was on the other line. His heart skipped a beat as he expected the worst.

"I need to take this."

He stood from his chair and turned his back to Digby. Not that he needed privacy, but so he wouldn't see his hand shaking.

"Steele is at Trafalgar again," his assistant said. "He's hanging around the lions like he did yesterday."

"Send your men in right away. Arrest him. I'll be right there."

Weaver hung up.

"That's Steele. He's back at it. I've got to go."

"Good luck."

"Thanks. You've been a big help. I'm going to arrest him right now."

"Good. I hope the charges stick. What kind of man lets a woman get stabbed right in front of him? Or lets a model get her whole life ruined? A scumbag if you ask me."

"The lowest of the low," Weaver said. "I don't know who's worse. The terrorists or Steele."

20

Trafalgar Square

M y timing had to be perfect.

Considering I was guessing and going on assumptions that may or may not be true, my chances were next to impossible to get it right. Curly wouldn't like my plan. From my vantage point, I saw no other choice.

I said a quick prayer. Why I didn't do that more often, I wasn't sure. If I ever needed help from God, this was one of those times.

The plan was to lure the vest bomber to Trafalgar Square. I showed my face on the security camera hoping to accomplish that goal. The problem was knowing when he would arrive. I couldn't be there. If the bomber had confirmation that I was in the square, all he had to do was detonate the bomb and dozens would be killed or injured, and I would be placed at the scene. I had to be long gone.

Not long gone, but out of the square before he arrived. But I couldn't leave too soon. That's where the timing was critical. I needed to be far enough away from the bomber that he wouldn't detonate, but close enough to entice him to follow me. Impossible, considering I had no idea if he was even coming, much less when or from what direction.

If the plan didn't work, it wasn't because I wasn't prepared. I'd studied the details until my eyes hurt. I felt comfortable in my assumptions and had to tamp down my concerns. The arrival time of the bomber was an educated guess. Based on yesterday, it took the acid attacker eighteen minutes to arrive from the time I showed my face to the time he entered the square. In my estimation, today's bomber would probably take longer.

The likelihood was that there were only two vest bombers as opposed to a dozen or more acid attackers. Finding the materials to make vest bombs wasn't as easy as filling up a squirt bottle full of acid. So, they'd be spread out. One close to the hotel and one in a central location. Probably a twenty-minute walk from me. Pok wouldn't expect me to come back to Trafalgar. Curly would like that part of the plan. *Always do what your enemy least expects you to do*, he said more times than I could remember.

That little bit of indecision would work to my advantage. From the time Pok spotted me, notifying the bomber and for that person to make his way to the square, unnoticed, would take several minutes. Vest bombers were careful for obvious reasons. They didn't walk as fast, and they moved hesitantly. Human nature. Even though they intended to blow themselves up, they weren't generally in a rush to do so. Unless the bomber was in the direct vicinity of Trafalgar Square, his arrival time would be between fifteen and thirty minutes.

I needed to leave the square four to five minutes before he arrived.

Curly was right.

This wasn't a good plan. Or at least the Curly who was always in my head and offering the criticism of it.

The problem was obvious. Even if I left at the right time, I needed the bomber to follow me. My plan was so detailed and intricate that I had to lead him to a predetermined point through a maze of streets. All the while, keeping my face on the camera so Pok could help the man keep following me, but making sure the bomber wasn't close enough to set off his bomb. At least the path would lead us through less populated areas. I always had my gun, and could kill the man, but the bomb would still go off. He was going to die anyway.

I had to make sure he died at a time and place of my choosing, not his.

I also had Weaver to consider. He was watching as well. I was certain of that. If my plan worked, he'd realize that I'm one of the good guys and that I had saved lives by stopping the attacks. Not that I wanted to be a hero or wanted any recognition. I didn't choose this battle. The whole thing looked fishy to him. I wanted to prove to him that I was helping him. He still needed me. There was the dirty bomb at the royal wedding to consider.

Part of me wanted to tell Weaver the whole story. I couldn't. Brad wouldn't back me up, and Weaver would arrest me on the spot for hacking into the London security camera system. This was the only way. I began to get antsy again.

The timer on my watch read ten minutes. That's how long it'd been since Pok saw me on the cameras. The urge to leave was overwhelming. I had to force myself to wait. The plan couldn't fail because I suddenly lost my nerve and couldn't control my impulses.

That's why I needed divine intervention to show me the right time. Thinking about God would distract me for a few more minutes. A few months ago, I read an article about a person who'd had a near death experience. He was swept out into the ocean by a rip tide. It took rescuers more than ten hours to find him. Many times, he'd given up hope. Treading water for that long took every ounce of energy from him. The man related in the article that he pleaded with God to save him. Even admitted he made a number of promises to God that he'd already broken.

"Save me, and I promise to be a better husband and father," he said, while in the ocean. "If you'll rescue me, I promise I'll go to church every Sunday for the rest of my life."

That article hit close to home for me for different reasons. Many people turn to God when they're facing death's door. The rest of the time, God's on the backburner. Prayer is only turned to when they really needed it. I wasn't judging. I did the same thing. Just the opposite, though. I faced near death experiences all the time. Because I was so well trained, I often relied more on my own abilities and forgot to ask God for help. I'd faced death four times in the last forty-eight hours! More times than I could count if I included the last four years. This was the first time in London, I'd thought to ask him to help me.

Maybe I had become too used to the danger. Looking back, I remembered many times when it felt like God was protecting me, even if I wasn't acknowledging it or pleading with him. It wouldn't hurt for me to remember that more. In my line of work, I needed his protection every day. All of us do in our own ways, but today, I needed him more than ever.

Too many things could go wrong with my plan. My angst returned with a vengeance.

Show me the right time to leave, I prayed.

At eighteen minutes, I couldn't resist the impulse. I probably should've waited another five minutes but didn't. It seemed like the right time. Almost like I could sense the bomber's presence drawing near to the square. I stretched my arms, trying to look nonchalant, casual even. Like I was about to go for a stroll without a care in the world.

Choosing which direction to leave the square was preplanned. Truthfully, I didn't know if I was making the right choice. In a way, the odds were fifty-fifty. If I chose wrong, I'd run directly into the bomber, and my plan would be for naught. I hoped and prayed I was right.

Maybe the odds were better than fifty-fifty since the odds were good that the bomber would come from the same direction as the acid man. A reasonable assumption, which was the best I could do under the circumstances.

I forced my feet to start walking.

I was on the move.

* * *

Iran

The timing has to be perfect, Pok thought to himself.

Halee was standing in Trafalgar Square. Niazi had a man with a bomb on the way. Two bombers were in London ready to go. One was at Halee's hotel, the other in a central location of London. Pok was shocked that Halee had gone back to Trafalgar, and that threw him off at first. It took extra time to scramble the man and get him headed to the square. Pok could only hope Halee would wait for him to arrive.

So far, so good.

Halee had been in the square for a good fifteen minutes and didn't appear to be leaving anytime soon. As long as Pok had eyes on Halee, all the bomber had to do was enter the square and detonate the bomb. Halee was standing next to the lions. He wouldn't be harmed, but he'd be in the camera shot. Once again for the authorities to see.

The bomb would do significant damage, and there'd be loss of life. Niazi explained how the bombs were made and why they only had two available. Basically, the men took a special vest with shoulder straps and sewed shrapnel, steel ball bearings, and various other objects such as nails, brads, etc, into the pockets of the vest. They weren't easy to make. The explosives connected to a detonator in the bomber's hand which he kept in his pocket and had to be armed carefully so the bomb didn't explode prematurely.

More sophisticated devices could be set off with a cell phone from a remote location. These devices were simpler. The man had his finger on the button. He released the button and the vest exploded. If the target were within thirty yards, the bomb would do serious damage.

Halee was making it easy for them.

"Just a couple more minutes," Pok said aloud to Alex.

Niazi entered the room. "Are we a go?"

"Everything still looks good. I'll signal you when to detonate." Pok had a split screen on his computer. He could see both men. Halee by the lion. The bomber walking down the street toward Trafalgar.

"Just two more minutes," Pok said. "Two more minutes."

Pok felt like he was watching a rocket launch. The same type of anticipation with a countdown.

This was going to be more exciting than anything he'd ever seen before.

* * *

MI5 Headquarters

The timing had to be perfect.

Weaver was back in headquarters monitoring the security cameras. He had a SWAT team on go a block away from Trafalgar Square, hidden from view. They were prepared to move at his command.

Not too early, but not too late. That's why the timing was critical.

At the moment, Alex Steele was standing in the square by one of the lion statues. Just like yesterday. Weaver was tempted to rush in and apprehend him but sensed that something else was about to happen. Maybe another attack. This was a chance for him to take another bad guy off the street.

If he moved too soon, the terrorist would get spooked and disappear without being spotted. If they waited too long, then Weaver ran the risk of the attack happening before his men could stop it.

Just a couple minutes more, he thought to himself. That's how much longer he was willing to wake. His case against Alex would be advanced even more if Weaver had evidence of a fifth attack about to take place in the square. No judge in London would believe that Alex being present at the attacks was coincidental. If nothing else, they had probable cause to hold him until after the wedding.

His heart pounded in his chest. He tried to slow it by taking a sip of coffee. His hand was shaking so much, he almost spilled it on his shirt. This was probably what Bond Digby felt when he was on a mission. This was the most exciting case he'd worked since he started at MI5, years ago.

Weaver kept his eyes peeled to the screen.

Alex stretched his arms. It looked like he was getting ready to move.

Indecision gripped Weaver like a vise. A quick glance around the square confirmed that there wasn't a bomber in it.

Should we go in or wait?

Alex was walking now. Toward the northeast corner intersection.

Weaver had SWAT on a direct line.

"We have a visual," the SWAT team commander said. "Do you want us to grab him?"

Weaver hesitated.

"No. Let him go. Follow him. Let's see where he takes us."

"Roger that."

Weaver hoped he made the right decision.

"Where are you going, Alex Steele?" he said to the screen.

21

Iran

From Pok's perspective, the plan could not have gone any better. He couldn't wipe away the smug look on his face which even Niazi commented on. His plan was brilliant, even by Pok's high standards. From the safety of Iran, he was able to follow Halee and the vest bomber every step of the way, even through the maze of London streets.

The bomber arrived in Trafalgar Square two minutes after Halee left. At first, Pok panicked. He regrouped and worked the plan. All he had to do was go camera-by-camera and follow Halee's every move then relay it to the bomber.

The longer the chase continued, the closer Niazi's man got to Steele. The gap was narrowing with every turn. Now, he was closing in. Halee entered an industrial complex. The bomber was about fifty yards behind him. The area wasn't a good place to detonate the bomb. There were no people around.

According to Pok's maps, Halee was cornered, and there was only one way out. From the looks of it, Halee was leading the bomber right into an area with a crowded street on the other side of the complex. On the wall behind the televisions was a row of clocks set at different time zones. London time was at lunch hour. People would be filing out of the industrial complex in droves to get something to eat.

The thought caused Pok to fill with emotions, although he knew better than to celebrate too soon. He kept his eyes focused on the screen. They had come too far to lose Halee now. The bomber would be in range within a minute or two, and Pok would give the order to detonate. Then he would celebrate. Not a second before.

Pok was in the main room where all the workers were congregated to watch the scene unfold on the many television screens. Tension filled the room like a London fog. All eyes were riveted to them with anticipation. Halee walked behind the building and turned the corner. From what he could tell, the bomber already had him in his sights because he quickened his steps.

Within seconds, Pok would give the order.

The bomber slowed and peered around the corner. Pok watched him round the corner and come into view on another camera. He turned his head and then started walking again. With purpose. Halee was not in view of the camera. Pok wasn't sure what the bomber was seeing. Pok looked at the next camera. Just ahead was the street. That must be where Steele was headed.

Pok prepared to give the order to detonate. The bomber only needed to be a few feet from the crowd in order to inflict maximum damage. The street camera should pick up Halee's image any second.

A fireball suddenly erupted on the television. It brightened the room as the image of the orange flame appeared on hundreds of screens at once. Then the TVs went dark as a black plume of smoke covered the lens. The camera actually shook from the concussion.

A cheer went up from the throng of people in Pok's cyber lab.

Niazi thrust his fist into the air.

Pok wasn't celebrating just yet.

He wasn't sure what just happened.

***

MI5 Headquarters

"What just happened?" Weaver asked the room full of people watching the cameras following Alex Steele.

He'd just given the order to the SWAT team to move in and arrest Alex Steele. They'd followed him from Trafalgar Square a few miles east through a maze of streets into an industrial complex. Weaver ordered them to stay back and out of Steele's sight. He was watching Alex in real time and told the SWAT team which path to take to follow him.

Shortly after entering the complex, Alex disappeared from the camera view. That's when Weaver acted and ordered the men to move on Steele.

Seconds later another man entered the picture.

A middle easterner.

Wearing a jacket.

He had all the mannerisms of a terrorist.

A bolt of panic shot through Weaver as he shouted on the radio, trying to warn the SWAT team of the potential danger.

The words had barely come out of his mouth when a fireball erupted. A black plume of smoke filled the area, and the camera shook from the concussion.

A gasp went through the crowd of people watching as tension filled the room like a dark storm cloud.

"Did you see that?" the SWAT team commander said over the radio with panic in his voice.

"What happened?" Weaver asked.

"A guy just blew himself up."

"Any casualties?"

"My men were not in the blast radius. It looks like a war zone down here."

The man was practically shouting. Weaver could hear screaming in the background.

"Get emergency personnel down there right now!" Weaver shouted to anyone who could hear him.

He wasn't sure what to do. Should he go down there himself or keep watching the screen? Staying was the better option for now until he knew what he was dealing with. When the smoke cleared, he could assess the situation. He had men on the ground already. Not knowing, though, sent bolts of fear and trepidation through him like the fireball he'd just witnessed. His hand was shaking.

"Do you have eyes on Steele?" he asked over the radio.

"Negative."

"Was he caught up in the blast?"

"I'll get back to you on that. I can't tell you anything until the smoke clears."

Suddenly, Weaver was worried. Had he arrested Steele when he had the chance, none of this would've happened. If an innocent bystander was killed, he had no way to explain his actions. Also, if Steele died, he'd probably never know the truth. Why were the terrorists following him?

A plan was already forming in his mind to justify his actions. They were doing reconnaissance. Fact gathering. He had no idea a bomber was following Steele. Now he was kicking himself. He never thought to look at other cameras for additional threats for fear of losing Steele.

What a disaster.

His plan couldn't have gone any worse.

* * *

Industrial complex
Downtown London

My plan could not have gone any better.

I left Trafalgar Square on foot, hoping the vest bomber was right behind me. To most people, it might've seemed strange walking through the streets of London, not knowing if I was fleeing from a ghost. Such was counterintelligence. Many times, we employed tactics in the field to expose a tail, not knowing if one was there or not. That sometimes took hours to do. It meant making all kinds of evasive maneuvers. Going in and out of businesses. Starting. Stopping. Changing direction on a dime. All the while having no clue if anyone was actually tailing you.

That's what this felt like. Except for the starting and stopping. The route was preplanned. All I had to do was judge the pace. I needed for the bomber, if he was really behind me, to slowly catch up. Not too fast, but not too slow either. I had to time it so that he entered the designated area shortly after me.

I entered the industrial complex as adrenaline pulsed through my body like a fire hose spraying it out of my heart. Every one of my senses was heightened to their maximum intensity. With every fiber of my being, I hoped and prayed the bomber was behind me, but not too close. Sometimes, a fine line hung between mission success and disaster. I'd been on that line many times and knew what it felt like. It never felt good until I knew the outcome.

One way or the other, I'd know the outcome of this plan soon. I was near the point where I'd confront the bomber. If there was a bomber.

When I rounded the corner of the office building, I left the view of the camera. That was by design. It took me hours to find it. No eyes were on me then. I sprinted to a place behind a large metal trash container. Just ahead on the left was a busy street. Dozens of people were walking on the sidewalk. Just out of harm's way. Thankfully.

I waited.

I didn't have to wait long.

The man emerged from the side of the building cautiously. My heart did a gymnastics routine when I saw him.

Middle eastern

Wearing a jacket. His right hand was in his pocket.

The bulges of the bomb could be seen pressing against his shirt.

No doubt in my mind who he was.

I shouted out to him. "I'm over here," I said.

The bomber was still in the camera view. That was for Weaver and Pok's benefit. I wanted them to see the whole thing. Everything, except what I was about to do.

The bomber took ten steps toward me.

I raised my gun and fired.

A fireball erupted.

I ducked behind the dumpster as shrapnel and ball bearings pinged against it causing a loud clamor. I could feel the heat from the blast.

The shot had been pre planned as well. I aimed for his chest. At the detonator. The bomb would destroy any evidence that a bullet was fired. Vest bombs were strange in how they operated. They blew the person's head completely off his body. Separated, but fully intact. As if it had been severed by a sharp guillotine blade. Most of the time, the man's head could be found dozens of yards away, but with no noticeable injuries. Had I shot the man in the head, the bomb would have exploded, but Weaver would've known he'd been shot. I'd be the obvious suspect.

Pok would be watching as well and would realize I'd set off the bomb. I needed him to think the man exploded the bomb prematurely or maybe even on purpose. Pok might even consider the bombing a success. He wouldn't know if I was caught up in it or not.

Weaver would see it as a success as well. He would conclude that I led the bomber away from the crowded square. Saving lives. He'd never know about the gun. England had some of the toughest gun control laws in the world. I couldn't let Weaver see me shoot the guy. I'd be arrested on the spot. The fact that I killed the terrorists might only knock a couple of years off my lengthy prison sentence.

Weaver also couldn't know that I had hacked into the camera system. Another major offense which would get me locked away for years, regardless of the motive. Weaver needed to believe that I was being targeted by terrorists for some reason. When questioned, I would even argue that I was the victim who needed protection.

Of course, I would deny involvement. I was just walking the streets of London, minding my own business. On my honeymoon. For some reason, the terrorists were after me. Maybe seeking revenge for me maiming one of their own. That explanation had just popped in my head. It sounded believable to me. I suddenly had a defense that made sense. Weaver wouldn't believe it, but at least he had no reason to arrest me.

If I worked for the CIA and was on a mission, all of these offenses would go away. I had done England a favor. I still looked at it that way, even if they didn't.

A terrorist was dead. This was no small victory in my book. No civilians were injured. But I knew the war had just started. I won this round, but tomorrow's terror was car bombings. How would I stop those? The next day after that was the royal wedding and the dirty bomb. I had no idea where the bomb was or how they intended to set it off. I only had forty-eight hours to find out. Telling Weaver or MI6 wasn't an option. Then I'd have to explain how I knew.

While I was plotting my next move, I saw movement out of the corner of my eye. From a different part of the complex.

A SWAT team was approaching the area where the bomber had detonated the bomb. It looked like a war zone, and they looked like soldiers infiltrating it with their machine guns raised and wearing full combat gear.

They couldn't catch me with the gun. I was on the move. From my vantage point, I was able to make it to the street undetected and blend into the crowd. Within two minutes, I was in a cab on my way to the hospital.

Jamie was to be released at one o'clock.

Time to explain to her what was happening.

We had a mutual problem. Our honeymoon was ruined. Like it or not, we were on a mission.

And if my situational analysis was correct, there was one more vest bomber out there.

22

Royal London Hospital

When I got off the elevator, I could hear yelling all the way down the hall coming from Jamie's hospital room. My nerves were already frazzled from the confrontation with the terrorist and watching him incinerate right in front of my eyes. Adding to my angst was what we were facing over the next couple days. Another vest bomber, car bombings, and a potential dirty bomb at the royal wedding.

A problem at the hospital was the last thing I expected to encounter. Jamie was supposed to be released at one o'clock. I hurried to see what all the commotion was about.

When I entered the room, Jamie was standing up, although still in her hospital gown. The nurse had an exasperated, almost angry look. Her eyes were narrowed and her jaw clenched. They were standing toe to toe almost like two boxers about to square off.

"What's going on?" I asked, somewhat hesitantly. I took a couple long strides so I was next to Jamie. Her hands were still heavily bandaged, but her knee only had one layer of gauze wrapped around it. She was favoring her knee, but at least she was standing which seemed like a good thing to me.

"I'm glad you're here," Jamie said then glared at the nurse. "Maybe you can talk some sense into this lady."

"I'm trying to get your wife to put her clothes on so she can check out." The nurse put her hands on Jamie's arms, but she jerked them away.

The lady had no way of knowing that if Jamie didn't want to do something, not a man or a woman alive could make her do it.

The scene didn't make any sense. I would think Jamie would be dying to get out of there.

"I'm not going outside looking like this!" Jamie waved her big oven mitts in the air as it suddenly made sense. Being a tall girl, Jamie looked like a windmill with large, cup-sized blades twirling in the wind. I bit my lip to keep from smiling, knowing that might make her angrier.

"I thought the doctor said you could get your bandages off today," I said, still not fully understanding the problem.

Jamie threw her hands in the air. "I know! Tell that to Nurse Ratchett."

"It's *Ratched*," the nurse said sarcastically emphasizing the last syllable. "With an e and d. Not Ratchett. I've seen the movie nine times."

I didn't remember what movie they were talking about, but I remembered that calling a person "Nurse Ratched" was a highly derogatory term meant to offend. Which it obviously did based on the nurse's reaction.

"Whatever. I've never seen it," Jamie said. She turned toward me. "I want these bandages off. Now."

"The doctor said they had to stay on until two o'clock," the nurse retorted.

"That's so stupid," Jamie said. "I check out at one. What difference does another hour make?"

They were both now facing me, making their points like I was the judge and they were pleading a case. I wasn't sure I wanted to be in the middle of it.

"Those are the doctor's orders. I have to follow his procedures," the nurse argued to me.

"I won't be here at two o'clock," Jamie said. "I'm checking out at one. Tell her she's being ridiculous," Jamie said pointing her big bear paws at me.

Jamie had a good point.

The clock on the wall said one o'clock. I was tempted to take the knife out of my pocket and cut the bandages off. Then I wondered if I was allowed to even have a knife in the hospital. The nurse might try to have me arrested. That wasn't an option. Jamie and I were going back to the hotel, checking out, and going dark for the rest of our trip. The best way for me to find the dirty bomb was to work incognito. Dodging terrorists was getting old, not to mention extremely dangerous. Things went well with the vest bomber, all things considered. I didn't want to push my luck any farther. I also now had Jamie to protect who clearly wasn't yet one hundred percent.

Charm would be the better tactic with the nurse. I decided to sweet talk her since a confrontation obviously wasn't working. That would annoy Jamie, but it still seemed like the best approach.

"I know that you're just doing your job," I said in my most disarming voice. "But it's after one o'clock. Technically, she's checked out now. Could we compromise?"

It seemed to work, because the nurse's shoulders dropped slightly, and her jaw wasn't as clenched.

"She's going to need bandages on her hands," the nurse said. "They're going to be tender and sore for the next day or two."

"Can you wrap her hands like you did her knee? That way she can at least put her clothes on and have some use of her hands."

That argument seemed to work, because the lady instructed Jamie to sit down on the edge of the bed. She pulled a tray beside her and began clipping off the bandages with a pair of scissors. Jamie mouthed a "thank you" to me.

With the bandages off, Jamie's hands were still bright red which made me wince. At least the blisters were gone.

"The bright red is because her hands are healing," the nurse said, almost sensing what I was thinking. "That will go away in time. Just be careful not to touch anything over the next couple days. You can take a shower, but no baths. I put a small bottle of pain pills in your bag. Take as needed."

"I won't need them."

The nurse put a salve on Jamie's hands and then wrapped each one with a piece of gauze. Jamie grimaced a couple of times, telling me she was still in pain. Even so, she wouldn't take the pill. I probably wouldn't let her anyway. She needed to be fully alert for the next forty-eight hours.

"Get dressed, and I'll be back to collect you in ten minutes," the nurse said curtly as she walked out of the room. The woman's bedside manner could use some work. I could see why Jamie would have a short fuse with her. Getting there when I did was probably a good thing.

"I'm so glad to have those bandages off," Jamie said. "I couldn't even scratch my butt with those airplane wings on my hands."

"I'll scratch your butt for you anytime you want," I said boyishly, while wrapping my arms around her. "All you have to do is ask."

Jamie wasn't much for sexual innuendo and rarely appreciated my dry sense of humor, but sometimes I simply couldn't resist.

As expected, she rolled her eyes, but the smile on her face told me she'd be in a better mood soon.

At least until I told her what we faced over the next two days. For all practical purposes, our honeymoon was ruined. I'd wait to tell her until we were alone for an extended period of time.

We packed her things and waited for the nurse to return. When she did, she was pushing a wheelchair.

Jamie shook her head no.

"Hospital policy," the nurse said. "Every patient must leave the hospital in a wheelchair."

Jamie brushed right past the lady and started heading down the hallway. Still favoring her knee, but fast enough that I would have to hurry to catch her before she got on the elevator.

"Is your wife always this stubborn?" the nurse asked me.

"You have no idea," I said, letting out a deep sigh.

To me, that was a good sign. The old Jamie was back.

* * *

Site of the vest bombing

Weaver had never seen a bombing site in person. The closest he came was a training video which didn't even begin to capture the horror of the scene. The smell of explosives mixed with burning human remains was nauseating. The body of the bomber was unrecognizable as a human form, other than the head of the man, which was perfectly intact, a good thirty yards away from the initial blast. Forensic teams were already at work poring over the evidence.

Weaver was questioning Robert Manwaring, the SWAT team captain with a name appropriate for his line of work. Something Manwaring said was puzzling to Weaver.

"So, you think you heard a gunshot?" Weaver said in the form of a question.

"I think so, but I can't be sure. Things happened so fast."

"Walk me through it from the beginning."

"My men and I rounded the building." He pointed to a spot at the southwest corner of the scene.

"We saw the bomber. I immediately put my fist in the air for everyone to stop. We knelt down and focused our weapons on the man who had his back to us."

"Did you see anyone else? A tall man? Athletic build? American?"

"No. We didn't see Steele if that's what you mean. Or anyone else for that matter."

Weaver looked over the scene. He had clearly seen Alex Steele on the security camera, walk into the area shortly before the bomber. Alex didn't have time to make it all the way to the other side of the building.

The only place Alex could've been hiding was behind a large trash dumpster that was now dented in multiple places from the blast.

"What happened next?" Weaver asked.

"It sounded like a gunshot went off."

"What type of weapon?"

"Definitely small caliber. I did a number of tours in Iraq and Afghanistan. I know what an assault rifle sounds like. This was a handgun."

"Did you see where the shot came from?"

"Like I said, it all happened so fast. The bomb went off milliseconds later. We retreated back behind the building."

Weaver wondered if Steele shot the bomber causing the bomb to explode. When they retreated, that would've given Steele the opportunity to flee the scene. They also wouldn't have been able to see him with all the smoke.

"Thank you," Weaver said to Manwaring. "I'll be in touch if I have any more questions."

What to do next was obvious. He'd seen Alex Steele enter the hospital and then leave with his wife. Or whoever she was. He needed to pay them a visit at their hotel room and search the room for a gun. Steele may have ditched it along the way, but Weaver could tie him to the scene from the security camera.

No way Alex could explain his way out of this.

* * *

Iran

Pok was trying to do two things at once. Monitor Halee's location and watch the news reports from London to try and piece together what happened. The bomb had exploded prematurely. No one knew why. The Iranians thought it was a good thing, and a buzz of excitement filled the room. Pok wasn't so sure and wouldn't celebrate until he knew the end result.

When the London news reported that only one person was dead—the bomber, the jubilation in the cyber lab dissipated like a puff of smoke in the wind..

Niazi was furious. He pounded his fist into a wall so hard, it left a hole in the sheetrock. If Niazi noticed the blood on his knuckles, it wasn't obvious he even cared. His thirst for vengeance against Halee started raging out of control like a wildfire next to dry kindling as he filled the room with expletives in several different languages.

Pok needed to channel Niazi's hatred toward a productive end. Niazi's focus was still on Halee.

"We need to kill him," Niazi said.

"In due time, my friend. In due time."

"I don't understand why no one else was killed when the bomb exploded."

"Water under a bridge as they say. We need to focus on the next attack. Where is your other man?"

"He's outside Halee's hotel."

"Perfect."

Pok had seen Halee leave the hospital with his wife. He assumed they were headed back to the hotel. That would be confirmed soon as Pok had the security camera at the entrance pulled up on his screen.

"Forget the first bomber. He served our purposes and didn't die in vain. I have a plan," Pok said. "The second man doesn't need to track Halee. We'll hit him in his hotel."

"I like that plan." Niazi's demeanor changed immediately.

"Tell your man to get ready to move on my instructions."

"What do you want him to do?"

"Explode his bomb in the hotel lobby."

23

London

The ten-minute drive from the hospital to our hotel took a lot longer than that. Jamie asked the driver why the traffic was almost at a standstill. I thought I already knew the answer, which the driver confirmed.

"A suicide bomber blew himself up earlier this afternoon," he said. "That, and with the royal wedding this weekend, security is going to be tighter than my wife's pants for the next couple days. I'll be glad when everybody clears out of here." I got the feeling that wasn't the first time he'd used that" tighter than my wife's pants" line. What he said about wanting everyone to leave probably wasn't true either. The meter on the cab kept churning cash for him even though we weren't moving.

After he mentioned the bomber, Jamie leaned toward me and whispered, "Do you know anything about that suicide bomber, Alex?"

When I shrugged my shoulders, the look of resignation on her face told me she knew I was involved. A lot of things had happened while she was in the hospital, but I wasn't about to go into information about our mission with the driver within earshot. Another thing I didn't want to tell her was that when we got back to the hotel, we needed to pack up our things and leave as soon as we got there. Something she wasn't going to like which was why I hadn't already told her.

"Are we going to make love when we get to the hotel?" she asked in my ear, as she interlocked her arm with mine and snuggled her shoulder against me.

"I'm not sure you're up for it. Aren't you still in pain?" It hurt me to try and come up with an excuse.

"I'm fine," Jamie said.

As desperately as I wanted to be with her, we had to get out of the hotel and go into hiding. Pok's failure with the first bomber meant he was almost certainly planning another one right that minute. I didn't want to make us an easy target. He obviously knew about our hotel. Until we were off the security camera grid, I didn't plan on being stationary for any length of time. Even stalled in traffic was making me uncomfortable.

Unfortunately, going dark usually meant finding the seediest hotel in the worst part of town. One that took cash and didn't require a passport at check in. No security cameras would be operating there. The last thing the establishment wanted were eyes on who came and went on a regular basis.

Perfect for hiding but not great for romance and a honeymoon. Jamie wouldn't want to even lay on the bed, much less have sex on it.

She turned to face me. When she did, she suddenly cried out in pain. Our knees accidentally touched and, by the grimace on her face, I could tell the pain level was still high. Turned out, that made the argument for me even clearer. I couldn't imagine we could enjoy any type of intimacy with her hands and knees still that tender.

"See what I mean," I said, apologetically. "Your hands are so tender you can't touch me. How would I avoid hitting your knees? We're going to have to wait a day or two until you're healed."

"I still want to try."

"Let's see when we get there," I said, knowing it wouldn't be an option.

Neither of us said anything for a couple of minutes. We stared out the windows at the traffic, which was still at a standstill. I decided a little humor might break the monotony.

"I told you we should've joined the Mile High club," I said jokingly.

Jamie rolled her eyes and turned her head away from me to look out the side window. The same reaction I got the first and second time I brought up the subject.

The night before our wedding, Jamie was lamenting the fact that we weren't going to have a traditional wedding night. "Why do we have to wait for London?" I asked her. "We could join the Mile-High club."

I was only halfway joking.

Jamie's reaction was exactly what I expected.

"Alex Halee, get that thought right out of your mind!" she said emphatically. Her cheeks turned red.

"It'd be cool," I argued. "Something different. We'd always remember our first time."

"You'll always remember it anyway. Trust me." She had a seductive look on her face when she said it.

"Yeah, but this would really be different," I said, not willing to let it drop.

"I'm not having sex on an airplane with people around! Not going to happen."

"No one will be around. We're in business class. We have our own cubicle. It's an overnight flight. Everyone else will be asleep. No one will know but us."

"No! I'm not going to do it. What if a flight attendant walked by? Somebody might hear us. I'd be too embarrassed."

"Think about it. We'd have a great story to tell our grandkids."

"I'm not talking to our grandkids about our sex life!" Jamie said. "Have you lost your mind?"

"I'm surprised at you. I thought you were a risk taker. You parachuted into the eye of a hurricane. Now you're worried about what a flight attendant might think. Having our first time on an airplane forty thousand feet in the air would add to the adventure and make it exciting."

"It's going to be exciting anyway," she retorted. "I want it to be romantic. In a beautiful hotel room. With a glass of wine."

"Is that what's going to happen when we get married?" I argued. "We're going to become one of those boring married couples! Just like everyone else we know."

That argument resonated.

"I'll think about it," she said. "But no promises."

Of course, that plan was moot when our plane reservations were changed to coach instead of business class. That didn't keep me from bringing up the subject on the flight from our coach seats. About halfway through the flight, Jamie had said. "I'm going to the restroom."

A stupid thought popped into my head and I blurted it out before I could stop myself. "Do you want me to join you?"

Jamie's lips twisted into a look of disgust. "No," she said quickly and emphatically.

"Have you given any more thought to joining The Mile High Club?"

"In an airplane bathroom? Have you lost your friggin mind?" she said sternly but barely above a whisper so the other passengers wouldn't hear. "You've waited this long. You can wait a few more hours."

Neither of us could've possibly known that the few hours had turned into a few days. From the looks of things, it might be a few days more.

* * *

The taxi finally arrived at our hotel. Out of habit, I always check my surroundings when exiting a vehicle. It wouldn't be that hard for Pok to have a bomber waiting for us in front of our hotel.

Turns out, it wasn't a bomber. Agent Weaver was the first person I saw when we entered the lobby. Fortunately, he didn't see us. I took Jamie by the arm and ushered her quickly through the lobby to the elevators without Weaver seeing us.

When we got to our room I said, "We have to pack and get out of here."

"What's going on, Alex?"

I explained everything to her. The security cameras. Pok. The vest bomber. The trap I'd set. My suspicions that another bomber was lurking nearby. My discussions with Brad. The mission he gave us to find the dirty bomb.

"Weaver's in the lobby," I added. "That complicates things."

After showing her the laptop and the cyber lab in Iran, Jamie realized the gravity of the situation and immediately started packing. I scrolled through the security camera system until I came to the front of our hotel. I didn't want to be caught by surprise when we exited the hotel.

I also wondered where Weaver was. More than likely, he was throwing his considerable weight around with a manager to get a key to our room.

What I saw sent a chill through my spine.

Weaver wasn't our biggest worry.

A vest bomber was standing across the street. I was getting better at identifying Pok's men in a crowd. At the moment, he was only standing there. I suspected he was waiting for us to leave. With Weaver present, there wasn't time to create a plan to lead the bomber away from the hotel and into a trap. I wasn't sure Pok would fall for the same trick again anyway.

The best thing for us to do was to get out of there as soon as possible. Perhaps we could take the stairway to the parking garage and avoid running into Weaver. I thought about ditching my gun along the way but thought better of it. In case I needed it for the bomber.

I closed the laptop and threw my things into my backpack.

A knock on the door startled me.

Weaver!

I motioned for Jamie to remain still and quiet.

The banging on the door got louder. "Steele. I know you're in there. I heard you. Open the door. You're under arrest."

Jamie looked at me in disbelief. "Why are we hiding from him? You've done nothing wrong," she whispered.

"You heard him. He said I'm under arrest. I haven't done anything wrong, but if they take me down to the station, we'll lose valuable time. I've got to find out where that dirty bomb is and when and where Pok intends to detonate it."

When I heard Weaver inserting a keycard into the door, I realized that a confrontation was inevitable. When the door didn't open right away, I could tell he was having trouble with it. That bought me a few more seconds to think. What were my options? I could easily overpower him. Even pull my gun if I had to. That would only make things worse. The best thing was to try and talk my way out of it and force would be the last resort.

Rather than letting him open the door, I opened it for him.

"Sorry it took so long," I said. "We just got back from the hospital. I was trying to get my wife settled. What can we do for you, Agent Weaver?"

He brushed past me, knocking against my shoulder for emphasis and didn't stop until he was well into our suite. "What do you know about the suicide bombing earlier today?" he asked me.

"I heard no one was injured or killed," I answered.

"Don't play coy with me. I saw you on camera. You were there. What happened?"

"What happened was that no one was injured or killed thanks to me."

"Why are terrorists targeting you and your wife, if she really is your wife?"

I could tell that almost got a rise out of Jamie as her fists balled and her shoulders tensed. Fortunately, she chose not to respond.

"That's obvious, isn't it?" I said. Weaver was between Jamie and me. I'd prefer her next to me so we could make a quick exit if we had to.

"Why don't you explain it to me?" Weaver said.

"We maimed one of their guys at Kensington Park. They've been following us around ever since. Trying to get payback."

Jamie had the presence of mind to interject, "As you can see, Agent Weaver, all our bags are packed. We were just about to head to the airport and go home."

"Not so fast. Why are you running an operation on London soil without permission?"

"We're not," I said. "I told you we're not with the CIA."

"That's right you're not. Or at least you aren't," he said pointing at me. "I'm not sure about her." He turned his accusatory finger and pointed it in Jamie's direction.

"I'm not with the CIA either," she said.

"You used to be," Weaver retorted almost angrily. "Does the name Bond Digby ring a bell?"

I saw the flash of recognition on Jamie's face, but I doubt Weaver picked it up. Didn't matter anyway because Jamie said, "Okay. I used to be with the CIA. I know Bond. We worked together on a mission. Why are you harassing us? I'm sure he vouched for me." Jamie obviously made the call to reveal what Weaver already knew anyway.

"You, I'm not worried about," Weaver said, referring to Jamie. "It's you, Steele. You've been traipsing around London trying to be a hero. Putting innocent civilians in danger. What if that bomb had exploded in Trafalgar? Then what? Dozens of people could've been killed. And it would've been your fault."

"How's it my fault? They're obviously targeting *me*. I'm just trying to stay alive."

"How do you know when and where the attacks are going to take place?" he asked in an accusatory tone.

"I don't know. Like Jamie said, Weaver, we're leaving. We're on our way to the airport. We'll be out of your hair for good."

"You're not going anywhere. I'm taking you down to the station. We're going to sort all this out. I want to know what you know and who you're working for. Where's your gun?"

That threw me off guard for a second. I didn't know he knew about the gun which was in the front of my pants. There was no way we were leaving that hotel room without him searching for it. At that point, I made the decision that I was going to have to take Weaver down. Not hurt him but overpower him so we could get away. I looked over at Jamie and our eyes met. I could tell she was thinking the same thing.

Before I could take a step, the room suddenly began to shake.

Violently.

A loud noise followed. An explosion.

I pushed past Weaver to the window. Pillars of black smoke poured from the front of the hotel. Debris was blown out in the street. Several people looked to be injured outside the hotel.

The alarm in our room let out a deafening sound that echoed through the entire suite.

"What was that?" Weaver asked.

"Another suicide bomber," I shouted over the din. "In the lobby."

My worst fear had come to pass.

What do I do now?

24

The Palace Hotel

When the bomb exploded, what I did next was probably a mistake. Judging by Jamie's reaction, she felt the same way.

"Alex, what are you doing?" she cried out.

The gun previously tucked in the front of my pants was now pointed at Weaver. I relieved him of his weapon and searched him for any others.

"You're making a big mistake, Steele," Weaver said with his arms raised and his lips twisted in disdain.

I didn't doubt it.

"It's not my first and won't be my last," I said, realizing right after I did it that turning back was no longer an option. My only focus was doing everything I could to stop more bombings from happening. At the moment, Weaver was the one standing in my way and had to be dealt with. Getting arrested was not an option. Neither was hurting him.

I was walking a fine line.

"Let's go Jamie," I said. "We have to get out of here."

"We can't leave him here," Jamie responded. "Everybody needs to evacuate the building. There might be a fire. We don't even know if we can get out."

I hadn't thought that through. The elevators were programmed to go immediately to the first floor in the event of a fire or emergency. If the stairway were blocked with smoke, we'd have to evacuate to the top of the building and hope for the best. Hard to do with a hostage. Tying him up in the room wasn't an option. He could die from a fire or smoke inhalation.

I opened the door to the hallway. No smoke. "Weaver, you go to the left stairs, and we're going to the right. Don't try and follow us. Come on, Jamie."

Jamie limped toward me. I'd forgotten she wasn't moving well because of her injured knees. A quick getaway wasn't a sure thing as we'd have to take the stairs carefully. My plan was to take the stairs by the service elevator. The one in the back of the building the manager brought us up in when we first checked into the hotel. If I remembered the layout correctly, the stairs would bring us to the laundry area, which would lead to an employee entrance. Or if we went back toward the lobby, we could go to the parking garage. There we could commandeer a vehicle and get somewhere safe.

As we exited the hotel room, I pointed to the left and waved my gun at Weaver. "Don't follow us. Leave us alone. I'm trying to help you."

"You won't get far," he said and took off running for the exit sign.

We had to hurry as well. But we couldn't run. I took the time to give Jamie his gun just in case. I wasn't certain another bomber wasn't lurking in the building.

"Let's move," I said.

Going down the stairway, we didn't encounter any smoke until the fourth floor. Rather than turn back, we kept forging our way down along with a number of guests. So far, everyone seemed to have the same idea as us and kept plodding downward. The pace was slow. Women were clutching children. Some elderly were struggling with the stairs. Jamie winced with each step and let out an occasional cry of pain, but matched my pace as I went around everyone I could, taking two or three steps at time when possible.

As we neared the bottom, a familiar smell stung my nose and the chemicals from the bomb burned my eyes. Obviously made with the same materials as the one before. This time, though, it went off in the lobby of a hotel. I could only hope and pray it wasn't crowded. I wondered about the manager and the sweet young girl at the desk. I hoped they were off today or in one of the back offices.

When we reached the first floor, I decided to head for the parking garage. That meant we had to go by the lobby, but it seemed like the best idea. Weaver might be down there, but Jamie and I were both armed, and he knew that. My guess was that he'd call for backup and then tend to the injured. That would buy us some time.

I wasn't prepared for what we saw.

The lobby was unrecognizable. Hard to believe it was ever a five-star hotel. The huge chandelier that graced the entrance, now laid in a heap on the floor. Several people were crushed underneath it. Bodies were strewn everywhere. Some missing arms and legs. Most of the survivors standing or walking around had noticeable injuries. Cuts. Burns. Ripping of skin where steel ball bearings and nails had penetrated and left their heinous marks.

In a situation like that, called the fog of war, most everyone was in a daze. Moving in slow motion. Like zombies. In a state of shock. Dozens were clearly dead or dying. Many more injured. Some critically. First responders hadn't yet arrived. I desperately wanted to help them, but there was nothing we could do. Jamie and I had to get out of there.

We had two more days of this. Finding the car bombs and the dirty bombs were our top priority. If we weren't successful, then what we were seeing in the hotel lobby would pale in comparison to the destruction Pok could unleash on the city.

A quick glance around, and I didn't see Weaver and wasn't going to waste time looking any further. We quickly got away from the carnage to the parking garage. When we exited into the fresh air, I let out a violent cough to clear my lungs. The stench of bomb making residue and burning flesh would take longer to get out of my nostrils.

The valet workers had left their posts. Thankfully. I planned to steal a car but hoped not to do it at gunpoint. The box with the keys was locked so I busted it open using the butt of the gun. Various sets of keys hung on hooks inside the box. I rifled through and looked for a set from a rental car company. Meaning, it didn't have a ring of house or office keys. I'd take any car but preferred a rental. Adding grand theft auto to my list of crimes was the least of my worries, but I didn't want a family or couple to be left stranded without their car, considering what had happened. A rental car company could bring a replacement car in a few hours.

A black SUV with tinted windows was near the exit. Perfect for a getaway. There wasn't time to search through all the keys to find that one, though. When I hit the fob from the one chosen, a two-door compact car beeped. One of the many "green" cars people drove in London. It'd have to do. At least it was a vehicle, and we were out of time. If traffic were bad before, I could imagine it being worse a few minutes from now, when news of the bombing hit the airwaves. Weaver might even set a roadblock for us.

We sped out of the garage. No doubt the garage security cameras captured our faces as we left. Nothing I could do about that, so we didn't even try to hide from them. I'm sure we were already on camera breaking into the box.

"What's your plan?" Jamie asked in her calm and steady operational voice. She could've been asking when we were going to the grocery store.

"I need a place to work. I have to find where the car bombs are going off tomorrow. Then find the dirty bomb. Then I have to find Pok's location in Iran so Brad can send a cruise missile his way."

"That's all?" Jamie said sarcastically.

"Get my laptop out of my backpack, please. Pull up the security cameras and find me a route out of here. We need to get out of London and away from the bloody cameras."

I don't know why I used an English slang term like bloody. It just came out of my mouth like a burp.

Jamie was amazing. She found our location on the laptop right away and directed me around the traffic that was starting to pile up.

"I know of a safehouse," Jamie said. "I used it when I was on the mission to London. I needed to hide out for a few days. You can do your work there."

"Are we allowed to use CIA assets?"

"I don't see why not. Brad didn't say we couldn't. He wants us to find the bombs. That's the best place to do it. When I was there, it wasn't manned. Hopefully, no one's there, and we can hunker down."

A safehouse was much better than a sleazy hotel. It'd have supplies. Guns. A secure internet and phone connection. Weaver would have no way of knowing about it. It was called a safehouse for a reason. Generally, that's the safest place we could be in a crisis.

"Do you remember how to get there?" I asked.

"Of course."

"You have a great memory."

"That, and it was in the CIA briefing file I read on the plane. I memorized the directions."

"I sure do love you."

This was what we trained for. Things were working out better than expected. I wouldn't breathe easy until we were out of London. So many security cameras made it next to impossible to hide. Even then, we'd have to come back to London at some point. It occurred to me that we couldn't even go to the airport and get on a plane now. That's how compromised we were. Hopefully, Weaver wouldn't plaster our images on television, totally blowing our cover.

What a mess.

Our skills in tradecraft would be tested to their limits.

A gnawing feeling consumed me. Things were going to get worse before they got better.

25

Day Four

Iran

If Alex Halee were as good a hacker as he claimed, he'd walk into Pok's cyber trap. Probably already had. While Pok had no way to verify it, he was counting on Halee hacking into the London security camera system and following the breadcrumbs he left for him all the way to the cyber lab in Iran. All Halee had to do was follow the camera feed through the maze of cyber space until he found Pok's cyber lab. Then he'd have to go through the complicated work of accessing Pok's cameras on his computers.

Something difficult to do. Halee was the only other person alive who could do it, and Pok was certain he would try. So, he made it easier for him. Left off safeguards and firewalls that would've prevented it. Didn't send Halee on too many wild goose chases looking for his location. Left little subtle clues along the way.

Would Halee be suspicious that he could find Pok that easily? Perhaps. But Alex Halee had always been overconfident in his own abilities and underestimated Pok's. Halee's ego wouldn't let him think the success was anything short of his own brilliance. Or at least that was what he was counting on.

Pok adjusted the whiteboard on the wall behind his desk so it would be right in the line of the camera on his computer. An eerie feeling came over him as he wondered if his arch enemy was watching his every move. Pok could only hope he was.

He turned his attention to the information on the whiteboard. In clear display were the time, date, and location of today's car bombing. Like a piece of cheese in a mousetrap. Halee wouldn't resist taking the bait.

Day Four. Saturday.

Car bombing.

4:05 London time.

London Bridge.

All Halee had to do was act on it. Then Pok would know Halee was watching him. When the bomber arrived at London Bridge at that exact time, Halee would be ecstatic. Another bombing had been averted. Halee would think he'd won. That his intelligence was correct. Tomorrow, he'd be looking for the same thing. Information on the time and place of the dirty bomb.

Pok regretted the fact that he had to double cross Niazi to make his plan work. Something he did with tremendous trepidation. Niazi would be furious if Halee was somehow able to stop the car bombing. If Niazi found out Pok had fed him the information, he was as good as dead. Which was why his assistant, Heo Jin Su, was the only other person in Pok's office. One of only a handful of men he brought with him from North Korea—the only one he trusted with such sensitive information.

Heo and Pok grew up together in the upper caste of North Korean influence. The privilege gave them access to their parent's computers in their high school years. At first, they dabbled in hacking and learned how to infiltrate email systems just for fun. Back when very few people even had emails, and the systems weren't sophisticated at all. In college, they taught themselves how to write code from information they stole off the internet. Their mischievous pranks turned into petty crimes like changing grades and pilfering North Korean currency.

As their abilities became more refined, they became more brazen. When they were caught in the more serious crime of hacking into government accounts, the only thing that saved them from a life of hard labor in a prison camp was an investigator who took an interest in how they pulled off such a computer attack. When they showed him their vast skills and how they could be used for cyberwarfare, they were offered a job for leniency. They both took the offer, and North Korea's cyber warfare organization was formed.

Pok rose higher through the ranks more quickly than Heo, and his skills were more sophisticated. However, Pok managed to bring Heo with him every step of the way. Now they were in Iran together about to pull off the most ambitious plan to date. The launching of a dirty bomb at a London Royal wedding. If everything went as planned, Halee would get the blame and no one would ever know they were involved.

That all depended on one thing. Was Halee watching them?

Pok could only assume he was.

He adjusted his hair and began going over today's car bombing with Heo. They had to make the presentation seem believable. This exercise was nothing more than an acting job for Halee's benefit. If Halee showed up at the site of the car bombing at the time on the whiteboard, Pok would know he succeeded in hacking into his lab and was indeed watching him.

If confirmed, then the trap for tomorrow was set.

* * *

CIA safehouse
Twickenham England
9:09 a.m.

The safehouse had been a good call on Jamie's part. The location was secluded, and the house was full of food, clothing of all colors and sizes, weapons from small handguns to shoulder fired missiles, a hot shower, a king-sized bed, and most importantly, high-speed, secure internet.

From the kitchen table, I was able to monitor Pok and his cyber lab the entire night. A few minutes before, Pok and another man had gone over the plans for today's car bombings. I was never able to secure audio, but what I could see was chilling enough.

Pok intended to explode a car bomb on London bridge at five after four that afternoon, London time.

Before all the attacks had targeted me. Obviously, Pok had given up on that plan. Which made sense. How could he maneuver a car through London streets to a location and get close enough to me? Further complicated by the fact that I had disappeared and was no longer staying at the hotel.

Of course, Pok already knew that. No one would be able to stay there after the bomb ripped through the lobby.

There were a lot of things I assumed Pok knew. He had to know that I figured out he was watching me. Then I set the trap for his vest bomber in the industrial park complex. That much was obvious, and Pok had likely seen the entire thing on camera. That's why he sent the second bomber into the hotel. The ultimate retaliation. He knew there would be nothing I could do to stop it, and he never even gave me the chance.

That thought sent a flood of guilt through me like a lightning strike. The images from the carnage in the lobby were still playing in my mind like a movie and made me cringe every time I thought of them.

Jamie told me I shouldn't feel guilty. Curly had tried to prepare us for the fact that innocent people were going to die, and we couldn't prevent it.

Blame is lame, he used to say. In other words, it'll debilitate you. Blame would keep me from acting effectively and rationally the next time. If it got a stronghold, blame would make me wash out of the CIA altogether. Many a career had been short circuited because an officer was unable to handle the emotional turmoil caused from killing people and seeing innocent people killed.

"The only person to blame is the person who exploded the bomb," Jamie had reminded me before she went to bed the night before.

"And Pok, who planned it," I added.

So, overnight, I fought back the urge to feel sorry for myself and kept reminding myself it wasn't my fault.

Curly addressed that in our training as well. *Feeling sorry for yourself makes you a sorry person. Of no use to anyone.*

He was right. I had to snap out of it. We were in the middle of a war. There were casualties. I was still standing. So was Jamie. Many people had already been saved because of my actions. Many more would be saved if I could figure out a way to stop the car bombing today.

No matter how hard I tried, I couldn't think of a way to do that. Which was probably why I was feeling such a range of emotions. What good did it do to have the information if I couldn't do anything about it?

When the sun began to rise, so did my emotional outlook. When Jamie woke up, my spirits improved twofold. She made both of us a much-needed cup of coffee.

"Are you feeling better?" I asked her as she sat down at the kitchen table across from me.

"Much better," she said.

The bandages were off her hands, and she was actually holding the coffee cup fairly easily in one hand with the other resting against the side of it. The redness in her hands and fingers was almost gone. One layer of gauze was still wrapped around her knee, but she propped her foot up on the chair without grimacing, so it appeared that even her knee was feeling better.

"I need to talk to you about the plan of action for today," I said.

"I'm ready."

I knew what she meant. Not just ready to hear the plan, but ready to go execute it. I'd thought about that all night. I didn't want to put her in harm's way again until she was fully healed of her injuries.

"No, Jamie," I said matter-of-factly. "You need to stay here. Get completely one-hundred percent for tomorrow."

"Not going to happen. I'm going with you. I'll be fine."

Now was not the time to have that argument, so I didn't respond. I didn't even have a plan yet. If I didn't know what I was going to do, I certainly didn't know whether she would be able to help or not. She certainly could drive a getaway car. Shoot a gun. Or provide moral support.

Jamie took her foot off the chair and set it back down on the floor and then propped her elbows on the table and leaned toward me. I could see in her eyes that she was mentally ready for a fight. Even though she wasn't a morning person, she was ready to go kill some bad guys. I was sure the bomber at the hotel had a big impact on her emotionally as well, and she wanted revenge as much as I did.

"Tell me what's going on," she said.

"This is day four."

"Right. If I remember correctly, day four is car bombings."

"That's correct. I know where and at what time the car bombing is going to take place today."

Her eyes widened and her mouth contorted to the side in confusion, so I explained.

"As you know, I hacked into the London security camera system yesterday. Just like Pok did. I followed the link back to his cyber lab. That's how I tracked the vest bomber."

Jamie already knew all this, but for some reason I felt the need to remind her. If only for my benefit. So, my train of thought was sequential. I liked sharing the plan from the beginning, even if it wasn't fully formed.

"I'm following you."

"Overnight, I saw Pok in his office going over the plan with one of his men."

"Really? Right in front of the cameras?"

"I know! It was almost too easy."

"Maybe it was."

"No. Pok's always underestimated me. He thinks he's better than me and that I don't have the skills he has. Pok probably thinks I would try to find him by tracing the feed, but I doubt he thinks I would be successful. In reality, I'm probably the only person in the world who could actually do it."

"So, what's his plan?"

"He's going to strike London Bridge just after four o'clock, today."

"If you show up on London Bridge at four o'clock, isn't he going to know you've hacked into the cameras?"

"I hadn't thought of that. I was too busy trying to figure out how to stop the bombing."

That thought gave me pause. The information on the car bombing was a gold mine of intelligence. I still didn't know when and where they were going to explode the dirty bomb. If the car bomb information was correct, then I might be able to get the same information tomorrow. I needed to make sure Pok didn't know that I knew his plans ahead of time. We had to make it look like we happened upon the attack.

"That's a whole other problem in and of itself. How will we stop the car bomb? It's not like a person with a knife or even a vest bomber. A car is mobile."

"I've been thinking about that too. There's a shoulder missile in there."

It sounded as stupid when I said it as when I thought of it in the middle of the night.

"You're going to shoot a missile on a crowded bridge in downtown London?"

"No. I'm just spitballing here. I told you I don't have a plan. That's why I'm talking to you about it."

Jamie looked past me like she was deep in thought.

"Another problem is that I have no way of knowing which vehicle the bomb is in," I said. "It could be in any of them."

"It'll be in a van for sure."

"Or a moving truck. You know. Like a rental car van."

"The missile wouldn't work anyway," Jamie said. "Assuming you could get on the bridge with it, you can't fire it at the first van that comes on the bridge after four o'clock. It could just as easily be an innocent. Even if you did know which car, how would you get close enough to hit it? When was the last time you fired one? What if you shot wildly and hit an office building or something or blew a big hole in the bridge?"

"I know!" I said roughly. "I've already ruled out the missile. It wouldn't work. I've been sitting here racking my brain trying to think of something that would."

"You need to call Brad," she said succinctly. "This isn't our problem. We found the bomb. You found the bomb, I mean. We can't be expected to stop it. And if we don't stop it and it goes off, I don't want us to take the blame for it."

I didn't mind that Jamie was talking in terms of we and us. We were married now. Everything I did affected her and vice versa. And she was right. I already had the vest bombing in the lobby of the hotel on my conscience. Too many things could go wrong on this mission. I'd done my job and found the date and location of the bomb. London authorities needed to handle it.

"You also have Weaver to consider," Jamie said. "It's not safe to show our faces in London at the moment. If Weaver or Pok see you on a camera, who knows what might happen."

Jamie was right on all points. Talking to her had brought clarity to the situation.

I needed to call Brad.

He'd know what to do. And I'd better hurry. Four o'clock would be here before we knew it. Not much time, considering a major car bomb was about to explode on London Bridge.

26

I hadn't been this nervous since our wedding day. Which at this point, seemed like months ago. So much had happened since that day. Two knife attacks. Two acid attacks. Two vest bombers. And now, potentially a car bomb that could explode on the London Bridge at any time.

No wonder Jamie and I hadn't been able to consummate our marriage. Even though Jamie was feeling better, the topic hadn't even been discussed. The last thing on our minds was when we'd get the chance to have sex for the first time. After the car bomb crisis was over, the threat of a dirty bomb hung over us like a storm cloud about to unleash a torrential downpour. Or a tornado. Or a tsunami. Truthfully, we had no idea what was in store and I was dreading finding out.

After discovering the intelligence regarding the potential London Bridge bombing, I called Brad and discussed it with him. The decision was made that Jamie and I wouldn't go into London but would stay at the safehouse. While I wanted to resist, I knew we'd made the right call. We'd leave it for the British authorities to handle. They had the manpower and resources to deal with the threat.

Brad notified MI6 and gave them the intelligence information without revealing how I came upon it. The British intelligence service was very appreciative, and Brad even gave me a rare "atta boy." Compliments were few and far between when it came to Brad. While I appreciated this one, it seemed premature. I had no idea if my intelligence was correct or not. Curly drilled in us not to ever celebrate early on a mission. Success was never guaranteed, and a thousand things could go wrong. Save the pats on the back for when we were back home safely.

Brad also impressed upon MI6 the importance of making it seem like the security precautions were routine. While he couldn't reveal why, he hinted that we had someone planted in the terrorist organization. Close to the decision makers. If it were obvious we were on to them, we'd blow his cover. Brad told them the asset was too valuable to lose which warmed my heart since he was referring to me. He also relayed to them that his source had already confirmed the existence of a dirty bomb, and that if we played our cards right, we had a good chance of uncovering where and when it was going to detonate.

MI6 followed Brad's advice and played it the right way. They set up checkpoints at every bridge. A strategic move and one that would seem routine. After all, the royal wedding was tomorrow. Pok would know security would be tight. Traffic coming in and out of London would be monitored. It wouldn't seem at all out of the ordinary for the bridges to be the checkpoint for incoming traffic. Hopefully, Pok wouldn't make the connection to me.

I still had eyes on him in Iran. Nothing in his actions gave me the impression that he thought he was being monitored. No precautions were being taken. He could do something as simple as put a post-it-note over the camera on his computer, and I wouldn't be able to see a thing.

Pok did seem as nervous as I was. The closer it got to four o'clock our time, the more nervous he seemed. He was pacing back and forth like the Queen's guard in front of Buckingham Palace. That led me to believe the intelligence was real. Something was clearly about to happen. The fact that he was pacing and not sitting with his eyes glued to the screen told me we still had more time.

TERRY TOLER

My emotions were mixed. On the one hand, I had hoped I was wrong, and the bomb didn't exist. Innocent people could be hurt. Soldiers and policemen could get caught up in the blast. On the other hand, I'd be vindicated. Weaver would have to quit harassing me. I'd be free to continue my intelligence work and find the dirty bomb.

Something I was doing anyway, while I had the chance. The afternoon hadn't been wasted. During that time, I was able to find Pok's actual location. It took several hours, but I tracked him to a spot just outside Zahedan, Iran, near the border of Pakistan. I gave Brad the actual latitude and longitude of the cyber lab, much to his delight.

Brad rarely showed emotion. When I told him the location, he was almost giddy. This would be a big win for him with his bosses. A confirmation that keeping Jamie and me associated with the Agency was the right thing to do. Brad had stuck his neck out for us. Without him, we might not have AJAX, the money, the jet, or more importantly, the opportunity to do what we loved. If a car bomb attack did occur, in a strange and ironic way, Brad would be vindicated for putting his trust in us. We'd be given more freedom to operate in the future and keep doing what we loved and lived for. Stopping bad guys who wanted to kill innocent people.

Jesus once said, "The poor you'll have with you always." It seemed like it could also be said that the terrorists, we'll have with us always. Even though that was true, it didn't damper my motivation to get rid of those I could. Like others who were called to help as many poor people as they could. Even if poverty and terrorism couldn't be fully eradicated, at least we could make a dent and do our part to lessen the problem. Sometimes I wondered if we were making a dent.

Finding Pok's location made it seem like we were. Brad said the lab was already on his radar based on suspicious activity spotted from satellites.

"Any chance we can take out the lab before tomorrow?" I had asked.

194

"We're cutting it close. It'll take us twenty-four hours to move our submarine into place so we can launch a cruise missile. We also have to get an order from the President to strike. The powers that be are waiting to see what happens with this car bomb. If your intelligence is correct, I would imagine the order will be given right away. We're looking at tomorrow afternoon at the earliest."

More than likely, that would be after the dirty bomb strike, but not by much. Regardless of what happened today and tomorrow, at least we were prepared to deal with Pok once and for all. This time tomorrow, he'd be a pile of ashes somewhere in Iran, and I would be able to sleep better at night.

The thought occurred to me to get on a plane, fly into Iran, and take out the lab myself. That idea was quickly dismissed. Not enough time. Also, my time was better spent in London, helping MI6 find the dirty bomb. Even if I'm able to discover Pok's intentions tomorrow morning, that doesn't mean we could stop it. We didn't even know if we could stop the car bomb today.

We'd know soon.

The clock was ticking.

Slowly. But drawing closer to the time.

4:01.

Jamie and I had our eyes glued to my laptop. I felt utterly helpless to do anything about it and said as much to her.

"You did good," she said. "I'm proud of you. Regardless of what happens. You've done everything you could."

I turned my focus back to my laptop. Eight cameras were pulled up at once on the screen in separate boxes. British authorities had set up the checkpoint at Trolley Street—a good thirty yards before the entrance to the bridge. Authorities inspected vehicles and then allowed them to cross. A man with a long, metal rod with a mirror checked under cars for bombs. Foot traffic had been completely stopped, and the bridge was empty except for cars coming out of London and the periodic line of cars going in.

The problem with a checkpoint was that it became a target. There really wasn't anything the people guarding the area could do to stop a terrorist from driving a vehicle right up to their location and exploding a bomb. The best they could do was keep it off of London Bridge and away from as many people as possible.

4:08.

Each minute that passed was more agonizing than the previous.

The scheduled time passed.

Not surprising, considering the checkpoint had bottlenecked traffic in line to go across the bridge. I had a camera view going back nearly a mile on the road leading up to the entrance to the bridge. Jamie and I were scanning each camera angle, looking for any suspicious vehicles.

I was certain Weaver, Pok, and MI6 were doing the exact same thing.

We were looking for a van or rental car truck. That seemed to be the vehicle of choice for car bombers.

4:17.

Still no signs of any suspicious vehicles. I began to wonder if my intelligence was correct. I hoped it wasn't.

Then I saw it.

Not a van. Or a rental truck.

A two door older model pickup truck. Faded blue. It came to a stop at the end of the line of traffic. Then did a U-turn and sped away. Four men were sitting in the bed of the truck. The camera angle was from a distance, but the men had beards, longer hair, and looked middle eastern. No doubt in my mind, they were the terrorists with the bomb.

I hoped MI6 saw them as well.

The vehicle went out of camera view. Maybe they were abandoning their mission.

I had my doubts.

What was the truck doing? Were they leaving? Were they coming back? Were they going to a different location?

Before I could pull up another camera to track their location, the truck suddenly appeared back in the frame.

Going at a high rate of speed. At first, I thought it was going to ram the last car in line. Instead, it jumped the curb and drove on the sidewalk. The rims had sparks flying from them as the tires went flat.

Several pedestrians were in its path. Panicked bystanders struggled to get out of the way. One man jumped into the bushes. Another pushed a woman next to him out of the way as the truck barreled into him and dragged him several feet.

Adrenaline pulsed through me like a fire hose had been turned on at full pressure.

Jamie was on the edge of her seat. Her jaw was clenched. Her shoulders raised. Her fists balled. As if she were prepared to jump through the screen and stop the horror unfolding before our eyes.

The truck slammed into a concrete barrier a good fifty yards before the checkpoint. I grimaced as I half expected the truck to explode on impact.

The four men in the back jumped out of the bed and began running. Away from where the vehicle had come to a stop. The opposite direction of the bridge. Away from the waiting soldiers.

The driver of the vehicle tried to back up and get the vehicle moving again. The rims just spun on the concrete, sending more sparks flying. I kept expecting the explosion that hadn't come. The sparks alone could ignite the bomb.

Soldiers with machine guns closed in on the vehicle. They opened fire. The truck was still running, but I could see the driver slumped over the wheel. The windshield was riddled with bullets. More soldiers fanned out in the street to clear people out of their vehicles and away from the threat. We could see hundreds of people running for their lives.

They had to hurry. The bomb could explode at any time. I had no way of knowing if it was on a timer or a detonator. More than likely, it was attached to the undercarriage. For a second, I wondered if we'd dodged a major catastrophe, and the bomb malfunctioned.

As if on cue, a fireball erupted on the screen. A plume of black smoke filled the sky. The truck rose twenty-to-thirty feet in the air and landed in a crumpled mess almost in the same spot where it had crashed into the barrier. I almost jumped out of my chair.

When the smoke cleared, I had a better view of the scene. Fortunately, the blast was contained somewhat by being under the truck. Only the closest cars were affected. Windows were blown out of restaurants and shops.

The surrounding restaurants normally had outdoor seating, but the authorities had wisely evacuated those areas prior to four o'clock. If not, hundreds of people could've been in the bomb blast. The injured seemed to be limited to the pedestrians who had been on the sidewalk when the truck barreled through.

The four men.

Where were they?

It took me nearly a minute to change the camera views. I went from camera to camera, down Borough Street, searching for them. I saw them running in the same direction but at different speeds. They appeared to have knives in their hands. It appeared that they were headed for Borough Market. A highly trafficked tourist spot.

The nightmare wasn't over yet.

27

T he British response to the terrorist attack was impressive. Jamie and I were glued to the television for more than two hours. The four terrorists who jumped out of the truck had gone to the Borough Market armed with knives. Exactly what I'd feared. One of the men killed three people outside of a local bistro off Borough High Street. According to reports, the victims had just finished a late lunch and were exiting the restaurant when they happened upon the man. He attacked them before they had a chance to defend themselves.

The other three continued on to the market where they stabbed anyone and everyone in their way. Stories of heroism filled the airwaves as the attackers were ultimately confronted by individual bystanders who fought back. Londoners and tourists alike threw bottles and rocks at the attackers. A local restaurant owner hit one of the terrorists over the head with a chair. Another man fought one of them with his fists. He was stabbed repeatedly with a knife but kept fighting until he collapsed on the ground in a pool of blood. His condition was unknown.

A number of civilians were rushed to the local hospitals, and some were in surgery. According to the news reports, a call went out requesting blood donations, and lines were so long they were turning people away.

The four terrorists were ultimately shot and killed by British Transport Police officers who arrived at the market and confronted the men. Only eight minutes passed between the time the truck slammed into the concrete embankment, and the terrorists were killed. MI5 and MI6 had obviously kept some men hidden in the area, ready to respond. Something I was thankful for. As far as I knew, my cover was not blown, and Pok wouldn't suspect anything.

I looked at the feed of Pok's cyberlab and was sickened by what I saw. It looked like an office party had broken out. Pok and the Iranians were celebrating like their team had just won the Super Bowl. I wished that cruise missile could hit them right at that moment and ruin their celebration. The fact that they'd get theirs tomorrow was the only consolation. That and the bombing would've been a lot worse had I not discovered the plan in advance. The British authorities had mitigated the damages as well as could be expected.

Metropolitan police issued a "Run, Tell, and Hide" notice and sent it out through all of social media. The alert came on our phones within minutes of the attack. While the location of the threat was identified and we were miles away, everyone within a twenty-mile radius got the alert. An initiative put in place after previous attacks. Instructions were given to evacuate all the buildings near the London Bridge and stay clear of the area. Additionally, it said to remain calm and contact authorities if they saw anything suspicious. From the security camera feeds, I could tell people were taking their advice.

Authorities were worried about other potential attacks, but I wasn't. It seemed to me like Pok made the splash he wanted. Tomorrow was the big day. The last thing Pok would want would be to launch so many attacks that the authorities canceled the wedding. Or severely restricted access to the point that launching a dirty bomb would be impossible. MI6 could lockdown London in a second if they wanted to.

That would blow Pok's plan out of the water. I was certain he was done for the day.

Even with the limited nature of the attack, security was tight. The underground stations were closed and cordoned off. No one was allowed in or out of the subway station. Helicopters landed on London

Bridge, and a stream of what appeared to be SAS, Special Air Service military units, filed out. The men set up a perimeter.

Police boats filled the River Thames and for the first thirty minutes, organized chaos ensued. Now they were patrolling the river, just in case. More confirmation to me that we did the right thing letting the British authorities handle the threat.

When the smoke settled, the initial reports were that eight people lost their lives, not including the five terrorists. Thirty-six people were injured. Six critically.

It could've been a lot worse.

* * *

Iran

Things couldn't have gone better, as far as Niazi was concerned. British authorities set up checkpoints and limited the damage, but the bomb still exploded. Niazi seemed pleased which was all that mattered.

Pok wasn't as excited. He expected to see Halee somewhere at the site. Now he wasn't sure if Alex was watching him or not. If he wasn't, that would throw a serious kink in his plan.

Niazi was so pleased, he brought out alcohol and a party had ensued. Pok wasn't in the mood to celebrate. More work had to be done, and he needed another plan if Halee hadn't hacked into his camera systems. On Niazi's insistence, Pok reluctantly joined in and pretended to be having a good time. What he really wanted to do was go through all the logistics of his plan one more time.

"Relax, my friend," Niazi said, raising his glass in a toast. "Put a smile on your face. You did good. Today was a success. Tomorrow will come soon enough. Today, we celebrate a great victory over the enemy who has been brought to its knees. Let's toast to the men who sacrificed their lives for Allah."

Pok raised a glass, but his mind was elsewhere. He was thinking through everything that happened, looking for confirmation that Halee was watching him. The British police did react quickly. Could they have reacted that fast without some advance warning?

That thought moved him off the fence into the belief that Halee was watching him. Fortunately, Niazi hadn't associated the increased security to Pok's double cross. The fact that a number of people were still killed satisfied the man's thirst for blood. Not their most successful mission, Niazi commented, but better than most.

Pok took another sip of wine. The strong drink began to relax him some. Niazi was right. Things had gone well. Tomorrow would be another day.

The day he finally got his revenge against Alex Halee.

***

Safehouse

Jamie got up from her chair where she'd been watching the television, came over to the sofa, and sat on my lap.

"You know... we still haven't made love yet," she said in a sweet voice which was a stark contrast to the images we'd just watched unfold before our eyes. Curly had taught us to segment the mission from our personal feelings. Turn them on and off as necessary. Like a light switch. Apparently, Jamie was better at it than I was.

"We've been married four days," she said. "Don't you think it's time?"

I used my free hand to rub my eyes roughly. It'd been more than thirty-six hours since I'd slept, and now that the adrenaline from the bombing was subsiding, I was starting to crash. The thought of finally making love to my wife for the first time was countering the sluggishness somewhat.

I felt the sudden need to apologize. "I know. I'm sorry. First you got hurt. Then I've been consumed with finding Pok. I need to get up about three in the morning to see what I can find out about tomorrow."

She kissed me seductively on the lips. Clearly attempting to get my attention off Pok and the mission.

When the kiss ended I said, "I haven't slept in two days. I don't know how good I'll be."

I wasn't sure how good I'd be anyway. I'd never done it before.

"I have an idea," she said. "You go get in bed and sleep for about three hours. Set an alarm. At nine thirty, I'll come join you. Then you can sleep until three in the morning. You can get back to saving the world after you've spent time with me. How does that sound?"

"That sounds amazing."

Jamie gave me another kiss. Hard and strong. It sent chills down my spine. I wondered if I'd even be able to sleep after that. I decided to give her another kiss. Even deeper.

But before I could, Brad called. His distinct ringtone filled the room with an unwanted distraction.

"I'd better get this," I said to Jamie as she stood to get off my lap.

I picked up the call, but before I could say hello, Brad said, "The Brits seemed pleased." .

"Good. I'm glad. Too bad they don't know I deserve the credit. I'm sure they're still trying to find me and arrest me."

"You can stay at the safehouse until things blow over. How's Jamie?"

"I'm fine," Jamie said. I had the call on speaker so she could hear it as well. "Back to normal."

"You were never normal to begin with."

"Ha. Ha."

It felt good to hear Brad joking with us again.

"You two are the only ones I know who could turn a honeymoon into a mission."

"We didn't do it on purpose," I said.

"We're going to need time off from our vacation," Jamie quipped.

"Still more work to do," Brad reminded us. Not that I needed reminding.

Pok was still at the forefront of my mind so I ended the call so I could get to sleep as soon as possible.

Hopefully, the nap would wipe the mission out of my mind, and I could focus all my energies on my wife and our first time. I was half-way tempted to skip the nap, but I needed a shower first anyway. Maybe after the shower I wouldn't need a nap.

Jamie was probably thinking the same thing. I figured she needed me to sleep for a while so she'd have time to prepare. Take a shower. Primp. Do whatever it was she did to look so amazing. Hopefully, she'd put on that silky white nightgown she was wearing the first night, before I got distracted and ruined it.

The sooner I got to sleep, the sooner I would wake up and be with her. Something I'd been dreaming about for four years. I was within three hours of it happening and was determined that nothing was going to prevent it this time.

"I'm taking a shower," I said.

I gave Jamie a quick kiss on the cheek and bolted out of the room. After a hot shower, I felt better. As soon as my head hit the sheets, I was out.

* * *

I slept hard because when I woke up, I had no idea where I was at first. The alarm on my phone wasn't beeping but I could hear the shower running. Why did I wake up early? Something had startled me out of a deep sleep. It took a second to clear my head. I laid it back down to go back to sleep but then remembered why I was going to wake up. Jamie and I were going to make love for the first time. The anticipation must've awakened me early.

Jamie was obviously in the shower getting ready. When she was done, I needed to brush my teeth, and then I'd be ready.

The anticipation rose in me and overcame the grogginess.

Then I felt something. Again.

A presence.

Someone was in the room.

I knew that feeling.

Not Jamie. A threat.

I lifted my head off the pillow.

Slowly.

I wasn't sure why I was being so cautious.

I had a sudden urge to reach for my gun which was always on the nightstand. Making a sudden movement didn't seem like a good idea.

The lights in the room were off. The only light came from the bathroom where the door was slightly opened.

A man was standing at the foot of my bed. He held a gun pointed right at me. "Don't make any sudden moves, Alex," he said.

An unfamiliar voice. Not Weaver.

Who was he, and how did he know my name?

28

What I saw wasn't making any sense.

A man I didn't know was standing at the foot of my bed in the safehouse with a gun pointed at me. Even though I'd been asleep, I wasn't now. My senses were on full alert. Like a sports car, my heartbeat had gone from a resting sixty to one-twenty in the course of five seconds.

"Keep your hands under the blanket," the gunman ordered.

A smart, strategic move. My gun was on the nightstand next to the bed. Even back home, I always slept with it next to me. With my hands under the blanket, any move I made would be futile. An amateur could gun me down in the time it took to get my hands free, grab the gun, aim, and fire.

This man was no amateur. I took several seconds to study him. Made easier when he reached back and turned on the lamp on the desk behind him, fully illuminating the room. He was tall. Cary Grant handsome as Jamie would say. Forty-five to fifty years old. He wore a suit and a thin tie. Expensive suit and dress shirt. Designer cufflinks. Not a hair on his dark head was out of place. Dimples emerged on the side of his cheeks when he smiled. Which he did almost continually, like he was pleased he'd bested me.

I had to give him that. What he'd done was no small feat. To get to this position, he had to avoid the motion detector lights on the outside of the safehouse, pick the lock on a door or window, stealth into my room without waking me up, and then have the nerve to confront me with a gun while a gun was within my reach and Jamie was in the other room.

Brazen. Something I would do. I had to give him credit for that much, anyway. Even though I was going to kill him, I still respected his effort.

Neither of us said anything. I could only assume he didn't want to alert Jamie of his presence. I stayed quiet for the same reason. Until I had a plan in my mind, I didn't want her bolting into the room not knowing the nature of the threat. How could she know that someone was in our room with a gun? I didn't even know why and I was right there with him.

The man wasn't a terrorist. Not MI5. My first thought was that Weaver sent him. But men like Weaver and his ilk weren't that skilled. Only a professional operative with extensive training could do what he'd done. MI6 maybe. Probably. A James Bond type. He looked the part. Smooth. Demure. Confident in his abilities. Killing him wouldn't be easy. At the moment, I didn't see a way to reverse the situation. The only consolation was that if he had wanted me dead, he could have easily killed me already.

That would buy me some time. I wanted to warn Jamie, but she might be the best hope in this situation. Two against one would improve our odds. The shower was no longer running, and I could hear her moving around, probably getting into her white nightgown.

The alarm on my phone went off sending a bolt of anger through me for the first time since I'd awakened. I wasn't sure what was making me angrier. The fact that he had a gun pointed at me and was threatening to kill me, or that he'd ruined our plans which the alarm reminded me of.

"Ready or not, here I come," Jamie said, in the most seductive voice I'd ever heard from her.

The door to the bathroom opened. Jamie was wearing the white nightgown. She had a huge grin on her face. That turned to a twisted look of disbelief. Jamie was the best at processing a dangerous situation and acting on impulse which was almost always right And something she would do quickly.

As I expected, she started toward the man immediately. Almost running.

I prepared to remove my hands from under the blanket and grab the gun. The man's head turned toward her. The gun was still pointed at me. The brain couldn't process a threat quickly enough to do both at the same time.

Jamie was on him. Instead of commandeering the gun, she threw her arms around his neck.

"Bond Digby," she said, to my shock. "What are you doing here?"

Where had I heard that name, and why did this man have his arms around my wife?

They kissed both cheeks. He had his free arm around her waist and pulled her close to him. Out of instinct, I saw an opportunity.

Like a flash of light, my hands were out from under the blanket, and I pointed my gun at him. He had lowered his slightly, distracted by my wife's attention. I'd practiced the move a thousand times and had perfected it. I could've shot him, but Jamie was in the way.

Was this Jamie's plan?

I didn't like it, even though it was working. The two of them were much too friendly for my liking.

Who the hell is Bond Digby?

And... where have I heard that name?

Weaver.

I remembered him mentioning that name. MI6. Jamie had a mission in London and was working with a Bond Digby. He had vouched for Jamie and said she was the best operative he'd ever worked with. Some of it was starting to make sense. I still kept my weapon on him. That got his attention, and he raised his. To the duel position. Both of us stared at the other, totally fixated. Neither of us blinked.

Jamie seemed unconcerned.

"You two put down those guns before you hurt someone," she said.

I didn't move a muscle. Neither did he. I think if either of us twitched, we might've shot the other.

"Oh, for heaven's sake," Jamie said. "Alex, this is Bond Digby. He works with MI6. Bond this is my husband, Alex."

"So, you really are married?" Bond said. "I heard that, but I didn't believe it."

Bond hadn't released his grip around Jamie's waist. I didn't care if they were best of friends. If he didn't get his hands off my wife soon, I'd shoot him anyway.

"I don't see a ring on your finger," Bond said.

Jamie waved her ring hand in the air. "I got some acid on my hands. I haven't been able to wear my rings."

"I always thought you and I were going to get married."

Who is this guy? Why have I never heard of him?

"You're way too old for me," Jamie quipped.

"Ouch."

"I'm going to go change," Jamie said, as she finally broke free from his grip.

Digby and I still had our guns raised.

Jamie's eyes rolled and she threw back her head for emphasis.

"You two idiots try not to shoot each other until I get back," Jamie said, as she turned, walked back to the bathroom, and closed the door.

"You put your gun down first," I said sternly.

"You put yours down first," he retorted.

Jamie didn't see him as a threat, but I still did. The man broke into the safehouse. Held a gun on me. He didn't go to all that trouble for nothing. Weaver probably sent him here to arrest me. That couldn't happen. I had to find out what Pok was planning.

"Who are you and why are you here?" I said roughly, still holding my gun on him.

He suddenly holstered his. "I have the same question for you."

"I can't tell you why I'm here. That's top secret. Need to know basis."

"I'm here to arrest you."

"Good luck with that. You'll have to kill me first."

Bond let out a laugh. "I could've killed you ten times by now. While you were sleeping."

"You guys put your testosterone away," Jamie said as the door to the bathroom burst open and she emerged fully clothed clearly having heard what Bond just said. Then she started ordering us around.

"Alex, get dressed."

She looked at me somewhat apologetically. The moment was ruined. Again! I could tell she felt bad about that.

"Bond, let's go get some iced tea and get caught up," Jamie said grabbing his hand and pulling him toward the door.

When I came out of the bedroom, Bond and Jamie were sitting at the kitchen table drinking tea. Jamie was telling Bond about AJAX, which shocked me. I didn't think we were telling anyone. From Bond's demeanor, it might've been a good thing. He seemed much more at ease. When I sat down next to Jamie, it appeared that he no longer considered me a threat because he didn't tense up at all. In fact, they barely acknowledged that I was there. He seemed fixated on her now.

"I really am no longer with the CIA. Not technically anyway," Jamie said.

"That sounds interesting," Bond said.

"I was telling Bond about AJAX," Jamie said to me.

"I heard," I said, with a slight glare at Jamie to let her know I wasn't sure that was a good idea. Not that it mattered. She'd already told him.

Jamie was sitting forward with her elbows on the table, facing Bond with her back to me. He was sitting in my chair, in front of my laptop, which was thankfully closed. I hoped Jamie didn't take it upon herself to reveal my mission or that I'd hacked into London's security camera system.

Jamie leaned back and then turned slightly so she was facing me. "When you asked me, Alex, who I thought would be good to work for AJAX, Bond was the first person who came to mind."

That wasn't happening. This guy was much too flirty with Jamie. I could tell he had a thing for her.

I could see why she thought of him, though. Under different circumstances, he would've been perfect. He was good at his job and looked the part. Even through the suit, I could tell he was in excellent physical condition for his age. Fit. Muscular in a runner's sort of way. The way he handled the gun was top notch and professional. He was cool under pressure. It took restraint to keep from pulling the trigger when I had my gun pointed at him.

He also had a striking charisma about him. The same thing Jamie had. I was rough around the edges socially. More awkward. Jamie could talk to anyone, anywhere, at any time and make them think she was their best friend. That's one of the things I loved about her and one of the things that made her so good at her job.

Bond's face turned more serious as his eyes narrowed and his lips pursed.

"Tell me what you know about the dirty bomb," he asked me in a tone I didn't like.

"Tell me what *you* know about it," I said back in the same tone.

"I talked to your boss, Brad. He said he had a source for information. It didn't take me long to put together that you were the source. You seem to know about every terrorist attack in London before it happens. I want to know how."

"How do you know about the safehouse?" I asked.

"Bond dropped me off here," Jamie answered. "When I was on my mission to England, we made some serious enemies. I needed to go into hiding for a couple days, and this was the logical place for me to go."

"Your wife saved my life," Bond added.

"She's saved mine on more than one occasion too," I said.

Bond wasn't going to get distracted by chitchat. "What about the bomb? I'm under a lot of pressure here. My bosses want me to bring you in."

"If you bring me in, you'll never know the time or where the bomb is going to go off."

"Are you blackmailing me?"

"No. I'm just saying that you need me."

"You'd withhold information about a bomb that could kill millions in order to save your own skin?" He leaned back in his chair and turned his head in a look of disgust. "I was right about you."

"What's that supposed to mean?" I said angrily.

"I told them that you were doing this for attention. I figured you were washed out of the CIA. Probably for stealing money. You've been orchestrating these attacks so you can be the hero."

"It's more complicated than that," Jamie said, before I could defend myself.

"Where's the bomb?" he insisted, leaning forward in his chair almost standing.

"I don't know."

"I don't believe you."

"Give me time, and I'll know when and where."

He let out a big sigh.

"How much time do you need?"

"A few more hours. I'll know by morning."

"You have until morning. If you don't tell me by then, I'm taking you in. If you resist again, I'll kill you."

I believed him. No doubt in mind he would try.

29

Day Five

London Safehouse

9:00 a.m.

Two hours before the Royal Wedding

The computer screen on my laptop had been dark for six hours. My eyes hurt from staring at it all that time. There'd been no movement at all in Pok's cyber lab. I wondered if perhaps they'd closed it down.

The feed was still live. I could see Pok's office and the whiteboard in the background. All the lights were off, and not one person was in the office or the cyber lab. When I talked to Brad a few minutes before, he said the soonest the cruise missile could launch on the target was one o'clock London time. Two hours after the start of the royal wedding. I hoped we hadn't missed an opportunity to kill Pok. If the building were abandoned, the $1.5 million-dollar missile would be wasted. The lab would be destroyed, but Pok would live to continue to wreak havoc in the cyberwar.

If the lab had been closed, I would've thought Pok would've terminated the feed. That left me optimistic they were going to show up at any time. Maybe that was wishful thinking. If they didn't, I had no idea what I was going to tell Bond.

He had slept in the guest room. Now, he and Jamie were in the living room talking about AJAX and catching up on old times. I'd asked Jamie to keep him occupied so I could work on my computer in private. I wasn't prepared to tell him about Pok or the hack into the London security camera system. Although Bond was a smart man who played his cards close to his vest. I'm sure he had all kinds of theories floating around in his head about what I was up to.

My relationship with Bond was still tense. The prospect of giving him actionable intelligence was what kept him from arresting me. Without that information, I wasn't sure what would happen. Since he deduced I was the source for the intelligence on the car bombing, that's why he was giving me time to get him information on the dirty bomb.

That time was running out. The wedding would start in two hours. I'd asked him about cancelling the wedding. That wasn't an option. The Brits didn't shrivel up in fear from terrorists, he'd said emphatically. Besides, millions of people were in town. The economic impact of a royal wedding was incalculable.

The computer screen was still dark. No movement at all in the lab. Bond wouldn't let this go on much longer. I had no plan B, other than an agreement with Jamie that I would go peacefully if he tried to arrest me.

Jamie and I talked about it before she went to bed the night before. In the event that happened, I needed to give myself up without a fight. Explain my actions in detail to the authorities. Brad would have my back considering I'd prevented the car bombing and confirmed Pok's location. Not to mention a knife attack and a vest bombing that I had thwarted. At that point, I had nothing to lose. I'd tell them about Pok and the hacks and hope for the best.

The night had been excruciatingly long. Jamie slept in our bedroom. The urge to go in there had been hard to resist. I'd give anything to be with her. But I couldn't risk it. What if Pok came into the lab and I missed something? Once again, our plans for intimacy had been circumvented. I blamed Bond for that.

I was beginning to think we'd have to wait until we got back home. That's assuming I was even allowed to go home and wasn't rotting away in a prison cell somewhere. In that case, it could be years before we were together again. I wondered if they allowed conjugal visits. That thought almost made me laugh out loud.

Let's hope it didn't come to that. Regardless, no matter what happened, today would be an eventful day. For a lot of people. Not just for Jamie and me. The royal couple. The Queen. Several million people were lining the streets of London for the wedding. Innocent men, women, and children might have their lives turned upside down today if I didn't come through.

An incredible weight to carry on my shoulders, but one I was prepared to lift. *To whom much has been given, much is required.* That Bible verse had always been my motto. My fallback when I needed motivation to do the seemingly impossible.

Curly often said, "There'll be good days and bad days, and this is one of them." In other words, suck it up. Take whatever life throws at you like a man. I'd barely slept in five days. I'd been accused of treason. I'd witnessed two knife attacks, an acid attack, two vest bombings, and a car bombing. Considering all that, I think I should be allowed to wallow in a little introspection for a few hours. The eerie quiet in the safehouse and the dark night, only made the introspection seem more ominous.

When the screen on my computer suddenly lit up shortly after nine in the morning, so did my spirits. I went immediately into mission mode and pushed those negative thoughts from the past night to the deep recesses of my soul.

Time to go to work.

The cyber lab was suddenly buzzing. Workers filled the lab, and the television screens and computers roared to life. Pok entered his office and erased the whiteboard which still contained day four's information on it. The same man I saw yesterday was also in the office. That sent adrenaline through me like an energy drink which I could've used a few moments before but now didn't need. The scene was similar to yesterday when Pok and the man had gone over their day four plan. One which played out exactly as they had outlined it. I could only hope they were about to repeat the same process.

Pok began writing on the board and talking with animated gestures. He was standing behind his desk and in front of the board so I couldn't see what he wrote. I leaned into my computer as if it would give me a better look.

"Come on, you piece of garbage," I said to the image of Pok on the computer screen. "Move over so I can see what you're planning."

He wrote some more. When he was done, he sat down in the chair. I could see the board perfectly.

Day Five

Sunday

Dirty Bomb

St. Margaret's Church.

Organ Loft.

When the Queen arrives.

I closed the laptop and went to talk to Bond.

* * *

Iran

Pok finished writing on the whiteboard and then moved out of the way so Halee could see it. He sat down and pretended to have a conversation with Heo, his trusted assistant. After a few minutes of the charade, he got up and left the room to find Niazi. Pok found him in his office.

"Are we all set?" Niazi asked Pok.

Niazi knew nothing of what had just transpired in Pok's office. Not that he needed to know. That display was a private chess match between Pok and Halee. One in which today, Pok would take Halee's Queen. Figuratively and literally. After that, checkmate was inevitable.

The Queen had been the target all along. The disinformation was designed to throw the British authorities off the path. If Pok's intuition was right, Halee had walked right into the trap and was feeding the information to MI6 as they spoke.

"We're all set on my end," Pok said. "Is the bomb in place?"

"My man put it on the helicopter last night. I already have confirmation. He's good to go. Inshallah."

"Inshallah," Pok responded, even though he wasn't even sure what it meant or if he was supposed to say it as a non-Muslim.

Niazi didn't seem to mind, and Pok felt like the conversation was over. Niazi was a man of few words. All the better.

Pok had work to do and didn't have time for idle chit chat. He was a man of few words himself. He was most comfortable sitting in front of a computer, which he could do for hours and days on end with little to no sleep.

Pok went back into his office feeling refreshed and confident. He slept well the night before. Considering the complexity of his plan, things were going well. Now he was in the final stages. Time to put the finishing touches on it.

The first thing he did was kill Halee's connection so he could no longer see into Pok's lab. Then he went into the deep recesses of the London Security camera system code that he wrote to hack into the system. He left the code in place so they would know it was hacked but changed where it was pointed. A hacker left a footprint. A signature pattern. A location map really. The best hackers in the world were able to disguise their IP addresses and SSL certificates to make them look identical to a known IP address. For misdirection. Pok could hack into a system and make it look like it had come from a country or person of his choosing.

Many times, Russia or South Korea, and even Iran had gotten the blame for something he did. In this instance, he made it look like Halee was the only one who hacked into their system. He erased any evidence that he'd ever been there. Nothing could be traced back to his lab in Iran.

Satisfied, he activated an alarm in the software, alerting British authorities that their system had been hacked. Then he left them bread crumbs along the way so they could find the malicious code. Pok tried not to make it too obvious. It'd take some sophistication to find the breach. Twenty minutes was his estimation. That's how long it would take them to trace it back to Halee's computer.

He could hardly contain his laughter.

Today was a defining moment in his career. The dirty bomb would explode in downtown London which would appease the Iranians. The Queen and scores of others would be dead. The bomb was retaliation for the sanctions put on the Iranian government by England and the United States. Not his battle, but one he was willing to lend his considerable skills to. Since they couldn't carry out an attack on U.S. soil, Britain was the next best thing. They couldn't have done it without Pok's help which he was more than willing to give. Pok didn't care about sanctions, and political maneuvering or even terrorist attacks. He cared about one thing. Bringing down Halee.

The British authorities would piece together the facts. Halee gave them the bad information. When they found out he was the one who hacked into their security cameras, they'd be furious. When the bomb exploded, and they couldn't stop it because of Halee's disinformation, Pok wasn't sure what they'd do, but it wouldn't be good for Halee's reputation and career, whatever it was.

The Queen would be dead, and the Brits would need someone to blame.

Pok provided them someone. Halee was their scapegoat.

Of course, Halee would be dead as well.

Pok was certain Halee wouldn't be able to resist the urge to go into downtown London to help stop the attack. Pok wished he could still see the security camera feed. He'd give almost anything to see that split second look on Halee's face the moment the dirty bomb exploded, and he realized his mistake.

30

I walked into the living room where Jamie and Bond were talking. Two chairs were against the far wall with a table between them. The conversation stopped abruptly as soon as they saw me.

"According to my source," I said hesitantly, "the bomb was placed in St. Margaret's Church. In the organ loft. It's set to explode right after the arrival of the Queen."

I didn't believe it when I read it on the screen, and I believed it less now after hearing the words come out of my mouth.

"That's impossible," Bond said.

"That's what my source is telling me. But I don't believe it either."

"That area has been searched a dozen times," Bond said what I had already presumed. "That church is right next to Westminster Abbey where the wedding is taking place. There's no way a bomb was planted there. We would've found it. The dogs would've picked up the scent."

I started to sit down on the sofa but had too much nervous energy. Instead, I just shifted back and forth between my two feet to keep from pacing.

"I don't disagree," I said. "But this is what I don't understand. If there's a dirty bomb in London, wouldn't the sensors pick up the increased level of radiation."

A dirty bomb was radioactive material wrapped around a conventional explosive. London had sensors throughout the city to detect any type of radiation. Most major cities had them. Terrorists weren't sophisticated enough to have the right materials to avoid detection. That's why a successful dirty bomb had never been exploded in a major city.

Bond hesitated. Like he was about to tell us something but wasn't sure if he should.

"We did pick up radiation," he finally said. "Two days ago. Just outside London. Then it disappeared, and we haven't seen a trace since."

"Could it have been a false positive?" Jamie asked. "Those sensors are extremely sensitive."

"That's what we thought, but then Brad called and said he had intelligence that a dirty bomb attack was likely in London. We didn't believe him but took precautions. When he gave us the intelligence on the car bomb, and it turned out to be accurate, that's when we put the possibility of a dirty bomb back on the table. That's why I'm here. I assume that intelligence came from you."

This time I hesitated. Not sure how much I could tell him. I decided that if he were going to lay some of his cards on the table and be honest then so would I. Not all my cards, but what he needed to know, considering we were in this together with one common goal. To stop the dirty bomb. This wasn't the time to be coy or let my ego get in the way. Sometimes on a mission, you didn't have all the pieces to solve the puzzle. Looking back, if a bomb exploded, and we each had pieces that would've solved it but were too stubborn to share it, then we'd have regrets for the rest of our lives.

I nodded.

"The intelligence did come from me. I was also the source for the car bombing yesterday. According to my information, a dirty bomb is going to be exploded at the royal wedding shortly after the Queen arrives. I think the threat is real."

Bond stood up. "I'll be back in a minute," he said, as he abruptly walked outside. Presumably to call his bosses.

I waited until he was out of earshot. "What do you think?" I asked Jamie.

"I don't know what to think."

"Do you remember what you said to me yesterday?"

"I said a lot of things. Can you be more specific?"

I walked over and sat down in the chair Bond had been sitting in. Then I leaned in so we would be closer together.

"When I found out about the car bombing, I said to you, 'it was almost too easy.' Do you remember what you said?"

"I said, 'what if it was.'"

"Exactly! It didn't register at the time, but what if Pok wanted me to find the information? What if it was too easy on purpose?"

"That's sort of what I meant. I've wondered all along if you were walking into a trap. All of this has been confusing. Like the knife attack. And the acid attacks. Why didn't they attack us? Why the people around us? Why didn't the vest bomber just walk into a crowd and blow himself up? Why did it have to be with you around?"

"I don't think there's any doubt Pok wanted me to know he was the one behind the attacks. I think he knew I'd figure it out and hack into the camera system."

"I'm beginning to wonder if he was behind all the crazy stuff that was happening with our wedding. The flowers and limo. And Curly. Maybe Pok sabotaged all of that for his own demented game he's playing."

"I've thought about that as well. I always assumed I was one step ahead of him. What if it's the other way around? What if he wanted me to find the lab and know the plans? He might be feeding me the information for some bigger purpose."

"Doesn't it seem weird to you that he would write out each day's plan on a whiteboard right in front of his computer?" Jamie asked.

"It seemed strange when I was watching it. It's almost like he was doing it for my benefit. But why tip me off about the car bomb?"

Jamie's eyes suddenly widened, and her mouth flew open. "So you'd believe the information about the dirty bomb!"

"That makes sense."

"But if the dirty bomb doesn't exist why go to all this trouble?"

"Because the dirty bomb does exist."

* * *

9:34 a.m.

Bond was gone for twenty minutes. When he returned, he had his gun drawn. Out of instinct, I reached for mine, but I didn't have it on me. It was in the kitchen.

"What are you doing?" I asked, raising my hands into the air.

"Bond!" Jamie said. "Put the gun down and let's talk about this."

"You're under arrest, Alex."

"Why? On what charge."

"There is no bomb in St. Margaret's church. We've searched that area. We also discovered something else."

"What's that?"

"That you hacked into the London security camera system. Our investigators traced the hack back to this location. Your laptop."

My heart sunk what felt like a couple of inches in my chest.

"There's been some mistake," I said.

I started to stand but Bond tensed up. His finger was on the trigger, so I sat back down, to make myself seem less threatening.

"Are you denying that you hacked into the camera system?" he said accusingly.

I didn't answer right away.

"That's what I thought."

"I can explain."

"You can explain down at headquarters. I've wasted enough time on you."

"You're making a big mistake," Jamie said. "There's a dirty bomb somewhere, and we can help you find it."

"Stay out of this, Jamie. This is between Alex and me."

He waved the gun in my direction. "Get on your knees and put your hands on your head."

"Do what he says, Alex!" Jamie said. Her eyes had a look of resignation as she gazed downward, and her shoulders drooped. "We'll sort all this out. Don't make things worse than they are."

"Listen to her, Alex. That's good advice. I don't want to kill you, but I will if you make me."

Reluctantly and slowly, I got down on my knees with my back to him and my hands up over my head. He roughly cuffed my hands behind my back.

"You're making a big mistake Digby," I said. "We're running out of time to find the dirty bomb. I know who's behind it."

"Who?"

I hesitated again even though it was time to put all my cards on the table. By the time I got down to headquarters, it would be too late.

"Pok. He's a hacker from North Korea."

"I know who Pok is."

"He's in Iran. I've been tracking him for more than a year. I almost had him in North Korea, but he got away. It's personal with him. He's trying to set me up. He's the one who's been orchestrating all these attacks. From a cyber lab in Iran. Talk to Brad. He'll confirm it. We're going to hit the lab with a cruise missile sometime this afternoon."

"How do you know Pok's behind it?"

"He's my source. He hacked into the London security system first. All I did was hack in to find him. Which I did. I can prove it."

"How?"

"On my computer. I've got a feed directly into his lab. I'll show you. You can see for yourself. Pok has a whiteboard in his office. On that board it says day five, dirty bomb. That's how I know about it. The location is St. Margaret's church. In the organ loft. After the arrival of the Queen. I'll show you on my computer. That'll give you all the proof you need."

"You've got two minutes."

I stood to my feet. Bond pushed me from behind toward the door. We walked into the kitchen.

"I'm telling you, Bond, Pok has a bomb somewhere in the city," I said. "You've got to believe me."

"He's telling the truth," Jamie added.

Bond took my arm and sat me down in the chair in front of my computer. "I'm going to free your hands, but don't try anything stupid."

He undid my handcuffs.

I powered up the computer.

Furiously typed in a few keystrokes.

I couldn't believe my eyes.

The screen was dark.

Pok had killed the connection to his lab.

I was screwed.

31

One hour and thirty minutes before the Royal Wedding

For the first time in my short marriage, I was going to defy my wife. Probably the first of many times.

I wouldn't go with Bond Digby peacefully. A dirty bomb was about to explode in London, and we were wasting valuable time. When he took the handcuffs off me, he'd made a critical mistake. With my hands free, he couldn't arrest me, even with a gun.

"You're coming with me," Bond said roughly, for what seemed like the tenth time.

"How are you going to make me?" I said defiantly, almost taunting him. I needed for him to move closer.

Jamie didn't say anything. Even her facial expression didn't give away what she was thinking. I was sitting in the chair at the kitchen table. I got the desired reaction. Bond was now towering over me waving the gun in my face. Jamie was behind him. She could disarm him in two seconds if she wanted to.

"Don't think I won't use this," he said.

"What are you going to do? Shoot two CIA Officers in a CIA safehouse owned by the United States government? Not even you are that stupid. You'll be the one arrested for murder."

"I thought you weren't with the CIA anymore. That you were with some AJAX corporation. Was that all a lie as well?"

"We are with AJAX, and we're still working with the CIA. Have you stopped to ask yourself why you found us in a CIA safehouse? Would we be here if we weren't still working with Brad and the CIA? You said I was the source of the intelligence on the car bombing. Brad's the one who fed you the information. Come on, Bond. Put two and two together. I thought you were good at your job."

"I am good at my job, and I have orders to take you in. That's what I'm going to do."

Bond's tough-guy routine was getting old with me.

"You're failing your job interview," I said, taking him by surprise, evident by his left eye suddenly squinting and his head shaking back and forth in disbelief.

"What the hell are you talking about?" he said.

"Jamie said you'd be a good candidate for AJAX. I'm not so sure about that. If you did come to work for us, I'd be your boss. It's not a good idea to threaten your boss with a gun, especially before he's even hired you. You're not making a good impression, I must say."

I was trying to bring some levity to the situation and calm things somewhat. That statement did take everyone by surprise, even Jamie who was forcing back a grin. It had such an effect that no one said anything for a good ten seconds.

"Bond would be good," Jamie finally said.

"I'm not so sure. At AJAX, we're flexible. We do whatever it takes to fulfill the mission. We don't worry about *orders*." I said the word with emphasis. "We do what the circumstances on the ground dictate. The reason you took the handcuffs off me and let me look at my laptop was because, deep down, you knew I was right. Dumb move, by the way. Two strikes against you now. One for being more concerned about what the suits would say rather than what the mission requires. Two, for freeing my hands. Let me show you what I mean."

Bond was less than two feet away from me. The gun was in his right hand pointed directly at me. The move had to be executed perfectly to avoid an accidental discharge of the gun. I brought my left hand up and forward, grabbed his wrist and twisted it to my left. The gun was now upside down. In one motion, I grabbed the barrel of the gun and jerked it upward, so it faced the ceiling and no longer pointed at me. If it fired, I'd get a nasty burn on my hand, but I'd survive, which was the main thing. That move put Bond's wrist in an awkward and painful position.

He let out a yelp.

Then I twisted the gun to the right. Normally, I would've twisted it to the left and snapped his trigger finger out of spite. In this instance, I gently slipped it off his finger and released his wrist, which he instantly grabbed. The soft tissue would be sore for a few days. I ejected the magazine and tossed the gun to Jamie which she snatched out of the air with ease.

She unchambered the round and handed the gun back to Bond.

"Now, sit down, Bond," I said firmly but in a less-confrontive tone. "Let's figure out where this bomb is. We're running out of time."

Still rubbing his wrist, Bond sat down in the chair at the head of the kitchen table. Jamie sat on the other side of him, across from me.

"I believe there is a dirty bomb. And that it's going to explode at the Royal Wedding sometime before the wedding. After the Queen arrives. My intelligence is correct. The only misinformation is the location. I think the time is dead-on accurate."

I looked at my watch. "That gives us less than an hour. The question is where and how are they going to get the bomb into London."

"It can't be there now," Jamie said. "If it was, the sensors would pick it up."

"So, how are the terrorists going to get it into downtown London in the next hour?" I asked. "What about by car or van?"

Bond still seemed hesitant to join in. I figured that would be temporary as his ego had taken a hit. But... he was a professional. This was what we lived for. Now that he didn't have the power, he really had no other choice in the matter but to help us. Which he could do. He knew London inside and out. Better than I ever would. I needed his knowledge. At some point, I would need his credentials to get us where we needed to go.

Finally, he answered. "All traffic is blocked. No vehicle can get in or out of London as of nine o'clock this morning. The bridges are all shut down."

"They didn't take it in before nine o'clock," I said. "Like Jamie said, the vehicle can't be downtown. Because of the sensors. What about by boat?"

Bond answered, "The river's blocked off as well. We have military patrols at each end of the Thames and points in between. No one can get within three miles of Westminster Abbey without being stopped."

"Submarines?"

"Sonar would pick that up."

"I doubt Pok has access to a sub," Jamie added.

I nodded in agreement. I already knew a submarine wasn't a possibility, but that's how my mind worked. Like a computer code. It had to follow a logical progression and rule everything out so I could get to the right thread.

I rubbed my eyes roughly. The adrenaline was overwhelming the fatigue, but I needed my mind sharper.

"What about the tube?" Jamie asked.

"Shut down," Bond said. "No routes into London are running after nine o'clock."

"Sewer systems? Water pipes?" she asked. We made a good team. She was taking up the slack at my momentary lack of focus.

"All were inspected again this morning."

"That rules out by land and sea. That leaves air," I said, although I already knew what Bond was going to say.

He shook his head no. Then rubbed his right wrist again. "Fighter planes are scrambled. The airspace is a no-fly zone. No planes are allowed to take off or land from any private area within a hundred miles until after the wedding is over."

"It seems like air would be the only way to get a bomb into London at the last moment," I said.

"We already know that air is the primary threat," Bond said. "After 9/11, we locked that down. Even commercial flights are diverted to the west. None can take off toward London. The only person allowed in the air is the Queen."

My heart did a couple somersaults. "What did you say?"

"Commercial flights can't take off toward London. If one were hijacked, our fighter planes would shoot it out of the sky before it got to London. There's no way a terrorist can fly a bomb into London on a plane."

"No. You said the only person allowed in the air is the Queen. What did you mean by that?"

"The Queen is at Windsor Palace. A helicopter will fly her to Buckingham Palace at around ten thirty this morning."

I suddenly bolted out of my chair as I remembered something. In the living room. I'd seen it on the television when I went in to tell Jamie and Bond about Pok. I practically ran in there. The TV was still on, but the sound was muted. On the screen was a picture of the courtyard at Windsor Palace. A blaring headline read that they were waiting for the Queen's departure to the wedding. Jamie and Bond entered the room and stood next to me, one on each side.

Sitting on the courtyard were four helicopters along with a number of armed soldiers guarding them.

"Why are there four helicopters there?" I asked.

"One will carry the Queen," Bond said. "The other three are decoys. That way if someone has a handheld missile or wants to attack the Queen, they won't know which helicopter she's on."

Jamie said, "We do that with the President of the United States. He travels in a caravan of several vehicles. For that very reason. Smart."

"Who flies the helicopters?" I asked hurriedly.

"They are selected by base commanders. One helicopter per base is chosen. It's a big honor to be selected."

"The bomb is in one of those helicopters," I said soberly.

"Those are military planes and pilots."

"I bet one of those pilots is locked in a closet of an airplane hangar, on a base somewhere. It's the only thing that makes sense. Somehow, those helicopters were compromised. Or at least one of them has been. Somehow the Iranians got a man on the inside. I don't know how, but I'm sure that's what happened."

Bond pulled out his phone. I put my hand on his wrist to stop him from making a call to his bosses.

"Don't call it in. The bomb could be on a detonator switch. If you send in the cavalry, he'll blow the whole thing up. The Queen is still in the castle. Depending on the size of the bomb, she could be killed. Not to mention those thousands of people in the streets waiting to watch her leave."

"What do you suggest we do?"

"Can you get us in that courtyard?"

"With my MI6 credentials, I can get us anywhere."

"Jamie, go change into a business professional outfit. Like a pantsuit or something. I'm going to put on a suit and tie."

"What's the plan?" Bond asked.

"I'll tell you in the car."

32

"Who flies the Queen's helicopter?" I asked Bond as we sped away from the safehouse.

"The royal pilot. He's been flying Her Majesty for years. That's never rotated. It's either him or his backup pilot."

"I think we can assume then, that the bomb's not on the Queen's helicopter."

"That's for certain. It's searched several times before she boards. I don't know if the other helicopters are searched. All they do is fly in formation. They're only in the air for less than ten minutes."

Bond was driving his car with Jamie in the back seat and I in the passenger seat. His car was equipped with sirens and lights. The lights were flashing, but the sirens were off. Bond was a good driver. He navigated the streets with skill and expected us to arrive at the castle within fifteen minutes.

"I assume there are no radiation sensors in Windsor," I said.

"That's correct. Too expensive."

Dirty bombs were difficult to attain and to make. Terrorists weren't going to waste one on a smaller area, even if the blast radius included the Queen. The conventional thinking was that they would only be used on high-value targets with huge population centers like London, New York, Paris, and similar cities. Bang for their buck, so to speak. Figuratively and literally.

"So, that leaves the other three helicopters," I said. "The bomb is on one of those. There are three of us."

Then a question popped into my mind that I hadn't considered. One that would blow my plan apart. "Do you know how to fly a helicopter?" I asked Bond. I knew Jamie did, although it'd been a while since she'd flown one.

"Of course. I'm not that proficient though."

I breathed a sigh of relief. "Okay. Here's my plan. When we arrive, you need to get us into the courtyard," I said to him.

"That won't be a problem. Although, I'll need to give them a good reason why."

"Tell them MI6 sent us to accompany the pilots into London. As a secondary security precaution."

"I can try. No guarantees, though."

"We'll act like it's business as usual. Like we're supposed to be there. You'll have to be persuasive. If push comes to shove, tell them about the bomb. At least they might have a chance to evacuate the queen. Let's assume the best-case scenario and they let us in. Each of us will board a helicopter. I'll go to the one that looks the most likely to have the bomb."

"How will you know which one that is?" Bond asked.

"I'll know. I'll be able to tell by looking into the pilot's eyes."

"I should be the one who gets on the helicopter with the bomb," Bond said. "After all, this is my country and my Queen. It's my job to protect her."

I shook my head no. Violently. Side to side, so he'd get the point. "This is my fight with Pok. And I'm the best pilot. I flew a helicopter a few months ago in the middle east."

I waited for an objection. When one didn't come, I continued on with my plan. Before I could, Jamie asked the obvious question haunting my mind.

"Then what?" Jamie asked, once again proving she was usually a step ahead of me. "Let's say you get on the helicopter and it does have a bomb. What are you going to do with it?"

"I don't know. Any ideas, Bond? What do I do with the bomb? Obviously, get it as far away from people as possible."

My mind was wildly speculating and running through all the scenarios. It seemed overwhelming. How do I commandeer the helicopter, fly it safely away from population centers, and ditch it before I get caught up in the blast? A daunting task under any circumstances, much less with so much on the line and so little time to plan the operation.

As Bond took a curve at a high rate of speed, the tires squealed, and the back of the car fishtailed. Even I was uncomfortable with how fast he was going. Probably wouldn't be if I were driving. My experience was that things seemed scarier from the passenger's seat than if I was actually driving. The thought occurred to me that what to do with the bomb was moot if Bond wrapped us around a tree.

When Bond didn't answer right away, Jamie asked, "What about the ocean?" She didn't have her seatbelt on. She clutched the back of our seats as her body leaned into each curve. Those same hands that were burned by the acid. They must be better. Either that, or the adrenaline of the moment was blocking the pain.

Bond shook his head no, as he leaned into another curve. Both of his arms were taut, and he was straining with all his might to keep us on the road. I wanted to tell him to slow down.

"That won't work," Bond answered. "The ecological damage would be catastrophic if that bomb goes off in the ocean. Our fishing industry would be devastated. The fallout would wash up on shore and contaminate beaches and reservoirs. Not an option."

"Where then?" I asked. "I'm open to ideas. We have to get it as far away from London as possible."

"Do you think the bomb is on a timer or a detonator?" Bond asked.

"That's a good question. We'll have to play that one by ear. My guess is a timer. They wouldn't want to risk the bomb going off prematurely. Since they have an approximate time, I think it's scheduled to go off right after the queen lands at Buckingham Palace, give or take a couple extra minutes."

"The Queen runs a tight schedule," Bond said. "They would know that she's not going to be late or early. And the wedding starts at eleven. They know she has to be in her seat before then. A timer makes sense."

"I guess, we just fly the bomb out into the countryside as far as we can," I answered my own question since Bond wasn't going to.

"How do we get away from the bomb before it explodes?" Jamie asked. "Will we have enough time to get away from the blast? If I land the helicopter in a sparsely populated place, there won't be any shelter to get away from it." She was obviously still considering the possibility that she could be the one who ended up on the helicopter with the bomb. She was bringing up a concern for all of us, but I'd thought about that already.

"You'll have to land the helicopter and get the bomb off," I answered. "And then get out of there as quickly as possible. Before it explodes. Hopefully, the timer will be in clear view, so you know how much time you have."

"The best bet would be to fly south," Bond said. "To South Downs National Park. That's basically a preserve. Not many people live there."

The road was straight now, and Bond floored it. I estimated we were going well over a hundred miles per hour. The houses and trees were whizzing by in a blur.

"No, wait. I just thought of something," Bond said. "Go northeast. About fifty klicks north is an abandoned missile testing site. We haven't used it in years. Top secret. Very few people even know about it. There's a big cavern there. It will absorb a lot of the blast. We tested nuclear bombs at that site back in the fifties."

"That's like our Area 51," Jamie said.

"Exactly."

"Will I have enough time to get there?" I asked, assuming I'd be the one in the helicopter with the bomb. If I did my math right, fifty klicks was about eighty miles.

"You'll be cutting it close. These are military choppers. They can travel one-hundred eighty miles an hour. You can get there in under thirty minutes."

"That means I'll have to act as soon as we take off."

The MSO were getting lower by the minute. Mission Success Odds were what Curly taught us to use to determine whether or not we should continue on with a mission. The lower the odds, the less likely the mission would be successful. In this case, we had no choice. We continued on with the plan even if the odds were close to zero.

At that moment, all I could think of was Jamie. Maybe she was thinking the same thing because she was suddenly resting her hand on my shoulder. An overwhelming sadness came over me like a punch in the emotional gut. Was I going to make her a widow five days into our marriage? Having never even had the chance to be intimate with her?

Too late now.

Bond pulled up to the security gate at Windsor Castle.

He flashed his credentials. The guard waved us through.

We were in.

* * *

The helicopter with the bomb was obvious. The one in the far back of the formation was the only one with a middle eastern pilot. Racial profiling wasn't the only reason. The man was nervous. Fidgeting in his seat. I saw him wipe his brow several times. Look over at the soldiers. Then the other helicopters. Then the door where the Queen would exit. Then his watch. His eyes were beady. His beard and mussed hair seemed out of place for a soldier of the royal guard. I was surprised no one else had noticed.

My impulse was to go right to the helicopter, but I couldn't. We had exited our car and were at the entrance to the heavily guarded courtyard. Bond was talking to the security supervisor. Jamie and I were standing next to him although we weren't doing any of the talking. The supervisor seemed confused. Like he wasn't happy with the sudden change of plans. Bond was smooth and persuasive and tried his best to convince him.

"I'm just following orders, sir," Bond said. "The Director wants a man on each helicopter. Just in case there's any breach in security or something goes wrong. Just an added precaution."

I realized at that moment how far Bond was sticking his neck out. If we were wrong, this might cost him his career. A momentary flash of guilt shot through me as I remembered how I had questioned his nerve to go against orders back at the safehouse. Bond was like Jamie and me. We'd sacrifice our careers for the good of the mission. In fact, we had. That's why we were no longer with the CIA. That brazenness was why we were the best in the business. Bond had that potential.

If we did hire him at AJAX, he'd have to quit flirting nonstop with my wife, though.

The man in charge wanted to call the higher ups. Somehow, Bond talked him out of it.

"Go ahead," the man said reluctantly, waving his hand in the air like he wanted to be done with the whole conversation. It had worked to our advantage getting there at the last minute when he didn't have time to check out our story.

Jamie went to one helicopter. Bond went to the other. I went straight to mine. The pilot had a sudden look of terror on his face as his mouth flew open and his eyes widened. More confirmation that he was the man with the bomb.

I flashed him a reassuring smile.

The helicopter was idling in place. I ducked my head to avoid the rotor blades and went around to the passenger side. My tie blew out of place and over my shoulder at the sudden rush of wind. I put my right hand down to make sure my gun stayed in place. One I had taken from the safehouse. A glock. One magazine and a clip attached to my belt.

I opened the door, climbed in, and said in my most British accent, which Jamie hated, "Hi, mate. My name's Alex. How are you today, bloke?"

I stuck my hand out for him, and he reluctantly shook it.

"It's blimey hot today, isn't it, mate?" I asked.

Then I playfully punched him on the arm. What I really wanted to do was coldcock him in the jaw. He still hadn't said anything. The impulse for violence was tamped down. Whatever I was going to do had to wait until the bird was in the air. I didn't see a detonator in his hand or anywhere on his body, but I couldn't be sure. At that point, I hadn't even confirmed the bomb was on this helicopter.

The door to the castle suddenly burst open, and an entourage of armed men exited the building. Wearing suits and sunglasses. Like our secret service. I pointed that way. The pilot turned his head to look.

I took that opportunity to look in the back. The seats were missing. On the floor was a suitcase-looking, metal container wrapped in explosives. A timer on the outside was facing toward me, counting down. A green light signified my worst fear.

The bomb was activated.

The countdown had begun.

29:15... 14... 13... 12... 11.

Bond's words echoed around in my head and sent chills down my spine. *You have thirty minutes to get there.*

That's not enough time.

33

Indecision can be a good thing or a bad thing.

Curly's words whirled through my mind like the deafening sound of the blades of the helicopter resounding in my ears. He clarified the statement about indecision during one of his many lengthy lectures on operational decision making. *If a mouse is looking at a piece of cheese in a trap, indecision will save his life if he does nothing. If he's caught in the trap, and does nothing, he'll die. Are you trapped or are you about to be? That's the most important question to ask in a life or death situation.*

In my current predicament, I wasn't sure. Hence the indecision. The one thing I did know was that indecision had already cost me valuable time. I'd boarded the helicopter at Windsor Castle. The terrorist and I were now flying in formation toward Buckingham Palace with the Queen's helicopter and two other escorts. Our bird was loaded with a dirty bomb that would kill millions of people, including the Queen, the Vice President of the United States, and the other dignitaries who were attending the royal wedding..

My intention had been to attack the man as soon as we reached altitude which was a little over a thousand feet. Simply pull out my gun and shoot the jerk in the head and take command of the craft. A number of factors caused me to rethink my plan. The first being that the controls on my side of the cockpit had been disabled. For whatever reason. I hadn't expected that. Consequently, the terrorist had full control of the craft, and if I wanted it, I'd have to take it from him.

Killing him or knocking him unconscious wasn't the problem. If I incapacitated the man, the helicopter would go into a ninety degree roll within seconds. By the time I undid his seat belt, opened his door, and pushed him out, it'd be too late to regain control of the helicopter. I'd have to undo my belt, climb over the center console, avoid hitting any of the many buttons that controlled vital functions, get into his seat without hitting any of the control mechanisms, then bring the bird under control before I crashed into the ground. Which I figured would take about twenty to thirty seconds from the moment I acted. If I could even do it considering I'd be tossed around the cockpit like a rag doll. In the best case scenario, it'd take about six to ten seconds for the hovercraft to fall to the ground.

The autopilot was within my reach, and I could activate that, which seemed like my best option. The problem was that all the pilot had to do was move one steering mechanism, and the autopilot disengaged. For that plan to work, I'd have to engage the autopilot and shoot him within fractions of a second of each other. All kinds of things could go wrong. If he slumped down, he'd fall on the cyclic and cause the helicopter to veer out of control. If he slumped backward, his feet would hit the pedals and send us into a spin. Even if neither of those things happened, when I tried to push him out of the plane, I had no doubt his left leg would hit the cyclic and disengage the autopilot, and I'd be in the same predicament.

If I only had one control to worry about, it wouldn't be a problem. I had three to concern myself with. The cyclic stick came up from the cockpit floor and sat between the pilot's legs. That was what enabled the pilot to tilt the craft to either side or forward and back. The foot pedals controlled the tail rotor. The right pedal turned the helicopter to the left and the nose to the right. The left pedal did the opposite. It would take several seconds for me to gain control over those pedals. They were the only things controlling the torque.

The collective lever was at his left side—within my reach. That lever controlled the altitude and the throttle attached to the lever and controlled the speed. So, I could control altitude and throttle. But that was like controlling the accelerator of a car, but not the steering wheel. What difference did it make? The only thing I controlled in that instance was how fast I was going when I died.

I stared at the man.

He stared back.

Like he knew what I was thinking.

In his beady, steely eyes, was the same indecision.

The difference between us was that he already had a death wish. He was prepared to die either way. I wanted to stay alive. He wanted to kill millions. I wanted to save as many people as possible. He thought seventy virgins were waiting for him in heaven. I wanted to go home safely and be with my one virgin.

A stalemate ensued.

Time to act to break it.

Make a decision, even if it's wrong.

I pushed the altitude hold button and the heading hold button activating the autopilot. As expected, he moved the cyclic, and it disengaged. I pulled out my gun and pointed it at him.

The terrorist jerked the cyclic to the right and the helicopter banked sharply. In essence turning me on my side. Unexpected The gun was still firmly in my grip, but if I pulled the trigger, we'd fall out of the sky in seconds.

Fortunately, he still had the helicopter under control and hadn't decided to end it all right there. But I had no way to engage him. The only thing I'd done was play my hand. He now knew my intentions. When he yanked the cyclic back to center, the craft stabilized. Apparently, he was at least committed to trying to get the helicopter to downtown London so the bomb would kill the most people.

That was the opening I needed. Either way, this helicopter was never going to London. I reached out to push the buttons again, this time ready to fire the gun as soon as the autopilot was activated.

Before I could, he jerked the bird to the left causing us to go into a roll. My heart felt like it was suddenly in my throat. A roll in a helicopter was a one-way ticket to disaster if you didn't know how to get out of it.

He didn't.

Whether I lived or died was now totally out of my hands.

I grabbed the collective and pulled back on the throttle. That got us out of the roll, but the idiot overcorrected, causing us to begin to spin uncontrollably and lose altitude. Alarm buttons sounded, sending sirens echoing through the cockpit. Trying desperately to get the helicopter under control, the inexperience of the pilot was evident as we pitched back and forth. If I didn't act soon, we'd go into a death spiral and crash.

I didn't want to risk firing the gun and have the bullet go in the fuselage or the gas tank. Instead, I brought my right arm up and backhanded a karate chop into his chin. I'd take my chances with no one controlling the helicopter as opposed to that yahoo. The blow was glancing as the helicopter torqued just as I began my motion. The blow was enough to stun him, though, at least momentarily.

Before the helicopter began to roll again, I activated the autopilot. The bird stabilized, although we were flying dangerously low. I didn't want to give it any throttle because the autopilot would disengage.

I had to hurry.

My heart was pounding. The change in altitude and jerking motion caused my ears to pop and sound like gunfire. Then came the trickiest part. I undid the terrorist's seat belt and reached across him and opened his door. Only then did I undo my seat belt. On my knees, I lifted the man's torso straight up in the air. One wrong move and we were both dead.

I was totally at the mercy of the movements of the helicopter. The slightest jerk one way or the other, I'd be plastered against the wall or thrown out the opened door. I swung the man's legs around. They were facing me. His back was to the open door and his head was leaning out the side of the helicopter. The air rushed by with what sounded like the force of a hurricane.

The man's eyes twitched. Then they opened. He recovered enough from the blow to his chin to realize what was happening. His eyes widened. I saw in his face a sudden steely resolve and a decision to kill me.

He lifted his body like he was doing a sit-up. With one flick of my wrists, I sent him tumbling out the door to the ground below.

Already half-way into the pilot's seat, I climbed the rest of the way to the right side of the craft, careful not to hit the collective or the cyclic. When I got into place, I moved the hand and foot controls deactivating the autopilot. The helicopter lurched, but her course was stable and true.

For the first time since I had moved on the man, I looked out the cockpit window. What I saw was horrifying.

A cell phone tower was dead ahead. Coming at me like the iceberg toward the Titanic. If any part of my bird hit that tower, I was a goner. I banked hard to the right to miss it and then cringed halfway through the maneuver, expecting the collision or a blade to clip the top of it.

When it didn't, I let out a huge breath of air. I immediately pulled back on the collective and began climbing. Then turned to the northeast. I entered the coordinates of the missile-testing site that Bond had sent to my phone. Then put the machine on full throttle. Open. As fast as she could go. The helicopter literally lurched in the air as the powerful engines thrust us forward with the same determination I felt inside.

Only then did I look back at the timer on the bomb.

00:23: 7... 6... 5... 4... 3.

I had twenty-three minutes to make a thirty-minute flight. I could only hope that Bond's estimate was at normal speed. I hit the throttle harder. Trying to get every mile-per-hour possible out of her. She responded and gave me more. The bird creaked and moaned as her limits were tested. I figured based on the size that she'd do 175 mph at top speed. That wasn't good enough. If we went 200 mph, I wouldn't make it in time.

The realization hit me. I wasn't going to make it. I'd have to ditch the bird before I could get to the missile site. My resolve was to get as far away from population as possible.

I put the helicopter in what I guessed was the most aerodynamic position. Then did the same for me, although, it wouldn't make any difference, except mentally. I got into a crouch. So that my eyes were barely looking above the dashboard. Like a soap box derby racer. Somehow, it made it feel like we were going faster.

Then I saw a flash.

Out of the corner of my eye.

Off the left side of the helicopter.

Then another one. To my right.

Two fighter planes surrounded me.

I'd forgotten about them. Bond mentioned them. They were patrolling the airspace over London. I could only imagine what they were thinking. One of the Queen's escorts broke formation. The door opened and a body flew out.

This was not good.

They must think I'm a hostile.

They began taking evasive action to force me down to the ground.

If I didn't, I knew exactly what was going to happen if they didn't give me time to explain.

They'd shoot me down.

34

The fighter jet to my right was so close, I could almost reach out the window and touch it. The pilot of the jet shook his fist at me and pointed his thumb down to signal for me to land. I could only imagine his confusion. He'd no doubt seen my helicopter break formation from the Queen's escort. Then fly wildly out of control and almost hit a cell tower. Right after a person was thrown out of the plane to his death.

Now he saw me speeding away from London. The picture probably didn't make sense to him or his commanders. I figured, the only reason he hadn't shot me down was because of that. As long as I was moving away from populated areas and not toward them, they had time to try and figure out my erratic behavior.

I pointed to my headset, so he'd know I wanted to communicate with him. When he pointed at his like he couldn't hear me, I realized the radio wasn't on. The terrorist must've turned it off sometime before he met his demise. In all the chaos, I hadn't noticed. Immediately upon turning it on, the man's voice erupted in my head.

"What are your intentions?" the fighter pilot said.

"I have a dirty bomb on board."

I immediately realized how that must've sounded to him. Like I was making a threat. Before he could respond, I clarified that statement.

"What I mean is that this helicopter had a terrorist on it who intended to blow up a dirty bomb at the royal wedding and kill the Queen. I eliminated the threat, and I'm flying the bomb to the abandoned missile site just ahead."

According to my computer screen and radar map, I was still ten minutes away. A quick glance back at the bomb confirmed my worst fear. Only eight minutes until detonation. Time to consider other options.

"We'll escort you."

"Negative. This thing is going to blow in eight minutes."

"You won't make it to the missile site."

"I already know that. Any other ideas?"

"What about a parachute? You could put it on autopilot and jump."

"I already thought of that. This bird's been stripped bare of everything. There's not even a fire extinguisher on board."

That thought almost made me chuckle, even in the tense situation. What good would a fire extinguisher do me now? I needed a release, as the soberness of my fate became clearer every second that clicked off the doomsday clock in the back of my helicopter. That provided me one, if only for a few seconds.

A different voice crackled through my headset. I assumed the pilot on my left was the one speaking.

"There's a canyon just ahead. Two o'clock. Four minutes away. You can land there. It has steep cliffs on all sides. That'll control the blast radius."

"There won't be a shelter in there," the right side fighter pilot said. "Or enough time to vacate."

His words only confirmed what I already knew. This was a one-way trip. Of the thousand regrets I'd have if I allowed myself to think of it, the main consolation was that at least I saved the life of the Queen and the scores of thousands who would've been in the blast radius had it gone off in downtown London. That was my job. It came with the territory. I always knew at some point I might be required to give my life to save others. It just sucked that it was on my honeymoon.

"You guys high tail it out of here," I said. "Get far enough away so you're not affected by the blast."

A sober silence filled the airwaves. Suddenly the man on the right waved to me and then banked hard and peeled off. I assumed the other guy did the same.

"Good luck and Godspeed," the man said. "And God save the Queen."

He had.

With my help.

That was the only thing that brought me comfort. Of all the things on my mind, Jamie rose to the top. Her face was all I could see. I pushed her out of my mind. I needed to focus on landing the helicopter.

The canyon was just ahead to the right. I turned the craft slightly so I could come in over the top of the highest ridge. In my mind, I pictured that would have the steepest cliffs. As I rose over the cliff and started into the valley, I felt my breath leave me. Under any other circumstances, the view would be postcard worthy.

I broke hard and reduced my speed. Then began to hover and set the helicopter down perfectly and gently like I was making a moon landing. I shut it off. Then took an inventory of my surroundings, looking to see if there was any possible shelter.

Nothing but steep cliffs on each side.

Maybe a large boulder or two. If I could run fast enough to get to them. I wasn't sure it was worth the effort. I looked back.

00:02:07... 06... 05... 04... 03.

The bomb timer clicked away. I'd never known seconds to go by that fast. Less than two minutes left. I unbuckled my seat belt and considered going in the back and trying to disarm the detonator timer. It was probably rigged to blow if it was messed with. What difference did it make? The only difference was that the odds were better that the detonator switch was defective. That happened every so often when amateurs tried to put together a bomb. It would be the worst irony if I detonated a defective bomb by trying to disarm it.

That didn't mean I was going to sit there and die. I intended to run as hard and fast away from the bomb as I could, hoping upon hope that somehow, I survived the blast. Or the bomb was a dud and didn't explode.

I had to do something first, while I still could. "Hey guys," I said on the radio. "Can you still hear me?"

"Roger that, mate."

"My wife's name is Jamie Steele. Give her a message for me. Tell her that Alex loves her with all his heart and that I'm sorry things turned out this way."

Tears had welled up in my eyes and my voice shook as I said it.

"Does this mean I can have her since you'll be out of the picture?" a familiar voice said. Startling me and shaking me out of my pity party.

Bond.

"What are you doing here?" I asked.

"I came to save you, buddy. But we lost you. Where are you?"

"I'm in a canyon. North of London. I didn't make it to the missile site."

I still didn't understand how my radio transmission could travel all the way to London where I assumed he was.

"Turn on your transponder," he said.

I reached over and put it on. The terrorist must've disabled that at some point as well. Maybe before I even boarded.

"Okay! I've got you," Bond said. "We'll be on the ground in less than a minute. The cavalry has arrived as you Americans would say."

"Negative, Bond. The timer is coming up on one minute. You'll never get out in time."

"Get your arse out of that helicopter! I'm picking you up in less than thirty. Don't make me wait for you. I might not."

No man left behind.

That's what Curly always said.

I'd do the same thing if the roles were reversed.

As much as I couldn't stand the guy, I'd still risk my life to save his life, if I had to.

I pushed the door open.

The distinct drone of the rotor blades neared. I couldn't see the helicopter, but I could hear it. Suddenly it appeared over the canyon cliffs. Coming in at a high rate of speed.

"Don't crash the thing, Bond," I shouted even though I knew he couldn't hear me.

The bird landed hard but intact. The back door flung open.

I sprinted. Faster than I'd ever run in my life.

I dove into the back. Sprawling into the back compartment. A sofa was on the right up against a wall that separated the area from the cockpit. Cushy seats were on the left. This was what my helicopter was supposed to look like before the terrorist took everything out and replaced it with a bomb.

"Go! Go! Go!" I shouted not knowing if they could hear me.

The pilot lifted the helicopter faster than it was designed to function. Up and to the left. Away from the bomb. The bird hesitated slightly but powered on. Building speed. I wasn't sure which would be best. Going up as high as possible or trying to get as far away as possible. The pilot chose the latter.

We were almost skimming across the ground barely above any tree line. Clearly, he wanted to get out of the canyon and behind the mountains.

Then I heard it.

A loud explosion. So loud it even drowned out the noise of the helicopter.

By this time, I was in one of the seats, fastening myself in for the anticipated bumpy ride. Looking back, I could see the mushroom cloud. Not as big as an atom bomb, but bigger than anything I'd ever seen before.

Within seconds, the helicopter began to rock back and forth as the wind from the blast reached us. It felt like we were in a wave pool at a waterpark.

The pilot held steady and banked hard to the right as we exited the canyon. The air stabilized.

I put on my headset so I could hear what they were saying in the cockpit.

"That was too close for comfort," Bond said.

"Thanks for the ride," I said.

"Are you okay?" Bond asked.

"Never been better," I said.

My hands were shaking. My knees were knocking together. Adrenaline was shooting through me and building up like a geyser getting ready to blow. The pounding heartbeat in my ears almost drowned out Bond's words.

"I owe you one, Bond," I said.

"How did I do on my job interview?" he asked.

"Not bad," I said jokingly, flashing a grin that he couldn't see but he could hear in my voice.

"Does this mean I'm hired?" he asked.

"I'm still considering it."

35

Buckingham Palace

Our helicopter landed in London about thirty minutes after the dirty bomb detonated in Northern England. Jamie stood at the landing area waiting for us. As soon as I exited the helicopter and cleared the rotor blades, she came running at me and jumped into my arms. Smothering me with kisses. Every square inch of my face was the recipient of her affection. My heart warmed at how happy she was to see me. While she didn't know all the specifics, the situation with the bomb was one of my closest calls with death.

Bond watched the effusive display with a disgusted look on his face. As he started to walk away, Jamie jumped down out of my arms and ran to him and hugged him. Actually, picked him up off the ground in a bear hug.

"Thank you for bringing my husband back to me safely," she said.

"I did it for you," he replied.

I held my hand out to Bond. He reached out and shook it. When our hands gripped, I pulled him toward me and gave him my own aggressive hug.

"You're okay in my book, Bond."

"Like I said, I did it for Jamie. I couldn't care less what happens to you."

His sly grin told me he was only kidding.

The British higher ups from MI6 were there to meet us and ushered us inside. To what appeared to be the office side of the Palace. They led us into a conference room, filled with water, food, and a restroom, which I needed to clean up.

A doctor was also there, who after examining me, gave me a clean bill of health. As a precaution, he gave all of us potassium iodide pills to counteract the potential exposure to radiation. For more than thirty minutes, they questioned me about the bombing, what I knew and when I knew it and the details of what happened on the helicopter with the terrorist. Bond had already been whisked away.

I learned a lot from the questioning. By that time, the press had been alerted, and the story was all over the news. My part in it wasn't revealed to protect our cover. Early reports were that the fallout from the bomb was negligible, and the steep walls of the canyon prevented a major environmental catastrophe. No loss of life. Even the mushroom cloud dissipated quickly and didn't seem to enter the atmosphere or travel beyond the general vicinity of the blast.

When we were done with the questioning, I called Brad. Everyone else left the room except Jamie so we'd have privacy.

"You're just in time," Brad said. He never answered with a greeting.

"Why's that?" I asked.

"Do you want to see Pok get what's coming to him?"

"Yes!" I'd forgotten all about the cruise missile to be fired into Iran.

Brad put me on speaker and turned his phone so I could see the big screen in the front of what I recognized as the situation room at Langley. In the picture was a large building with few windows but with several large satellite dishes on the top of it. I assumed that was the cyber lab where Pok had been conducting his cyberwarfare.

"The missile should hit in about ten minutes," Brad said.

"Say hi to Jamie," I said as I hit the speaker button on my phone so she could hear.

"Hi, Brad."

They chit chatted for less than a minute. Mostly about how she was doing with her injuries. When they finished, I proceeded to tell Brad about the day's events. Most of which he already knew.

"I've told MI6 to keep your name out of it and not to ask too many questions," Brad said. "The last thing we want is to have your cover blown before you even go on your first AJAX mission."

"Sure feels like I already have," I said.

The background noise coming over the phone suddenly stopped. Even Brad quit talking as the room became eerily quiet.

"What's going on?" I whispered. Not sure why, since I wasn't in the room.

"Thirty seconds to impact," Brad said.

I brought the phone in closer so I could see better.

"What's that car driving away?" I asked.

On the screen, I could clearly see a vehicle leaving the building and driving off.

"I don't know."

A fireball erupted. A strange sight considering there was no sound. I'm used to watching movies on a big screen with state-of-the-art surround sound. All we could see from the overhead drone was a large, black plume of smoke with orange balls of fire inside it.

A cheer erupted in the room as the dust and smoke cleared and the leveled building came into view.

I wanted to join them in the celebration but didn't want to make a commotion in the Palace. Instead, Jamie and I high fived a couple times, although, I was careful not to hit her hands too hard, concerned they might still be a little tender from the acid. She didn't seem as worried about that as I was.

The building was rubble. Completely demolished. Nothing left of it. That wasn't my focus. I was searching for the car. The vehicle I'd seen driving away was no longer visible on the screen. A weird feeling came over me. What if that was Pok?

"We need to take out that car," I said excitedly.

"We can't," Brad said.

"Is the drone armed?"

"Yes."

"That car came from the lab," I argued. We need to take it out. Pok could be in it."

"I don't have the intelligence. Anyone could be in that vehicle."

"I have a feeling Pok's in that car."

"We don't act on your feelings," Brad said. "It might be a maid and her five-year-old son. Could be a spouse of one of the workers. We're not blowing up a car without knowing who's in it."

Brad was right. That didn't make it any easier. Now I'd never know for sure if Pok was dead or not. I'd always be wondering if he escaped. He'd be more dangerous if he were operating in the dark with impunity. Especially if I assumed Pok was dead and quit looking for him. On the other hand, if he were dead, I could waste valuable time and resources searching for a ghost.

Nothing I could do about it now. More than likely, Pok was in the building and was nothing but ashes now. I'd have to put my worries aside.

If nothing else, the lab was destroyed, and no one would be tracking us around London. That would have to be satisfaction enough. That meant Jamie and I could start our honeymoon in earnest. As soon as we were done at the Palace. Someone had mentioned giving us a tour which Jamie was especially excited about. She wanted to see the various pieces of art in the Palace dating back centuries.

Shortly after we signed off with Brad, an official-looking man entered the room. Dressed in a tuxedo and black tie. I suddenly felt underdressed. The man was very British in sophistication and tone. Clearly one of the royal subjects. *Do they call them subjects? Servants?* I made a mental note to ask someone later. He introduced himself, but

I didn't catch his long title which had at least five words in it. "Of the Queen" was the only thing I heard leading me to believe he worked for her in some official and close capacity.

Confirmed when he said, "Her Majesty is greatly appreciative of your actions today and would like to thank you personally."

I looked at Jamie and could tell she was fighting back a squeal of delight. I think that meant we were going to get to meet her.

"It's not necessary," I said. Jamie gave me an unapproving glare. "It's our job. But we would love to meet the Queen," I added for Jamie's benefit.

"We're not dressed for it, though," Jamie said. "I can't meet the Queen looking like this."

The royal whatever waved his hand dismissively.

"Actually, it will not be a personal meeting."

"What will it be?" I asked.

"Mr. Steele, the Queen would like to bestow knighthood on you, for your bravery and courage and contribution to the monarchy."

Knighthood. Are you kidding me?

My jaw would've hit the floor if not attached to my head. I didn't know what to say so I said that.

"I don't know what to say."

"You don't have to accept it," the man added. "This is an honorary knighthood and is totally voluntary on your part."

"Of course, I'll accept it! I'd be crazy not to. I'm honored. Thank the Queen for me."

"You'll be able to thank her yourself. She'll be the one bestowing the honor. Actually, it was her idea. This is quite unusual. Normally, these honors are awarded by a committee. And there's a long process. It takes months for someone to be approved for medals and honors. Of course, Her Majesty has the authority to grant knighthood to anyone she chooses, subject to the traditions of the throne."

"I'm proud to accept."

"Marvelous. I'll let the Queen know so the arrangements can be made forthwith. You'll be made an Honorary Knight Grand Cross of the Most Honorable Order of the Bath."

"Try saying that three times in a row," I said.

Jamie jabbed me in the ribs.

"What?" I didn't know why she was poking me.

"It's the highest honor that can be awarded to a foreigner," he added. "From what I hear, you're very deserving. We all might be dead if not for you."

"He is deserving," Jamie said. "I'm very proud of him."

"Brilliant! If you'll come with me, the Queen is going to hold a private ceremony in the Palace ballroom. No press allowed. Her Majesty understands your need for anonymity."

We exited the room, and the man led us through a maze of halls. Along the way, the man gave us a history lesson on the various rooms in the Palace as we passed them. We came to a room with double doors, and when we entered the massive ballroom, my breath almost left me for a second time. The room was clearly set up for an event associated with the wedding later that day. I'd never seen such an elegant dinner display.

The royal advisor—subject, assistant, whatever he was—told Jamie and me to stand in front of two massive double doors. Facing it.

I suddenly felt nervous.

"What do I do?" I asked. "Do I, like, kneel and stuff, and she'll tap me on the shoulder with a sword?"

"That's only for British subjects," the man explained. "You have to be a citizen of England to be eligible for actual knighthood. Yours is an honorary knighthood. Here's how it'll work. The Queen will enter. A band will play the British National Anthem. You don't have to do anything. A consort will announce your honor. Her Majesty will approach you and hand you the insignia of knighthood."

"Will she pin it on me or something?"

"She'll hand the insignia to you. It's in a royal binder. Inside will be a star, badge, and crimson silk sash. Try not to drop it."

"I'll try," I said, although my hands suddenly felt clammy. I wish he hadn't said that.

"You'll have forty seconds with the Queen. She'll ask you a question. If she wants to speak to you longer, that'll be up to her."

"Got it. Stand still. Wait for her. She'll ask me a question. I have forty seconds to answer. I can do that."

Jamie took my hand and squeezed it.

"Should I answer in a British accent?" I asked the man jokingly.

"No!" Jamie said. "Don't you dare."

"She might like to hear me talk British," I said. I was only kidding, but Jamie acted like she didn't know I was.

"Try not to embarrass us," she said.

"I'll try. No promises, though."

Before I had a chance to get any more nervous, the doors opened, and the Queen appeared and walked through the huge double doors.

An hour ago, I was thirty seconds away from being blown up by a bomb. No problem. I dealt with it. Now I'm about to faint at the sight of the Queen of England.

36

Two guard-like people in royal military uniforms walked at the Queen's side. A small band entered from behind her. The Queen wore a teal dress and hat. When everyone was in position, the band played, and I stood at attention. Not really sure exactly how to act. Jamie and I had been holding hands but were no longer.

When the band finished, the man who'd helped us motioned for me to step forward. When I didn't immediately start walking, Jamie gave me a slight nudge forward. My knees suddenly felt weak and wobbly. I did manage to walk a few steps before he motioned for me to stop. The Queen approached, holding something in her hand. It looked like a college graduation degree folder, only fancier, and with a royal insignia on the outside.

She stopped right in front of me, and we made eye contact for the first time. She smiled. I tried to force my upper lip to stop quivering. I had no idea what to do, so I just stood there. Probably with a goofy looking grin on my face. My heart felt like it wanted to do laps around the ballroom.

A man read from a piece of paper in his hand. "Mr. Alex Steele. For bravery and courage in the face of an enemy on behalf of Britain."

I wondered if the honor counted since that wasn't my real name. In my role with the CIA, I could never tell anyone about it anyway. Except the people I worked with. That'd be satisfaction enough. Brad wouldn't be impressed, but a lot of my fellow officers would be.

Does this mean everyone has to call me Sir?

The Queen handed me the binder. My hand shook as I reached out to take it from her. I opened it and was instantly overwhelmed with a sense of pride that rose up inside of me and warmed my heart. I stared at it for several seconds, although it seemed like several minutes. I bowed my head slightly toward her in the same manner I'd seen someone else do it a few seconds before when the Queen entered the room.

The Queen had a pleasant smile and looked me right in the eyes. She reached out her right gloved hand, took my right hand in hers, and held it in place. Her grip was surprisingly strong. "Thank you, Mr. Steele, for your courage and bravery," she said. "You've done a great service to our country and to me personally. A tragedy was avoided today because of you."

"You're welcome, Ma'am. Er. My Queen. Er. Your Majesty." I wasn't sure how to address her. I added, "Thank you for this honor. I accept it on behalf of my country. I'll never forget it."

At least that's what I think I said.

"Is that lovely lady your wife?" she asked, gazing at Jamie.

"Yes... she is, and she'd love to meet you."

The Queen motioned for Jamie to join us.

Jamie approached cautiously and then curtsied. Awkwardly. We both faced down terrorists for a living, but we'd never faced anything as intimidating as the Queen of England.

Although, she was nothing like what I was expecting. She was charming and soft spoken and clearly trying to make us feel comfortable.

"Your husband is a very brave man," she said to Jamie. "You must be extremely proud of him."

"I am," Jamie said. "Although now that he's been knighted by the Queen of England, he may be harder to live with." Jamie smiled in her unassuming way as she said it.

I was suddenly the proud one. Jamie continually amazed me with her ability to adapt to every situation. Standing here in front of the Queen of England, she handled it with grace and poise and immediately knew exactly what to say to ease the tenseness of the situation.

"All men are hard to live with as it is," the Queen leaned in toward Jamie and quipped. I was pleasantly surprised that she was joking with us. Maybe I could pull out my British accent after all.

"How long have the two of you been married?" the Queen asked.

"Five days," we said in unison.

Her Majesty chuckled.

"Honeymooners," she said. "I should've known by looking at you. You both seem very much in love."

"We are," I said, taking Jamie's hand and giving her a quick glance. She didn't look my way but kept her focus on the Queen.

"It's been an eventful honeymoon for sure," Jamie said. "Hopefully, the rest of our trip will not be as trying."

"Where are you staying?" the Queen asked. It seemed like we were well past forty seconds, but I had no intention of cutting the conversation short.

I looked at Jamie and she looked at me. I wasn't sure where we were staying tonight. We hadn't even talked about it. Although, the thought did occur to me that Jamie and I would finally be able to have our wedding night. Uninterrupted. We should find a really nice hotel.

"We're not sure," Jamie said. "We don't have a place at the moment."

"Well, that will not do," the Queen said. She suddenly turned and summoned one of her subjects. Assistants, I decided. It would be politically incorrect to call the help subjects or servants.

A man stepped by her side within seconds.

"Has the Vice President and the Second Lady moved out of the Belgian Suite?" the Queen asked.

It sounded like she was talking about our Vice President and his wife who I knew were in England for the wedding. They must've stayed at Buckingham Palace as her guest. I hadn't seen any secret service, so I figured he was gone.

"Yes. Your Majesty. They left after the wedding."

"Splendid." She turned back toward us. "I'd love for you to be my guest for the night. You'll be very comfortable in the Belgian Suite. It's simply magnificent. It's named after King Leopold, the first of the Belgians. Queen Victoria's favorite uncle. Prince Andrew and Prince Edward were born there. Will you do me the honor of staying in my home tonight?"

She didn't have to ask us twice.

"Sure," we both said again in unison.

"It'd be our pleasure," I added.

"Then it's settled. Will you join me for breakfast in the morning?"

"Of course. It'd be our honor."

I could hardly believe what I was hearing. If I could, I'd pinch myself just to see if I were having a dream.

The Queen reached out her hand to shake mine again. Then Jamie's. "I'm so thrilled," she said. "I'll see you in the morning. I'd spend more time with you today, but I have a wedding reception to go to and dinner with the newly married couple." She waved her hand at the grand display behind us.

I wondered if we could crash the wedding later. That'd be something to tell our kids about.

"We perfectly understand," Jamie said. "And thank you for your hospitality."

The Queen turned and walked away.

Jamie and I both stayed perfectly still until she was gone.

As soon as the big doors closed, we danced around in a little jig as Jamie squealed like a schoolgirl. We were the only people in the room except for one other man.

He approached us.

"My name is Mr. Dorsey. I'm an assistant to the Queen."

He shook my hand and kissed Jamie's in a formal manner.

"If you'll come with me, I'll show you to the Belgian suite. Would you like to see the Throne Room first?"

I didn't think I'd ever hear those words in my lifetime.

"You bet... Yes sir, of course. We'd love to." I had to tone down my casualness. Everyone and everything was so prim and proper. Jamie seemed right at home. I felt like the proverbial fish out of water. I needed a quick lesson in how to act in front of royalty.

The walk to the Throne Room took nearly a half hour, as Mr. Dorsey stopped several times to point out various points along the way. He seemed knowledgeable about the history of Buckingham Palace and particularly the artwork which he and Jamie shared as a common interest.

We stopped in front of what he said was the Throne Room and Mr. Dorsey asked us to wait outside so he could check to see if anyone was in there.

After he was gone, I whispered to Jamie, "Do you think he'd let me sit on the throne?"

Jamie reached over and pinched my arm. Hard.

"Don't you even think about it," she said.

"You can't tell me what to do. I'm a knight now."

This time she punched me in the arm. Harder. "You might be a knight, but I'm a wife. Wife trumps knight."

"I'll have to check the rules on that."

"Don't get a big head. A knight is barely above a pawn in chess."

We both burst out laughing.

The man suddenly appeared and we both abruptly composed ourselves.

"Right this way," the man said pointing to the open doors.

I couldn't believe it. We were about to enter the Throne Room of Buckingham Palace.

Jamie entered before me.

I whispered in her ear, "I'm asking."
I never did ask. I was too much in awe.

The Belgian Suite

The guest suite at Buckingham Palace was more grandiose and magnificent than I imagined it would be. Mr. Dorsey told us several U.S. Presidents had stayed there, as well as many world dignitaries. None more important than us, he added. He thanked me profusely for my bravery and what I did for England and the monarchy.

I told him how thankful I was to be able to save so many lives. Including my own.

Mr. Dorsey was right. The bomb would've detonated in the courtyard of Buckingham Palace. Right at the Grand Entrance. Most of the staff were in the courtyard when the Queen arrived and would've been at the epicenter of the blast. I shuddered at the thought of how close we all came to a disaster of epic proportions.

He led us into the main living area of the Belgian Suite.

Jamie was immediately drawn to the artwork.

I merely tried to take it all in.

Mr. Dorsey wowed us with his knowledge of the famous paintings that lined each wall including a three-quarter-length painting of King George III and Queen Charlotte.

"These are works by Canaletto," Mr. Dorsey pointed out, more for Jamie's benefit than for mine.

"Diana and Acteon," Jamie said. "Gainsborough's most famous painting. Stunning."

I had no idea what they were talking about but kept nodding my head

"I'm impressed," Mr. Dorsey said. "You know your artists."

I was impressed with Jamie as well. Which reminded me.

"Where's the bedroom?" I asked. While I was enjoying the tour, my mind was elsewhere now.

"This way," Mr. Dorsey said. "I think you'll be pleased. It's quite opulent."

Opulent didn't begin to describe it. The room was sky blue. The centerpiece of the room was the massive king-sized bed with an elegant, gilded headboard. Draped by a crisp white, down-filled comforter with layers of starched, colorful spreads topped by two rows of the puffiest pillows with silk cases, standing at attention at the head of the bed. A huge, crystal chandelier was suspended high above.

While I was focused on the bed, Jamie and Mr. Dorsey were deep in discussion about the three portraits of Queen Victoria in the room.

After they were done conversing about art, Mr Dorsey said, "The suite has six bathrooms."

"Wow!" Now, I couldn't wait for the tour to be over, so we could start enjoying it.

Curly always told us to take everything in stride. To not give anything away. Act like we've been there and done that many times before. Whatever it was. He couldn't have imagined this. I couldn't help but show how impressed I was by my surroundings.

Before Mr. Dorsey had a chance to show us any of the bathrooms, we heard voices coming from the main room. We followed Mr. Dorsey back to the yellow room. Narrow corridors connected the rooms. The sound was coming from four staff members who were there. Upon seeing Dorsey, they suddenly became quiet and moved into formation. Three men and one woman. A younger looking lady. All dressed formally in black and white.

Mr. Dorsey gestured to each as he introduced them. "Ms. Tamara Gilbert will be Mrs. Steele's lady-in-waiting," he said. The young woman stepped forward.

"Please call me Jamie," my wife responded to the young lady.

"Ms. Gilbert," Mr. Dorsey said, "please show Jamie to the ladies' dressing area. I'm sure she'd like to get changed."

"I don't have any clothes," Jamie said, hesitantly. "We didn't come prepared to sleep over."

Mr. Dorsey answered, "Not a problem. We have a complete wardrobe closet for that very reason. I'm sure we can find something in your size. I'll tell you a funny story if you have the time."

I actually was starting to get anxious. We had the time, but I wanted to go back and try out the bedroom.

Mr. Dorsey continued. "A few years back, one of our clumsy footmen spilled a boat filled with gravy on the Grand Duchess of... I don't remember which country. Maybe she was a Princess. Or an actress. Anyway... it doesn't matter. It was quite the scandal. She was wearing an expensive dress. I believe her exact words to the footman was, 'I will thank you never to darken my Dior again."

We all burst into laughter. All except the staff. They maintained perfect composure as they continued to maintain stately decorum. Mr. Dorsey's laugh was deep and almost roaring. I bet he had a lot of juicy stories to tell. No telling what he had seen in his years of service.

"Right this way, Madam," the lady-in-waiting said to Jamie after the laughter died down.

Jamie looked back at me with what could only be described as child-like anticipation as they disappeared into another room.

As soon as they were gone, Mr. Dorsey continued. "Two footmen will remain outside your suite at all times," he said to me. "Twenty-four hours a day. If you need anything at all, don't hesitate to ask them."

"Can they bring us food?"

"Of course. The kitchen is open day and night. Just tell them what you desire."

"Nothing now. But perhaps in about an hour."

"We are at your service. I'm sure you will find the food exquisite." Dorsey gestured to another gentleman, still standing at attention. "Mr. Bennett Eland will be your equerry, Mr. Steele." A man stepped forward and gave me a slight salute. "He is one of Her Majesty's most trusted assistants and his family has served the Queens for three generations."

"I'm pleased to meet you, Bennett," I said.

"I'm at your service, Sir."

I wondered if he called me sir because I was a knight or if he called everyone sir. I was dying to know. So, I asked Mr. Dorsey. "Having been knighted by the Queen, does that mean I am to be called sir now?"

He shook his head no. "The titles of Dame and Sir are reserved for British citizens. Yours is an honorary title and does not come with the title of Sir. Nonetheless, you are an honored guest of the Queen. Our staff will address you in any manner you prefer."

"I prefer Alex."

"Alex it is. Make yourself at home, Alex. Should I be of further service to you, please don't hesitate to ask one of the footmen, and they will summon me at once."

"Very good," I said in my most formal voice. "I appreciate all your help. I don't expect that we'll need anything."

Mr. Dorsey clicked his heels, nodded his head, and departed the room. The two footmen followed him. Presumably to take their positions outside the room.

"Can I be of assistance to you?" Bennett Eland asked.

"I would like to get a shower and change clothes. Do you have a wardrobe for men as well?"

"We do, Sir. Right this way. I will help you get undressed and into the shower."

I had no idea what he meant, but I didn't like the sound of it.

* * *

Turned out the staff did whatever you asked them to do. After Bennett had shown me where to shower and change clothes, I asked Bennett to leave the suite and go join the footmen. I preferred to change in private.

The wardrobe closet did have things my size. Even size fourteen shoes. And underwear. At first, the thought of wearing used underwear gave me pause. Bennett explained that clothes were replaced after they were worn. Undergarments and socks were discarded. Dress clothes and shoes were donated to charity.

I intended to be in bed when Jamie came to the master suite, so I wouldn't be wearing much. The suite was stocked with every toiletry imaginable, and I was able to shave, brush my teeth, apply cologne, and fix my hair after taking a shower in the most luxurious bathroom I'd ever seen.

Then I settled into bed, even though only three in the afternoon. Hopefully, Jamie was thinking the same thing and would come back to the suite ready to finally consummate our marriage.

I heard a slight rap on the door, and my heart skipped a beat in anticipation. When the door opened slowly, Jamie was draped in a white, silk nightgown with a train. So stunningly gorgeous, she took my breath away and left me speechless.

"Do you like it?" she said as she slowly walked over to the side of the bed and climbed in next to me.

Before I could answer, she let out a pleasurable moan.

"I've never felt sheets so soft!" she said.

"I know. I feel like I'm lying on a cloud. In heaven. Can you believe it? And yes. I do like your nightgown. You look stunning."

She snuggled up next to me. Her hair, still slightly wet. I could smell a number of different fragrances. Her skin was soft like it had been woven from gossamer angel wings.

I said, "I can't believe our first time is going to be in the royal suite at Buckingham Palace."

"I know! I can't wait to tell our kids and grandkids this story. They won't believe it."

"I didn't think you were going to talk to them about sex. Remember?"

"Come on! We have to tell them about this. It's too amazing not to."

"I suppose."

I turned so we were facing each other and kissed her passionately.

"I told you our first time was going to be exciting," Jamie said.

And it was.

Not exciting like I thought it would be. Better.

More tender. Passionate. Romantic. Gentle. Slow.

I was so focused on Jamie I hardly noticed the suite.

I think it's how God intended it to be.

Without a doubt, the best moment of my life.

NOT THE END

GET YOUR FREE GIFT

As a thank you for finishing my book, I want to give you a free gift. Go to terrytoler.com and sign up for my mailing list and I'll give you the first three chapters of *The Launch*, a Jamie Austen novella free of charge.

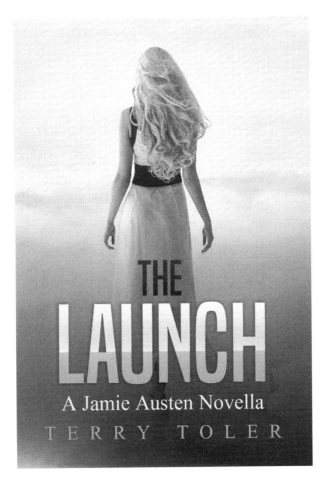

Terrytoler.com

SPY STORIES

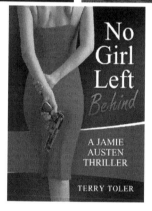

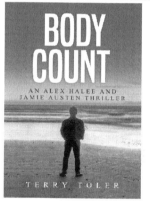

Thank you for purchasing this novel from best selling author, Terry Toler. As an additional thank you, Terry wants to give you a free gift.

Sign up for:

Updates
New Releases
Announcements

At terrytoler.com.

We'll send you the first three chapters of The Launch, a Jamie Austen novella, free of charge. The one that started the Spy Stories and Eden Stories Franchises.

BEHOLDINGS PUBLISHING

Made in the USA
Columbia, SC
04 January 2024

29831417R00167